**"Who are** Karen demanded.

"Keep your voice down," the man warned nervously. "Your friend is in grave danger. And you are not safe, either."

"What kind of danger?" Karen pressed.

The man leaned closer, his voice dropping to an urgent whisper. "You must find the Sospel connection. Look for Monsieur Henri. Tell him the dog is barking."

Then he left her, running like a madman. Karen tried to follow him, but it was too late. She didn't hear a shot, but as she watched in horror, he crumpled to the ground—dead.

And the only thing that kept her from screaming was the certain knowledge that she'd never stop....

## ABOUT THE AUTHOR

*Deathtrap* is Deborah Bryan's first solo
Intrigue. Before that she and her mother
wrote under the pseudonym of Deborah
Joyce. They have four Superromances and
one Intrigue to their credit. For Deborah
Bryan, writing has always been a family
affair and now her daughter, Elizabeth, seven
years old, informs her she's going to be a
writer, too. Her first attempt, complete with
illustrations, cost Deborah one dollar to
purchase. Deborah says it's the best dollar
she's ever spent, but knowing her daughter,
it's only a matter of time until she discovers
inflation!

## Books by Deborah Joyce

HARLEQUIN INTRIGUE
37–A MATTER OF TIME

HARLEQUIN SUPERROMANCE
61–A QUESTING HEART
108–A DREAM TO SHARE
125–NEVER LOOK BACK
142–SILVER HORIZONS

# DEATHTRAP
## DEBORAH BRYAN

## *Harlequin Books*

TORONTO • NEW YORK • LONDON
AMSTERDAM • PARIS • SYDNEY • HAMBURG
STOCKHOLM • ATHENS • TOKYO • MILAN

Harlequin Intrigue edition published April 1987

ISBN 0-373-22064-2

# *Prologue*

Luke Donovan was not a man who believed strongly in fate. He liked to think he controlled his own destiny, that things happened because he made them happen, not because of chance or kismet or luck. But every now and then, when he reached a dead end in one of his investigations, something would come along to make him reconsider. This was one of those times.

He noticed her the moment he walked into the lobby of the dingy Rome hotel. But then, what normal, unattached, thirty-three-year-old American man wouldn't have? Her hair, tumbling in natural waves to her shoulders, was the pale blond color of corn silk. She was tall, almost as tall as Luke, and she carried herself with the poise and assurance of a woman who didn't much care what others thought of her.

As she turned away from the reception desk, he paused to watch in a shadowy corner of the tiny area that passed for the lounge of the Hotel Gran Duca. Her stride was easy and purposeful, and at first he thought she was heading straight for him. Then he realized that she hadn't even noticed him. As she drew closer, he saw that her brows were drawn together in a puzzled frown. But even the frown couldn't detract from her remarkable face. Her skin was almost translucent, pale against the olive green fabric of the jumpsuit she wore. Viewed more closely, her hair resembled a soft cloud of spun gold, a cloud that invited a man's touch.

She walked past him without sparing him a glance. As the lobby door swung shut behind her, Luke felt a momentary sense of loss. So much for relying on fate. It seemed they hadn't even been destined to speak.

Apparently he wasn't the only man whose attention had been caught by the blonde. A thin, balding man seated on the worn couch in the corner of the lobby followed her every movement over the top of his newspaper. He waited until the woman was out the door, then he rose and shrugged his hunched shoulders into a rumpled jacket. As he turned toward the door he paused, as if seeing Luke for the first time.

For a moment their glances locked and Luke read a challenge in the other man's eyes. Coolly and deliberately, Luke returned it, glaring back. He didn't like the idea of this unkempt slouch being interested in the blonde. She'd been carrying a large tote bag. He hoped she was smart enough not to keep her money or anything of value in that bag. Under Luke's scrutiny, the man in the rumpled jacket seemed to back down. He turned and left the hotel.

Luke considered tailing the man for a few minutes to make sure he wasn't following the blonde, then dismissed the idea. Most likely, he was simply imagining trouble where there was none. Or, to be honest, perhaps he wanted an excuse to follow the blonde himself.

Luke turned to find the reception clerk eyeing him suspiciously. He strolled over to the desk and leaned against it. "Do you speak English?"

"A little." The reply was given grudgingly.

"I'm looking for someone. A man named Mark Turner. I believe he stayed here a few weeks ago."

There was a long silence. "He might have. I don't remember." The clerk shrugged dismissively.

"Would you check your records?"

At first Luke thought the man was going to refuse. But then he reached below the counter and pulled out a tray stuffed with cards. "The name of your friend again?"

"Turner. Mark Turner. He would have been a guest here about three weeks ago."

For several minutes the only sound was that of the shuffling cards. At length the clerk produced one and read it over carefully. He glanced at Luke before shifting back to the card. "Yes, he was here. But he only stayed one night. That was on the fourteenth of May."

"Any idea where he went?" Luke straightened away from the desk. He stuck his hands in the pockets of his camel leather jacket and eyed the clerk keenly.

The other man nervously licked his lips. Luke grew impatient when the clerk said nothing. He glanced around the lobby to make sure no one was watching, then he dug his wallet out of his pocket, extracted a bill and laid it on the counter. "May I see the card?"

The clerk's gaze fixed on the bill. After a moment, he took the money and slipped it into his shirt pocket. Without saying a word, he handed the card to Luke.

There wasn't much information on the card, but Luke recognized Mark's name on the top line. Beneath it were two dates. Although Luke couldn't read the printed Italian words on the card, he assumed that these dates referred to when Mark had checked in and out. Near the bottom of the card, the name of another hotel had been printed in neat block letters. "The Hotel Azur," he read. "Nice, France." He looked up at the clerk. "What does that mean?"

The clerk reached for the card. His gaze flicked over it and then darted back to Luke. "He asked us to forward his mail there."

"Anything else you can tell me?" Luke leaned closer. "Was he alone? Did he mention why he was going on to France?" The clerk merely stared back at him, his expression carefully blank. But Luke caught the momentary darkening of his eyes. "You know something, don't you?" Harshness colored his voice.

"I'm sorry, I don't understand," the clerk said slowly. "I speak only a little English." His gaze shifted away, refusing to meet Luke's probing stare.

With a muttered oath, Luke reached for his wallet again and extracted another bill. "Will this improve your English?"

The man's hand shot out swiftly to take the money. "I know nothing, really," he said, shrugging again. "It's only the young lady, the one who just left . . ."

"Yes?" Luke was instantly alert.

"She was looking for a friend, as well." The clerk's gaze narrowed with suspicion. "You and the American lady aren't together?"

"No." When the man didn't go on, Luke leaned across the counter and glared at him. "I haven't got all day. Tell me about the American lady."

"As I said, she was looking for a friend, as well. Not your Mark Turner. A young American woman like herself. Her friend went to Nice, also. To the Hotel Azur."

"With Mark?" Luke asked, surprised.

"No, not together." The clerk pointed at the dates on Mark's registration card. "This Mr. Turner was here the day before the American woman's friend. It does seem strange, though, both of them going on to Nice, to the same hotel." He stopped speaking as the door to the lobby opened and an elderly man entered.

"It does at that." Luke realized after a moment that the clerk wasn't going to tell him anything else. "Thanks for the information," he said dryly. He shifted away from the desk and started across the lobby, lost in thought. It seemed he might have been wrong. The way things looked now, he and the eye-catching blonde were headed in the same direction. Maybe, just maybe, there was something to be said for fate after all....

# Chapter One

It must have been nearly midnight when the Milan-to-Nice train shuddered to an unexpected halt. There was a loud clattering beneath the floorboards of the tiny bathroom where Karen St. Clair stood brushing her hair. She braced herself against the sink and steadied her balance by putting one hand against the wall. The lights flickered ominously and in the small, grimy mirror she caught a glimpse of her own horrified expression.

For the past twenty-four hours things had definitely not been going her way. Normally, she was one of those people who had life completely under control. Friends envied her ability to always appear to be put together, to keep her town house in impeccable order, and to manage her money. Employers commended her on her take-charge attitude and calm efficiency. But in the past few hours her composure had begun to slip.

If she were to admit the truth, the first chink in her armor of control had been that damn perm last month, she thought. "Natural wave," indeed! The only thing that had been natural about it was its refusal to be tamed. After weeks of struggling with hot combs and styling mousses, she had finally managed to subdue those waves. Now she simply washed and occasionally brushed.

But it hadn't stopped there. Next had come that thoroughly unsettling telephone call from Diane Garrett, a close family friend. Karen had felt guilty as soon as she heard Diane's voice on the phone. Diane's father had died earlier in the year but after a period of being supportive and on permanent call for Diane, Karen had gotten too busy to keep in touch regularly and had let things slide between them. Her guilt had turned to anxiety when she heard what Diane had to say.

Diane had sounded elated as she told Karen about her plans to go to Europe. For some time, she explained, she had been corresponding with a man she'd met through a personals column. They hadn't actually met in person yet, but Diane had been convinced from the man's letters that he was wonderful and sensitive.

According to Diane, he was a minister. Karen had listened in silence while Diane explained that the man had written to her to say that he was taking a group of high school students from his church on a tour of Europe. Right after the group had arrived in Rome, the other chaperone had become ill and had had to return to the States. Diane's friend had sent her a telegram, suggesting that she come to Europe and take over the chaperone's job. He'd arranged for a ticket to Rome to be held for her at the nearest airport.

Diane had ended the conversation by saying that she planned to leave for Rome the next day. Karen had protested, trying to reason with her, but Diane wouldn't listen. Instead, she had promised to write to Karen as soon as she joined the group in Rome and, at Karen's insistence, had supplied the name of the hotel in Rome where the group would be staying.

Almost a month had passed since the call, and there had still been no word from Diane. Karen had grown increasingly worried about her and finally, with end of term approaching, no summer session to teach and no serious plans made, she had decided to come to Europe herself in order to make certain that Diane was all right.

Nothing about the trip so far had gone as expected. After wrestling with a traffic tie-up on the expressway, she had arrived at the Norfolk airport only minutes before her plane was scheduled to take off. Her car was now parked in a lot meant strictly for overnight travelers. But she had decided not to worry about that until she returned. How much could towing and storage fees amount to, anyway?

There had been nothing calming or reassuring about the flight itself. After bouncing over the ocean, buffeted by severe turbulence, the plane had crawled into a prolonged holding pattern at Rome's airport, socked in by bad weather. Throughout all of this, Karen had managed to maintain something of her usual poise. But her impressive ability to remain calm was being taxed beyond endurance tonight. Surely she wasn't now going to be involved in a train wreck?

With a great deal of groaning and screeching the train finally shuddered to a complete stop and an eerie silence settled in. Without the chug of the engine and the whine of the wheels as they rolled effortlessly over the gleaming tracks, the night seemed strangely empty. An acrid odor of warm tar permeated the air, so thick she could almost taste it.

Karen slung the strap of her canvas tote bag over her shoulder and wrenched open the lavatory door. The scene in the corridor outside was somewhat reassuring. Here the lights were bright and unwavering and a fresh breeze grazed her ankles. From farther along the train came muffled shouts and a distant rumble of conversation, but her own car was comparatively quiet. As she moved to step out into the passageway, a uniformed conductor pushed roughly past her from behind.

*"Excusez-moi,"* she called after him.

He turned and regarded her impatiently. His glance darted rapidly from her heavy shoulder-length blond hair to her olive-green cotton jumpsuit and casual leather sandals. "You are American, yes?" The words were spoken in English, clipped and carefully pronounced.

"Yes, how did you—"

He cut her off sharply. "I can always tell, *mademoiselle*. Go to your compartment and stay inside. We have a small delay. Nothing to worry about."

With that brief instruction he was gone, leaving her to stare after his retreating back. Why had they stopped so abruptly? Had the engine broken down or had there been a collision up ahead? Hijackers? At this point, nothing would surprise me, she thought. It seemed her whole trip thus far had been a succession of minor disasters. She considered hurrying after the conductor but it seemed a useless pursuit. He'd made it clear he didn't have time for explanations.

His automatic assumption that she was American didn't surprise her, either. Europeans had an uncanny ability to spot Americans. A French woman had explained it to her once, saying, "Americans are easy to pick out. You recognize them first by their attitude, forthright and brash. Then you look at their shoes. The shoes always give them away...."

Karen glanced down at her feet. Brazilian sandals, a dead giveaway, she thought ruefully. Maybe he'd just made a lucky guess.

Karen walked toward her own compartment. A quick survey from the passageway revealed only two other occupants. Two men stood near the opposite end, smoking calmly and conversing in rapid Italian. They seemed undisturbed by the train's lurching halt. She gathered a vague impression of finely tailored business suits and discreet gold jewelry.

One of the men looked up and smiled. In that manner peculiar to Italian men of all ages, he managed in one inoffensive glance to express appreciation for her willowy figure, from the curve of her slightly full breasts down to her long legs. She stopped and looked away, not eager to encourage him and knowing that unless she looked receptive, he would leave her alone.

Even though the conductor had told her to return to her compartment, she felt a need for further information before capitulating like an obedient little tourist. How long was this stop going to delay their arrival in Nice, for example? She considered asking the two Italian men, but then they would probably want to be friendly. And she was far too exhausted to respond to even the mildest of flirtations.

Back to her right were the connecting doors that led to the next car. Through the window, she saw that a knot of passengers, including several women, had gathered on the other side of the partition. Perhaps they would know what was going on.

Quickly she threaded her way to the doors. As she drew level with the last compartment, a spate of angry words arrested her progress, catching her attention because they were spoken in English.

She paused, compelled to listen even though she realized the words weren't directed toward her. "It looks like she suspects something," a man's voice insisted brusquely. It was a low voice, harsh and heavily accented. The speaker's native language wasn't English, of that she was certain. German, perhaps?

Privacy shades shielded the occupants of the compartment from her view. The door was pulled tightly shut. Another man answered now, but his reply was low and rapid, almost inaudible. The heavily accented voice responded. "Don't worry. We'll soon be rid of her. We can't afford to let anyone get curious now."

It was silent in the shuttered compartment after he finished speaking. Glancing back over her shoulder, Karen saw that the two Italian businessmen had disappeared. She hesitated, reluctant to move on. It was rude to eavesdrop, she knew, yet she found the conversation curiously riveting.

It was none of her business, really. And, even though the conversation had sounded odd, it probably was perfectly innocent. Two men talking, perhaps about the wife of one of them. Yes, that might fit. "It looks like she suspects something," he had said. Infidelity? A secret affair, perhaps? Whatever it was about, it did not concern her.

Not wanting to eavesdrop any further, she hurried toward the door at the end of the passage. The platform between the two cars was cold in contrast to the corridor she had left behind. A stiff breeze whipped her thick hair into unruly waves and brought spots of color to her high cheekbones. The smell of tar burned her throat and caused her eyes to water. It was a relief to step into the next car.

Several people crowded the narrow corridor. A well-dressed older woman stepped back to make room for Karen. Smiling reassuringly, she broke out into a flood of rapid Italian.

"Pardon," Karen interrupted when she got a chance. "Do you speak English?" The woman shook her head, and Karen tried a new tack. *"Parlez-vous français?"*

Again the woman shook her head. Karen glanced around at the other passengers, only to find them looking apologetic, as well. *"Inglese?"* one man asked. He shifted the tiny baby girl he was holding to his shoulder and patted her soothingly.

"American."

Five pairs of eyes regarded her anxiously. Karen racked her brain for the few simple Italian phrases she knew but drew a blank. The smattering of Italian she'd picked up in her travels had deserted her completely, or not quite.

"*Treno* . . . ," she began, recalling the word for "train."
She pantomimed the action of sudden stopping. Haltingly,
she tried out a few more half-remembered phrases. "*Quanto
tempo* . . . how long . . . *si ferma*?" Was that the right way to
ask how long the train was stopping? She wasn't sure, but
from the relieved smiles on the others' faces, she gathered
they had understood.

The young father consulted with his wife and then addressed Karen. "*Signorina*," he said with exaggerated care.
"*Treno* . . . train," he translated with a proud smile at her.
"*Albero—*" he stopped and pointed at the floor of the train
"*—sotto treno.*" Caught up in his narrative, he unleashed
a rapid spate of words that were unintelligible to her, although she thought she heard him use the word *albero* more
than once.

Karen regarded him blankly, so he patiently repeated his
words, accompanying them, this time, with broad explan-
atory gestures. It took her a moment to catch on that something was apparently under the train. That was why they had
stopped so abruptly. But what was under the train? *Albero.*
The meaning of the word escaped her. "*Quanto tempo?*"
she repeated.

He shrugged. "*Una ora, signorina.*"

One hour. She must have looked worried because he
spoke again.

"Okay, *signorina*. Is okay." He smiled at her. The older
woman, who had been the first to speak, disappeared into
the compartment behind her and returned a second later
with a loaded picnic basket.

"Oh, no, I couldn't." Karen was touched by her kindness. "*Grazie,*" she murmured.

After thanking them all again, she crossed the windy
platform to her own car. It was apparent that these people
thought the mystifying *albero* would not cause much of a

delay. She fervently hoped they were right. The sooner she arrived in Nice, the better.

When she returned to her own car, the corridor was darker, one of the lights apparently having burned out. Her gaze was drawn automatically to the compartment in which the conversation she had overheard had taken place. The door stood open and the interior was empty.

At first she thought she was alone in the corridor. But as her eyes adjusted to the dim light, she realized there was someone else there. Near the outside windows, a man was standing alone. Karen couldn't see his eyes. Yet she felt instinctively that he was looking directly at her.

Karen found nothing particularly unusual about his scrutiny. Men usually noticed lone women travelers. European men, especially. Yet somehow, this man's regard seemed threatening. Perhaps it was something in his stance, the tension in the way he held his body, that made her uneasy. Or maybe she was remembering that heated exchange of words behind a closed compartment door. Had it been this man's voice she'd heard?

His face was in shadow, but she could see the outline of a strong, angular jaw and prominent brow. There was quiet determination in that face, and power emanated from his body.

Karen's pulse raced. She dreaded having to walk past him in the narrow passageway. Should she speak or simply pretend not to see him? Chances were he wouldn't speak English. French, perhaps? If so, then language wasn't a barrier. Her French, though not fluent, was certainly adequate for casual conversation.

She glanced down at his shoes as she walked toward him. Dark leather loafers. Italian. Expensive. Not much to go on there. She wasn't sure how you judged a person's nationality by his shoes, anyway. Perhaps it was an inborn knack, one she didn't possess. All she could tell was that he had money and taste and could be Italian. Or French. Or American, for that matter.

As she drew closer, she could see him more clearly. Thirtyish, she guessed, and very, very sure of himself. A buttersoft, camel leather jacket hugged his broad shoulders and corduroy slacks outlined well-muscled thighs. He radiated an aura of rugged strength and cool assurance.

But it was his face that inevitably captured her attention. Her gaze drifted over his features in pleased surprise. His skin was smooth and warmly tanned, clean-shaven, with only a hint of darker shadow on his jawline. Straight, dark brows were set well apart above his hazel eyes and his thick, brown hair was brushed casually back from his forehead. Everything about him was appealing except for the hard set to his mouth.

They stared at each other for a long moment. Only two or three inches taller than her own five feet eight inches, he seemed solid and well built. From across the small distance that separated them, Karen inhaled a faint aroma of subtle masculine cologne. Nothing obtrusive, simply a fresh, outdoorsy, clean scent. As if conscious of her unwilling interest, he smiled, the faintly mocking curve of his lips setting her on edge.

Karen's gaze was the first to drop. Normally she would have smiled briefly, or murmured a polite greeting—anything to break the awkward silence. But she felt oddly ill at ease, and instead stepped quickly past him without speaking, hugging the wall opposite him in a blatant effort to avoid contact with that powerful body. As she squeezed past, she could feel the heat of his stare.

When at last she reached her own compartment, she dived inside. There was really no reason for her discomfort. For a woman who normally managed to handle male interest with casual aplomb, she was acting suspiciously like a fool. So she'd caught a man staring at her. Was that so unusual? No, but her response to the situation had been. Even now, her pulse throbbed alarmingly quickly.

The woman in the compartment looked up from her magazine as Karen entered. "You're back. I wondered what had happened to you." Irene Miller had shared the compartment with Karen since Milan. A widow from Detroit, she was on her way to Menton, France, to visit friends. Karen guessed her to be about sixty, but as the night had worn on, her energy had shown no signs of flagging. Despite the late hour she exuded cheerful enthusiasm and lively curiosity.

"I was trying to find out why we've stopped." Karen tossed her tote bag onto the empty bench seat that faced Irene. Although the compartment was designed to seat six, she and Irene had had it to themselves so far.

"Any luck?"

"Apparently there's something caught under the train. I guess we're waiting while they clear it away."

"You spoke with the conductor?"

"Sort of." Karen explained as she sat down. "He didn't tell me much. But I was able to find an Italian family in the next car. Unfortunately, my Italian is rather spotty so I know that there is an *albero* under the train, but not what that is. You don't happen to speak the language, do you?"

Irene shook her head. "Not a word. I do hope we'll be on our way soon. I left Venice early this morning and don't feel I've made much progress." Her salt-and-peppery gray hair was flattened where she had been leaning back against the seat. But her soft blue eyes still gleamed with alert interest. She groped through her voluminous handbag and produced a roll of mints. Before taking one herself, she held them out to Karen.

"No, thanks." Karen flashed her a brief smile. After several hours in Irene's company, she was no longer surprised by what the other woman managed to pull out of her luggage. That straw bag on the seat beside her held enough picnic supplies for a family of four. And her purse was loaded, as well. For some reason, Irene seemed to feel she had to travel equipped with a stockpile of food. Karen suspected she was leery of the local cuisine.

Paper rustled as Irene unrolled a mint. "You've been to Europe before, you said?"

"Several times. My first trip was a high school graduation present from my father." Even as she gave the polite reply, Karen groaned inwardly. The question had the earmarks of a preamble to a cozy chat and Karen was not in the mood for one.

"And to Menton?"

"Yes, it's a lovely old town and a good base from which to visit all the art museums in the area. Last summer I brought a group of my students to France, and we stayed a week in Menton."

Irene delved into the straw basket for a bottle of mineral water. "Now, what did you say you teach?"

"Art history. I'm an assistant professor at Hamilton College. It's a small private school in Virginia."

"You came from Rome this morning?"

"Yes... Well actually, I came all the way from Virginia." Karen pushed her hair back from her face and sighed. "My plane got into Rome this morning and I caught the afternoon train to Milan."

Irene's clear blue gaze sharpened. "Seems like a long way to travel by train. Wouldn't it have been easier to fly directly into Nice?"

Karen hesitated before replying. Irene's constant questions were putting her on the defensive. Still, she could scarcely be rude to the woman. Taking a deep breath, Karen attempted to inject a friendlier note when she spoke again. "I was supposed to be meeting a friend in Rome, but when I got there, I found she'd left and gone on to Nice instead.

I'm hoping to catch up with her there. Today's connecting flights to Nice were booked up, so I was forced to take the train.''

"Too bad. I bet you're exhausted. Maybe you should try to get some sleep." Irene settled back against her seat and picked up her magazine. Before opening it, she asked, "If you'd rather, I can turn off the overhead light."

"It doesn't bother me, but thanks for offering." Karen leaned back and closed her eyes. Her body was keyed up, tense from the abuse she had forced on it these past few days, and her mind refused to idle. Too much coffee and not enough sleep were a lethal combination.

Almost against her will, an image of the man in the corridor rose in her mind. Polished, ruggedly good-looking and tough, he wasn't to be easily forgotten. Maybe she should have lingered in the corridor. He'd been interested, she was pretty sure of that. After all, she deserved some reward for the horrors she'd endured on this trip so far.

With that thought, she immediately felt guilty. Diane should be her sole concern right now, especially after that futile attempt to find her in Rome.

Locating Diane's hotel had been next to impossible. When she'd finally found it, tucked away in a warren of narrow, confusing streets near the main railway station, she had been horrified. She could not imagine Diane staying there. From the state of the lobby it was not hard to imagine how horrible the rooms would be. With all of the delightful, reasonably priced hotels to be found in Rome, it seemed unlikely that Diane would settle for such a seedy place.

But Diane had been there, and gone. To Nice, the hotel clerk had finally admitted after Karen pressed him for information. His manner had irritated her. From the moment she had mentioned Diane's name, he had behaved oddly, inspecting her with suspicion and what seemed like

*Deathtrap*

unwarranted curiosity. But he had given her a forwarding address. "Miss Garrett said she would be staying at the Hotel Azur." The experience at the hotel had done nothing to alleviate Karen's worry about Diane, and she had elected to go straight on to Nice, rather than stopping for a night in Rome. She had anticipated being able to sleep on the train, not counting on sharing her compartment with a talkative American. And she certainly hadn't expected the train to be delayed.

Karen's mind wandered over familiar territory as she fought it to relax. It seemed ridiculous to be chasing after Diane; after all, the woman was twenty-four years old, an independent adult, she thought. Then her mind switched course: Diane's recent behavior had been unusually impulsive; she was not herself after losing her father, and Karen owed it to her, and herself, to make sure Diane was all right.

Her next thought was more disturbing. At the rate this train was going, Diane might already have left Nice by the time she arrived. No express trains had been available, so Karen had been obliged to board a local route. Throughout the evening, the train had barely gathered speed before slowing for another stop. At each station, the silence of the night had been punctuated by loud bellows from public-address systems as the various stationmasters called out the names of the towns. And now it seemed they were making unscheduled stops, as well.

Irene snapped her magazine shut and rose to her feet. She retrieved a heavy blue cardigan from the upper rack and threw it over her shoulders. Seeing that Karen's eyes were open, she said, "I'm going to walk around a bit. My legs need stretching. Care to join me?"

"I think I'll stay here." Karen smiled encouragingly, feeling relief at the prospect of having the compartment to herself for a while. "Don't go too far, though. European trains have a habit of splitting at various points along the route and I'm not sure all the cars on this train will be stopping in Menton. You don't want to get caught in the wrong car when we start up."

For a moment Irene looked doubtful. "Maybe I shouldn't go."

Karen regretted her warning. Irene was anxious enough already. This was her first trip outside Michigan, she had confided earlier. "I didn't mean to worry you. You'll be fine as long as you stay within a car or so of ours." Irene nodded slowly, as if she was memorizing the instructions, and left.

Enjoying her newfound privacy, Karen rummaged through her tote bag until she found the slim wallet that contained her travel documents. A quick inspection revealed that her passport, traveler's checks, cash and credit cards were still inside. She pulled out a beige linen-blend jacket and slipped it on over her jumpsuit against the chill that was settling over the motionless train. Shoving her wallet into a jacket pocket, she stood up and unkinked her legs.

The delay was making her edgy and the privacy she had welcomed was making her claustrophobic. At least out in the corridor, she could move around, she thought. Leaving her tote bag on the seat, she stepped outside.

The corridor was empty. There was no sign of the man in the leather jacket. She hadn't admitted to herself that she was hoping he would still be here, but disappointment stabbed her when she realized he was gone.

Feeling oddly isolated, Karen walked rapidly up and down the corridor. All the compartments she passed appeared to be empty. There was not even a suitcase or a jacket to indicate that they might be occupied. And there was no sign of Irene.

Reluctant to go inside and sit down again, Karen leaned against the outside wall and pressed her forehead against its wide glass window. Beyond the glass, the night stretched empty and black. There were no twinkling lights to indicate a nearby town, no signs of life anywhere. She shuddered, the isolation chilling her even more than the crisp June air.

She had no idea where they were. The train was supposed to take them along the coast once they crossed into France. Peering into the dark night, she could see no sign of water. And since no one had come to check passports, she assumed they hadn't yet crossed the border.

Turning away from the window, she paced back and forth restlessly. Right now, she would give almost anything for a hot, soothing bath, a comfortable bed heaped with blankets, and ten free hours to enjoy it.

It was silly to stand watch out in the corridor like this, she decided, and pacing only gave an illusion of purposeful motion—it wasn't going to make the train get under way again. She had a thick new paperback tucked away in her tote bag. With any luck, the novel would capture her attention so completely that she wouldn't notice how long they were stopped.

She had just entered her compartment when the lights flickered and died. "Oh, great," she muttered aloud. So much for the novel. She waited hopefully, but blackness prevailed and the only sound was the beating of her heart.

Although she didn't ordinarily frighten easily, Karen felt a coil of tension knot in her stomach. There was something about the darkness and the silence that was oddly threatening. She found herself hoping Irene would return soon. Even her chatter would be better than this feeling of total isolation.

Despite the coolness of the air, Karen felt uncomfortably warm now. Nerves and exhaustion, she thought. She took off her jacket and then groped for a spot to put it on her side of the compartment.

In the distance she heard a door open and close with a soft whoosh. Irene, returning from her walk? No, the footsteps sounded too heavy to be Irene's. Someone else must have entered their car.

Karen held her breath, listening intently. Her pulse pounded in long, slow thuds and she drew in a quick, impatient breath. There was no reason to be afraid. Yet she felt a sharp surge of something almost akin to terror.

The footsteps echoed along the corridor. Karen's nerves bristled. The darkness pressed in on her from all sides and the air seemed suddenly thick and oppressive.

Then she heard it—a slight rustle right outside her compartment, followed by a heavy tread. She felt, rather than saw, someone enter through the door behind her. "Who is it?" she asked loudly. "Is that you, Irene?"

There was no answer, only the quick, shuffling sound of movement. Then, like a scene in a nightmare, a hand covered her mouth. Strong fingers bit cruelly into her skin, blocking off her air and stifling the scream that rose to her lips.

Karen fought back instinctively. She reached up to the hand at her mouth and scrabbled at it futilely with her nails. As she struggled, another hand came around, this one circling her throat. She felt the warmth of a body behind her. Her fingers closed around a muscular arm and she pulled frantically at the rough-textured fabric that covered it. The arm clamped hard around her neck and she was pinioned against a solid, rock-hard chest. She tried to drag in breath through her nose but instead inhaled a suffocating odor. Dry-cleaning fluid? Yes, and something else, an odor she couldn't quite identify.

Tall as she was, her assailant was taller, and as his arm tightened around her throat, she felt her ability to resist ebb away. Her thoughts blurred hazily and her lungs ached with the need for air. Still he continued to choke her, ruthlessly increasing the pressure against her windpipe. Karen sagged against her assailant.

*Someone is trying to kill me.* The thought was incredible yet undeniably real. *I must keep fighting.*

Relentlessly, his choke-hold tightened. Karen made one last attempt at escape. Kicking as hard as she could, she managed to connect with his shin. Through the deepening fog that encased her mind, she thought she heard a muffled oath. Then she was falling, losing her grip on consciousness, sliding slowly and inexorably to the floor....

## Chapter Two

Light. There was light all around her. It burned into her eyes when she tried to open them. Karen gave up for a moment, shutting her lids tightly. Her throat ached abominably. She tried to draw in a deep breath, but the effort brought tears to her eyes.

She was lying on the floor. She could feel it, hard beneath her back. The train had stopped, she remembered. But no, that had been earlier, before...

*Someone tried to kill me!* The events of the past few minutes flooded back with painful recollection. A noise caught her attention, and for a moment she stopped breathing. She heard the noise again, louder this time. Then she heard a man's voice. "What the..." There was a muffled curse, in English, and in surprise she opened her eyes wide.

The harsh light from the compartment's overhead light blinded her momentarily. Then a man's face swam into view, coming closer as he knelt beside her.

"My God, lady, what's happened to you?"

She should have known it would be him. She recognized the soft leather jacket, the corduroy trousers, the thick, dark hair and the handsome face. His dark eyes inspected her carefully, his expression showing kindness and concern.

Karen made an effort to sit up, but dizziness forced her back. Every breath she drew burned like fire in her throat. Pain stabbed her temples. Bringing a hand up to her neck, she tentatively explored her tender skin. She felt bruised, sore.

"Don't try to sit up yet." The man's voice rang with authority. She felt his hand brush against her forehead as he smoothed back her hair. "What happened? Who did this to you?"

"Someone tried to choke me." Karen's voice came out sounding weak and husky, and her throat muscles tightened painfully. "It was a man, I think, a tall man. The lights were out, but now they're back on, so I guess it's been a while since it happened."

Involuntarily her mind reviewed those frightening moments in the dark. Her attacker had been a little taller than she was. About the height of this man. Her gaze flew to his jacket. She stared at his sleeve, noting the smooth, buttery leather. Could her mind have played tricks on her? But no, she clearly remembered the feel of rough wool fabric, the distinctive chemical odor of fabric that had been recently dry-cleaned.

He leaned over her, so close that she felt the smooth brush of his leather jacket, the radiated warmth of his body. She inhaled the fresh, tangy aroma of his skin.

Dark hazel eyes regarded her intently. He moved his hand to trace the marks on her throat, and she flinched at his touch, her body reacting instinctively. "Don't," she said. "Please..." For a moment she relived those moments in the dark. Dizziness and nausea assailed her, and she trembled with delayed shock.

The sharp hiss of air indicated he had been holding his breath. "What kind of animal did this to you?" The controlled fury in his voice was impressive in its restraint. Without waiting for her to reply, he slid his arm beneath her.

"You'll be more comfortable on the seat. Here, let me help you up."

Karen put her hands against his chest. "I can manage by myself." She twisted her body away from him, fighting back a wave of dizziness as she forced herself to sit upright.

"You look like you could use some help," he insisted.

"I'll be all right if you just leave me alone a minute," Karen retorted. She was aware that his gaze followed her every movement as she lifted herself to the seat. Leaning back against the seat, she closed her eyes, willing the dizziness to pass.

"Do you feel faint?" she heard him ask, and she shook her head.

"I'll be okay." She forced the words out through dry lips.

There was a rustling noise, and then she felt him wrap something around her shoulders. Her eyes fluttered open, and she saw that it was his leather jacket. "That's not necessary," she managed to whisper.

"Take it easy." His hands were gentle but firm as he pulled the jacket closer around her. "Don't try to talk. Just rest a minute." He sounded as if he would take no argument, as if he was used to giving orders and having them obeyed.

She wanted to protest but couldn't muster the energy for it. She closed her eyes again. His footsteps receded and a moment later she heard him yell, "Conductor!" and then a muffled "Damn," before he turned back to her. "There's no one in sight," he said, then asked again, "Who did this to you?"

"I don't know."

"Why would anyone want to hurt you? Are you in some kind of trouble?"

"Maybe he wanted to rob me. I can't think of any other reason." Karen opened her eyes and looked around for her jacket, relieved when she saw that it was still on the seat where she'd left it earlier. She reached out and dug in the pocket. Yes, her wallet was still there. With shaking fingers she pulled it out and examined the contents. Passport. Cash. Credit cards. Traveler's checks. Robbery had not been the motive.

The man was watching her closely. His dark gaze met hers as she looked up. "Everything there?"

"Yes." Karen's lips barely moved.

"Did you see the man?"

"No." Karen shook her head and then winced. The slightest movement made her throat muscles tighten in a spasm of pain. "The lights flickered and went out. I heard the door open at the end of the corridor and I thought it was Irene, the lady who was sharing my compartment."

"But it wasn't her?"

"It was a man."

"You sound pretty sure of that."

"A woman couldn't have done this to me. Besides, I could just tell it was a man. He was wearing a jacket..." Instinctively her gaze flickered to the sleeve of the jacket she was now wearing. "It was a wool jacket," she said slowly, "some sort of nubby tweed, I'm fairly certain. It smelled like dry-cleaning fluid."

He hadn't missed her furtive glance at his jacket. Some of the warmth disappeared from his gaze, and she was fairly certain that he resented her suspicion. But he didn't comment on it. She recognized that hard set to his mouth she had noticed earlier. His features were lean and slightly tough. Whoever he was, this man wasn't someone to be trifled with.

Squirming with discomfort under his intense scrutiny, Karen was suddenly struck by how odd this conversation was. Why was a total stranger so interested?

"You're American," she stated abruptly.

"Yes." He nodded impatiently. "And you?"

"From Virginia." Karen paused, then added, "I thought you might be Italian when I saw you earlier."

"Italian?" The hazel eyes grew softer, registering his amusement.

"Your shoes," Karen said crisply, looking down at them.

Now his gaze was openly questioning. "What's wrong with my shoes?"

"Nothing's wrong with them. It's just that they're Italian." When his mouth twitched at the corners, she said crossly, "Never mind. It's not important."

"I'm flattered to know that you were inspecting my shoes so closely. Should I take that as a sign of interest?"

Karen regarded him coolly. "Take it any way you want." She fought back an urge to say something hateful. If this man thought she was interested in flirting with him, he was sadly mistaken. Right now, the only thing on her mind was the fact that someone had just tried to kill her. She put a hand up to her throat to massage the taut muscles and winced.

He noticed her movements, his expression becoming serious. "How are you feeling?"

"Terrible." Karen reached for her tote bag. Pulling out a compact, she flipped it open and studied herself in the tiny mirror. Four red splotches were spaced along the left side of her throat and on the right side, just below her jawline, a bruise had already started to form.

"Someone definitely had a hand around your throat." He spoke decisively. "From the spread of those marks, I'd be inclined to agree that it was a man. Whoever it was, was no amateur."

"He meant to kill me. I'm sure of it." Karen lowered the mirror.

"He wanted you to think that."

"What do you mean?" Karen felt a twinge of alarm. He spoke as if he knew something she didn't.

He shifted until he was kneeling on the floor in front of her. Taking the mirror from her hand, he held it up so she could see her throat again. "See this mark?" His forefinger brushed against her skin, outlining the mark.

She looked in the mirror, but instead of her throat, she saw his hand reflected. Nicely shaped, tanned, with tapering fingers unadorned with rings, it was an intensely masculine hand. Strong, too. Without wanting to, Karen found herself mentally measuring its spread against the marks on her throat.

As if he had read her thoughts, he spread his fingers, letting his whole hand rest against her throat. "I didn't do this, you know," he said quietly.

Karen found her voice at last. "And you don't think that someone actually meant to kill me?"

"If he'd wanted to kill you, he would have. Instantly, silently, with no mistakes. A quick application of force here—" he gently placed his thumb over one of the marks on the left side of her throat "—you would have been dead within seconds. It's probable that he merely wanted you to black out, so he put pressure on these two arteries to stop the blood to your brain. If he'd wanted you dead, he'd have used a locking stranglehold and snapped your neck at the same time."

Karen fought back a swift surge of nausea. She'd been so close to death! "Perhaps he thought I was dead. I told you, I fell to the floor of the compartment. In the dark . . ."

"No." His denial was immediate, final. "If your attacker had wanted to kill you, you'd be dead."

"But why?" Karen shrugged helplessly.

"You aren't in any kind of trouble?" he demanded bluntly. "Gambling? An angry husband or lover?" He paused and then added, "Drugs?"

Karen sat up abruptly. "No!"

"Don't get so uptight," he responded softly. His eyes were cold and hard, belying his soothing tone. "Someone tried to attack you. And it's been my experience that people don't get mixed up with professional killers unless they're in some sort of trouble."

"Wait just a minute." Karen sat up straighter and glared at him. "What gives you the right to question me this way? Who are you?"

"My name is Donovan," he said quietly. "Luke Donovan. And I'm asking the questions because I want to help you."

"I can take care of myself, Mr. Donovan."

"Really?" He raised his eyebrows, looking as if he was about to say more. At that moment, the door at the end of the corridor whooshed open. The sound of light footsteps followed.

Irene stopped abruptly inside the doorway. Her gaze shifted rapidly from Karen to Luke, taking in every detail of the scene. When she spoke, her voice sounded harsh and faintly out of breath. "Karen, what's happened to you?"

THE STALLED TRAIN sat in lumbering silence along the curving steel tracks. Near the engine, lanterns flickered and men called orders back and forth as they struggled to cut through tangled branches and brush. In the distance, the foothills of the Northern Italian Alps loomed against the moon-shadowed skyline. A chill breeze whipped around the train, hissing beneath the shadowy cars and buffeting the man who stood waiting.

He pulled a heavy tweed jacket more closely about his thickset body. Gravel crunched underfoot as he shifted his weight impatiently, trying to ease the ache in his shin where the American woman had kicked him. A moment later, his face was lit in the eerie yellow light as he put a match to his pipe, drawing forcefully and inhaling the pungent, acrid smoke of a cheap Turkish tobacco.

Another man hurried along the tracks, keeping to the safety of the shadows. When he saw the man in the tweed jacket, he stopped abruptly and then moved slowly toward him.

"Giovanni." The name cut through the cold air like a knife. After he spoke, the man with the pipe took several more deep drags.

Giovanni waited silently, his tall, thin body hunched against the chill night air. He tried unsuccessfully to fade into the shadows, but the other man's relentless gaze followed him.

"You little fool."

The words were followed by a loud crack as a powerful fist impacted with Giovanni's face. Blood began to trickle from the thin, Italian man's nose and sweat broke out on his balding forehead. He cowered backward and raised his arm as if to fend off another blow. It didn't come.

"You have almost ruined everything." The heavyset man regarded him impassively. Taking another deep draw on his pipe, he exhaled an unpleasant cloud of smoke and looked down at his feet. A frown creased his face as he saw that a small hole had begun to wear on the toe of his right shoe. They were flimsy, made of an inferior black leather that never lasted long. As he looked at them, he made a note to pay a visit to the man in East Berlin who'd sold them to him.

Giovanni began to dab his nose with a grubby handkerchief. His rumpled jacket seemed to hang from his narrow, hunched shoulders. "It was not my fault," he said at last. His voice was low and apologetic, his words carefully enunciated in English but spoken with the musical phrasing of a native Italian. "The hotel clerk is to blame. How was I to know the American woman had left a forwarding address?" He flinched as the larger man stepped toward him.

The man in the tweed jacket was also speaking in a language foreign to his own. His English was heavily accented, but he had no trouble getting his meaning across. "I should kill you right now, you idiot." As he stared at Giovanni, his rage grew. It irritated him that they'd had to use this man. He was unreliable, a cocaine addict who followed orders for money only.

"I should have known better than to trust you with even so simple a mission, Giovanni. You were hired because I needed someone who could speak both Italian and English. But you couldn't do the job." Gravel crunched again as he paced beside the track.

"I watched the hotel as you instructed," Giovanni said hastily. "The blond American woman was the first person to ask about those other Americans. I followed her to the train station and I called you."

"And I had to fly to Milan immediately." Rage creased the heavyset man's face. "I had to come myself because you also told me the American woman was on her way to Nice. Don't you understand that if someone got near us now, the whole plan could fail?"

"But soon it won't matter." Giovanni spoke quickly, as if eager to change the subject from his own failings.

"Until the operation is completed, we must not let down our guard." The heavyset man smacked his fist into his palm and Giovanni flinched, stepping backward. "I will not tolerate any more mistakes."

"You said you would take care of the blond woman." Giovanni attempted to change the subject again.

The heavyset man regarded him contemptuously. "You will be sorry that I have had to come here tonight. I have given the American woman a reason to reconsider her trip to France. I trust that she will decide to go home. But if she persists..." He let his words trail off, but the unspoken threat was clear.

"I will keep an eye on her." Giovanni straightened his shoulders in an attempt to reaffirm his competence.

"Report her every move to me. And don't make another mistake. Next time I will not be so patient." He tamped out his pipe against the side of the train and then strode off into the shadows, clambering aboard the train when he reached the last car.

IRENE WAS PATENTLY SHOCKED by the story of Karen's ordeal. While Karen filled her in on the details, Luke went to get his bag from his compartment. "I'm headed for Nice. If you don't mind, I'll move up here to sit. I don't want to leave you alone." Before he left, he paused at the door. "By the way, you haven't told me your name."

"Karen St. Clair." He repeated her name after she'd introduced herself. "I like that." Before she could respond to that cryptic comment, he was gone.

He returned moments later and stowed an expensive-looking leather bag on the rack above Karen's head. Irene waited until he was seated and then grabbed her straw bag, riffling through its contents. A moment later, she offered Karen a small plastic tumbler filled with clear liquid.

Karen took a quick gulp, expecting mineral water and swallowing a mouthful of gin instead. She coughed as it burned a fiery path down her raw throat. "My God, Irene. What haven't you got in that bag?"

Irene didn't seem to hear her. Since her return, she'd seemed distracted, but Karen supposed she was upset by what had happened. "We'll need to report this to the authorities. But the conductors are all up in the front of the train, trying to clear that brush from the tracks." Looking over at Karen, she explained. "That's what your word meant. You know, *albero* or whatever it was. A tree. Actually there was a fall of brush across the tracks and the train couldn't stop in time. When we ran over the brush, it tangled beneath the train and forced us to halt.''

"Did you find out where we are?"

"Apparently we're quite near the border," Irene answered. "We should be on our way again any moment now." Irene paused. "I feel awful that I left you alone. It's just that I didn't think anything would happen...."

"Of course you didn't," Karen said briskly. "If you had been here, I doubt you could have done anything to prevent this. Why don't you check your bags, just to make sure nothing is missing."

Luke helped Irene retrieve her suitcase from the upper rack. After a quick check, Irene announced, "Nothing's been touched."

"Whoever it was, he wasn't much of a robber." Karen attempted a laugh but stopped as pain shot through her bruised muscles.

"I'm going to find that conductor." Luke's sharp gaze missed nothing. His eyes darkened broodingly as he studied the bruises on Karen's neck. "I'd like to get my hands on the bastard who did this to you." His hand rested briefly on her hair, an oddly gentle touch that eloquently expressed his helpless anger. Then he strode out of the compartment.

Karen leaned her head back against the seat. Her body felt numbed with shock and fatigue. Unwillingly she began to mentally go back over the events of the evening. At the back of her mind, a memory nagged. A closed compartment door. A muffled, strangely disquieting conversation. "She suspects something," a man had said. "We'll soon be rid of her." Was it merely coincidence that only minutes after she'd overheard that conversation, someone had tried to kill her?

The thought was at once ridiculous and chilling. Why would anyone want to harm her? And if indeed those men had been talking about her, what did she suspect? Was all this somehow tied to Diane's abrupt departure from Rome? If so, she couldn't afford to waste a minute getting to Nice.

The train suddenly rumbled to life beneath them. Karen's eyes flew open.

"We should be at the border soon," Irene commented. "I hope your Mr. Donovan has found a conductor."

They traveled for eight or nine minutes before the train slowed to a halt again, this time on the crowded tangle of tracks that marked the border crossing into France. From outside the train came the faint glow of a spotlight. Through the window, Karen glimpsed the outline of another train, standing silent and empty on the adjacent track.

Noise in the corridor outside heralded Luke's return. Two men accompanied him. One of them was an older man, slightly worn looking, his face lined and tired in the uncompromising glare of the compartment's lone light. His gray uniform identified him as a conductor. Karen recognized him as the man she'd questioned earlier when the train stopped.

"I've done my best to explain what happened to you." Luke stepped into the compartment. "He speaks English."

"This is terrible." The conductor bent over and examined Karen's throat. "We must arrange for a doctor at once."

"That's not necessary." Karen sat up straighter. "I'm fine. Just a little sore."

"We will call the police at once, *mademoiselle.* When they arrive, you may make a report of this. Meanwhile, if you will get out your passport, we'll take care of the border formalities."

The other man, who was apparently one of the border officials, stepped forward and examined her passport. Karen waited until he had finished before speaking. "I'm anxious to go on to Nice."

The conductor frowned. "Perhaps it would be easier if you left this train. We could arrange a place for you to stay until this matter is cleared up."

Karen's heart sank. After she'd spent two days traveling, the thought of a tiresome delay and a hassle with bureaucracy was more than she could bear. "You don't understand. I must continue on to Nice. I'm meeting a friend there, and I might miss her if I don't get there this morning."

"But the police..."

"Couldn't I make my report to the police once I get to Nice? I've already been delayed by this unexpected stop."

The man who had checked her passport interrupted at this point, arguing with the conductor briefly in French. At last the conductor addressed her. "When we arrive in Nice, I will arrange for you to speak to the proper authorities. But you must promise you will report this matter to the police."

"Of course." Karen felt a surge of relief.

"Very well. I will check on you during our transit to Nice. Once we get there, do not leave the station until I come for you."

"I understand." Karen put her passport away. The two officials checked Irene's and Luke's papers and then departed.

"Are you sure you shouldn't stay here and wait to make a report to the police?" Irene said abruptly. "I'd be happy to stay behind with you."

"I'd rather go on to Nice." Karen's determination expressed itself in the tension that marked her words. She glanced at Luke as she made the statement. His dark eyes were watchful, his gaze fixed on her. She stared back at him coolly, meeting the challenge in his eyes with a firm deliberation of her own. Whoever this man was, she had no intention of letting him interfere in her plans.

DESPITE THE PRESENCE of Luke and Irene, Karen still felt nervous. Every time she closed her eyes, she relived those moments of terror in the darkness. Again and again, she asked herself why it had happened. And more often than not, she found herself wondering whether it had any connection with Diane or that partially overheard conversation.

After a prolonged and futile attempt at relaxation, Karen gave up and half-opened her eyes, observing the other occupants of the compartment from beneath her eyelashes. Irene sat in the opposite corner, staring out the window. From this angle, her face appeared tired and tense.

Luke Donovan shared her own side of the compartment. He was seated nearest the door that led to the corridor. Karen had wedged herself back into the corner by the window, pointedly placing her tote bag on the seat between them.

Luke's eyes were wide open, staring through the doorway. He seemed tense, almost as if he was on alert, but his body was still, except for the steady rise and fall of his breathing.

Beneath them, the wheels of the train hummed steadily on the tracks. In the daytime, Karen knew, the view through the window beside her would be breathtaking. Now, all outside was darkness. Somewhere in that blackness the Mediterranean glimmered and reflected the rocky promontories, luxuriant green vegetation and scattered houses that perched on the cliffs overhanging it.

As the train rounded a curve, Karen caught a glimpse of a flickering light ahead. Before long, they were slowing down for their arrival in Menton. The view outside the window changed rapidly. They slid past worn stone buildings and a billboard or two. And, as they neared the station, the area outside took on the false brightness that always seemed to surround railroad stations at night. Harsh floodlights beat down on the tracks, and Karen could see where the gleaming rails began to branch off in several directions.

With a short burst of its whistle, the train drew to a halt beside the station. A few people stood about on the platform, bags beside them, waiting to board. *"Le train pour Nice arrive sur la voie numéro deux,"* the stationmaster bellowed as the train came to a complete stop. Immediately there was a flurry of activity as passengers hurried to clamber aboard.

"Irene." Karen reached across and touched the other woman's arm. Irene looked at her distractedly, as if her thoughts had been on something else. "We're in Menton," Karen explained.

For a second Irene looked flustered. She reached for her purse and stood up. Immediately Luke was on his feet. "Here, let me," he offered, grasping her suitcase and hauling it down from the overhead rack. Irene collected her straw bag. "How long before the train will pull out?" she asked.

"Not long, I would imagine," Karen told her.

"Oh, dear, and I'd hoped to have a few more minutes to chat with you. I'm worried about you, Karen. Perhaps you should get off here in Menton with me. I could help you make that report to the police."

"It's kind of you to be concerned," Karen said. "But I really must go on to Nice. Diane is there, and now I'm obliged to the conductor to report to the police there."

Irene turned and considered her seriously. "I'd feel better if you promised to see a doctor when you get there."

"It's really not necessary."

Luke was listening to this conversation, his eyes dark and unsmiling. "I'll keep an eye on Karen. Don't worry."

Karen glared at him, not sure which of them he sought to reassure with this promise, but she could read nothing in his bland expression. Unlike Karen, Irene seemed grateful for his offer. "Thank you, Mr. Donovan. I'm going to hold you personally responsible for seeing that nothing happens to Karen between here and Nice."

"I promise to take good care of her," Luke said solemnly.

Karen was reaching the limits of her patience. These two were really no more than perfect strangers and yet they were discussing her as if she were somehow their responsibility. "You'd better hurry, Irene," she urged. "You don't want to miss your stop."

"I'll help you carry your bags to the platform," Luke offered.

Irene hesitated. "I'd rather you didn't leave Karen alone."

"That's ridiculous," Karen said firmly. "It's quite public here and the station is well lit. Besides, I hear other passengers out in the corridor now. I'm perfectly safe."

Irene was surprisingly brisk about her farewell, and soon Luke was following her out into the corridor. Karen stood up after they'd left, eager to stretch her cramped muscles. The ache in her throat had subsided to a bearable level, and her voice was starting to return to normal, but her stomach still felt queasy. A headache pounded at her temples, and for a moment after she stood up, she swayed dizzily.

Luke's jacket was still draped around her shoulders. She slipped it off, smoothing the soft leather with her fingers. It had been nice of him to offer it. She turned it over and glanced at the label. It bore the name of a New York designer, a well-known label that was available internationally. Nothing there to reveal anything about him.

Folding it carefully to avoid crushing the leather, she laid the jacket on one of the seats. Still unsteady on her feet, she made her way over to stand in the doorway of the compartment. Through the window on the opposite side of the corridor, she caught a better view of the platform. A motorized cart went past, heaped high with suitcases. Farther down the platform, a young girl and her boyfriend were wrapped in a passionate farewell clinch. She spotted Irene emerging from the train, followed by Luke. He set her suitcase down on the platform and they talked for a moment, Irene gesturing back toward the train. Then Irene grasped her suitcase, hitched her straw bag over the other arm with surprising strength and started toward the exit.

Luke looked up and down the platform before heading over to a cart where a young attendant was doing a brisk business selling rolls and coffee. He reached inside his jacket and pulled out a wallet, extracting a couple of bills and handing them to the boy. In a matter of moments, he had collected his change, tucked two rolls under his elbow and grasped two steaming cups of coffee, and was heading back to the train. Karen felt a quick surge of gratitude. Whatever else Luke Donovan might be, he certainly was thoughtful.

She was about to return to her seat when she caught a glimpse of Irene in the crowd on the platform. The older woman had apparently collided with a man and the two of them were in the process of collecting her scattered bags. As Karen watched, they appeared to be engaged in conversation, their faces unusually serious.

Irene seemed to be doing most of the talking. Occasionally she gestured toward the train, the man beside her nodding and listening intently. He was of medium height, probably in his mid-forties. His face was weathered from too much sun, with deep creases at the corners of his eyes and two slashing grooves on either side of his mouth. His dark blue trousers, slightly oversized and drawn in tightly at the waist, were topped by a gray cotton pullover. A pencil-thin mustache lined his upper lip and his coarse dark-brown hair looked as if it needed a trim.

While Irene talked to him, he attempted to wedge her bottle of mineral water back into the straw bag. At last he gave up and handed the bottle and the bag to Irene. Karen wondered what on earth they were finding to talk about for so long. And how were they bridging the language barrier? That man looked French.

Luke's return interrupted her thoughts. She shifted her gaze away from Irene to smile at him. "Is that coffee I smell?"

*"Oui, mademoiselle,"* he said with a flourish. *"Café à ton plaisir."*

Karen winced at his pronunciation. "Where did you learn your French?"

"High school," he said blithely. "Think I'll pass for a native?"

"A native American, perhaps," she replied dryly. Her earlier suspicions of Luke were dispelled by his cheerful friendliness. It seemed almost impossible that she had suspected him of being connected somehow with her ruthless assailant.

He stopped and regarded her carefully, a smile playing in his eyes. "Are you always so sweet this early in the morning? And to the poor guy who's bringing you breakfast?"

"I haven't noticed men standing around waiting to bring me breakfast at this hour."

"And no wonder," he retorted. "If this is all the thanks they'd get."

"I'm sorry," she said quickly. "And thanks for the coffee. It smells heavenly."

She backed away from the door, allowing Luke to move into the compartment. "Did you see that man talking to Irene?" she asked as they sat down.

"What man?"

"Out there on the platform. It looked like they'd collided with each other. Her bags were scattered on the ground. But they sure did seem to have a lot to say to each other."

Luke stood up and went over to look out at the platform. "She's not out there now," he said after a moment.

*"En voiture, s'il vous plaît!"* The loud call from outside the train heralded their departure.

"Better sit down," Karen urged Luke. "They're calling for us to get under way."

Luke offered her a thin, crusty roll after he sat down. "No, thanks," Karen said. "I doubt I could swallow it. But the coffee is wonderful."

"How's the throat?"

"Better," Karen replied, and then as he continued to look at her, she smiled slightly. "Well, not quite as bad as it was."

"I'm inclined to agree with Irene that you should see a doctor. How about if I help you find one when we get to Nice?"

"I don't think that's necessary. Anyway, you probably already have plans of your own." She paused, and then asked a question in what she hoped was a casual tone of voice. "Why are you going to Nice, anyway? Vacation?"

He took a long swallow of his coffee and then tossed the empty cup into the trash receptacle beneath the window. When he spoke, he appeared to be choosing his words carefully. "Business, of sorts."

"What sort of business are you in?" Karen asked.

Luke's eyes narrowed and he watched her as he spoke. "I'm a private investigator," he said. "I had business in Zurich earlier this week. Now I'm taking a few days off…" He paused and then added, "To look up an old friend."

Karen sat silently, absorbing this information about Luke Donovan. A private investigator. That explained the way he'd questioned her so professionally earlier in the evening. "What do you investigate?" she asked at last.

Luke looked momentarily uncomfortable. "Nothing exciting, I can assure you," he replied. "My company handles a lot of routine insurance investigations."

"Your company?"

"I have my own small operation in the D.C. area." He pulled out his wallet and extracted an ivory-colored business card, handing it to her.

She ran her fingers over the engraved letters, feeling the smooth, expensive finish of the card stock. Despite his casual air, there was nothing the least bit second-rate about Luke Donovan. His clothes, his manner, his good looks and now this very discreet but unmistakably elegant card. "Donovan Investigations," she murmured. "So you're used to being involved in all sorts of mystery and intrigue." She looked up and gave him a slight smile.

"Not quite. My work is usually very routine. Background investigations for potential investors and employers. Internal fraud in business or industry. Executive protection. The occasional criminal investigation for an attorney. And, as I've said, a lot of very boring insurance cases."

"Not like Magnum, P.I., then?"

He laughed. "Unfortunately, no. Yours is the most exciting case I've encountered in quite a while. Beautiful blonde attacked on a train at midnight near the Franco-Italian border. I can't wait to find out more."

The smile died on Karen's lips and when she spoke, her voice was considerably cooler. "I'm afraid there isn't any more. Certainly not enough to make a case." She wasn't sure she liked being referred to as a beautiful blonde. It reminded her of lurid paperback covers and the chauvinism they implied. His enthusiasm about her "case," as he put it, was a bit off-putting in that light and his curiosity unwelcome. She had no intention of confiding in him.

"I hope you'll let me decide that for myself," Luke replied, apparently unperturbed by her coolness. "Meanwhile, I intend to keep an eye on you. After all, I've given

Irene my solemn promise. And I always keep my promises."

"Always?" Karen raised her eyebrows.

"Nearly always," he amended with a quick grin. Despite her annoyance, she found herself smiling back at him. His unabashedness pleased her. She liked a man who wasn't afraid to laugh at himself a little.

"And what about you, Karen? What sort of a job do you have back in Virginia?"

"I'm a college professor," she said. "Art history. At Hamilton College."

He sat up straighter. "A college professor." He stared at her, obviously dismayed. "No, that can't be."

"What's wrong with my being a college professor?"

"Well, nothing, except you don't fit the image."

"I don't?"

"You don't look like a college professor."

"And how should a college professor look?" Karen asked with just a touch of humor.

"I don't know. Slightly dessicated, wan, pale, wearing glasses or something. I hadn't pictured you as being a college professor."

"I didn't realize you'd been picturing me at all," Karen murmured demurely. Her eyes narrowed, but she kept her tone light. "Should I take this as a sign of interest?"

Luke regarded her from beneath half-closed lids. He smiled slowly. "I don't think I'll answer that question."

A movement outside the compartment caught Karen's eye. She shifted her gaze away from Luke, her eyes widening as she saw that someone was standing in the corridor and staring in at them. It was the man she had seen talking to Irene.

For a moment their gazes locked. His eyes, dark and impassive, inspected first her and then Luke. Karen's breath caught in her throat.

After a moment, he moved on. She could hear his footsteps receding down the corridor. Glancing over at Luke, she saw that he was looking out the window. "Luke," she whispered urgently.

He seemed confused by her change of tone. "Is something wrong?"

She forgot about her resolution not to confide in him. "That man. The one I saw talking to Irene. Did you see him come by the compartment just now?"

"No." Luke looked at her oddly, as if not quite sure what to make of her.

Karen felt foolish suddenly. Why was she reading so much into such a simple incident? The man had probably been looking for a seat and, after the way she'd glared at him, he'd most likely moved on to find more congenial surroundings. "It's nothing," she said quickly. "Nothing to worry about."

DESPITE THE EARLY HOUR, the railway station in Menton was bustling with arriving and departing passengers. Outside a telephone booth, a man waited impatiently for his turn to use the public phone. There was a woman inside the booth, her blue wool cardigan making a bright splash of color.

Irene Miller wished she had removed the sweater before placing her call. The booth was hot and airless. Beads of perspiration glistened on her face, and she had to switch the receiver from one hand to the other in order to wipe her sweaty palm on the skirt of her dress.

"She's on her way to Nice." Irene made her report as rapidly as she could. "I've put Benoit on her trail. Your man pointed her out to me in Rome. He followed her from the Hotel Gran Duca to the train station. I kept an eye on her until we reached Milan and then managed to get a seat in her compartment."

"Wasn't there anything you could do to stop her?" The man on the other end of the line sounded impatient. "If she gets too close now, she could blow the whole operation."

"I did what you told me to." Irene's voice carried a sharp protest. "If you want her stopped, you'll have to use Benoit. There's a man with her now. She met him on the train. Luke Donovan is his name."

"Tall, dark-haired. Wearing a leather jacket?"

"Yes." Irene pressed the phone closer against her mouth and turned her back on a man who was motioning that he needed to use the phone. "How did you know?"

There was a long sigh on the other end of the phone. "He was at the Hotel Gran Duca, too. Asking a lot of questions."

"They'll have to be stopped." Irene wiped her forehead with the back of her hand.

"I know." When the man spoke again, his voice sounded hard and grim. "We can't afford to let them get close now. Too much is at stake. I'll contact Benoit when he reaches Nice."

## Chapter Three

It was nearly dawn when they pulled into Nice. As the train rumbled into the central railway station, Karen caught glimpses of the city through the window. Nice never failed to impress her with its beauty. Behind the city rose a backdrop of hills and mountains, covered with greening vegetation this time of year. In front was the lovely Baie des Anges, glistening with the reflected rays of the rising sun.

As the train neared the center of the city, the streets grew narrower, crowded with a jumble of old and new buildings. Near the station, the railroad tracks turned into a veritable maze of blackened rails and flashing signals that directed the flow of trains in and out of the city.

Karen felt she ought to make at least some attempt to repair her appearance. She smoothed her hair with her hands, making a face as she realized her nose was oily and her skin felt sticky. She found her linen jacket and pulled it on, doing her best to make herself look less disreputable. A bright red cotton scarf from her tote bag served to cover the worst of her bruises.

When she looked up, she found Luke watching her. "How are you feeling?"

"I'll feel much better when I've had a shower and some sleep."

"Where are you meeting your friend?"

"At her hotel," Karen said briefly. "Look, you really don't have to worry about me. I'll be fine. The conductor has promised to direct me to the proper police station and I won't have any trouble finding Diane's hotel."

"What hotel is she staying at?"

Faced with his direct question, Karen felt it would be rude to refuse to answer. Anyway, what harm could it do to tell him where Diane was staying?

"The Hotel Azur. On the Promenade des Anglais."

Luke's eyes widened with amazement. He looked surprised and then pleased. Yet Karen couldn't help noticing that his surprise seemed a little strained. "That's amazing. I'm going to the same hotel myself. That's where my friend is supposed to be staying."

Karen regarded him with frank suspicion. "Isn't that a coincidence?" she said acidly.

"A pleasant one, I hope."

Karen didn't reply. Inside, she was seething with unanswered questions. She wished now that she hadn't told him the name of Diane's hotel. She was almost positive that he was lying about that being his real destination. Yet she could hardly accuse him of that, could she?

She got to her feet briskly. Brushing the wrinkles in her jumpsuit, she avoided looking directly at Luke. "I'll probably see you there, then. Thanks for the coffee and all your help."

"Is that all the luggage you have?" He nodded toward her tote bag as he stood up, making the small compartment seem crowded. He didn't seem any the worse for having spent the night sitting up on a train. The rough shadow on his jawline, indicating that he needed a shave, gave him a slightly rakish look. Some men deliberately cultivated that look, she knew. But she did not think he was one of them.

"Thanks, again, for your help." She reached for her tote bag and slung the strap over her shoulder.

Luke reached over and put his finger under her jaw, tipping her head back. "Those bruises must hurt like hell."

"They're not too bad." She moved away from his touch. "I'd better look for that conductor." She was near the door when something caught her eye. A slip of paper lay on the floor. Karen reached down and picked it up. "Did you lose something?" she asked absently, unfolding the paper.

"What is it, Karen? . . . Karen?" Luke repeated her name twice before she recovered herself sufficiently to reply.

"This is odd," she murmured.

Luke stepped closer and looked over her shoulder. "What is it?"

"A hotel receipt." Karen struggled to absorb the implications of this new information. "According to this, Irene spent the night before last at a hotel in Rome. But she told me that she had come from Venice."

"Are you sure you didn't misunderstand? Anyway, what does it matter where Irene spent the night?"

"Why would she lie?" Karen read the information on the paper one more time and then shoved it into her tote bag. "I'm sure she told me she came from Venice."

"Don't worry about it." Luke was clearly puzzled by her fascination with the receipt. "You've got more important things to worry about now, like finding that conductor." Karen said nothing more as she allowed Luke to lead her off the train.

There was the usual rush to disembark that Karen had come to expect of European trains. Somehow, the corridors were never quite wide enough once they filled with suitcases and yawning passengers. Their car seemed to have picked up a few more passengers since entering France. This morning, the conversation was mainly in French, with only a few snatches of Italian and the occasional sounds of English. Karen found herself listening for the voice she'd overheard the night before, but heard nothing that resembled it.

The station itself was bustling with activity, despite the early hour. As she stepped down onto the platform, the ground shook with the arrival of another train on the next track. Karen's nostrils filled with the peculiarly distinctive odor of a rail station, the pungent, slightly burning odor of creosote.

She waited as Luke swung down beside her. It would be rude to simply walk off and leave him since he was making it clear that he intended to stick with her. Now that she had finally arrived in Nice, she was eager to find Diane's hotel. But she had promised the conductor that she would allow him to escort her to the police.

Men and women scurried past her, most of them headed toward the train on the next platform. Near the end of the train, she spotted a refreshment cart, surrounded by a knot of impatient customers. A pile of oranges on the cart was rapidly disappearing as the busy attendant pushed them through a juicer and dispensed small cups of thick, slightly reddish juice. From past visits, she knew the juice would be strong and refreshing and she longed for a cup to soothe her parched throat.

Luke was growing impatient beside her. "Do you think that fellow's forgotten you?" He raked his glance over the last of the passengers who were leaving the train behind them.

Karen spotted the conductor before Luke did. "There he is now." She pushed her way toward the man who was hurrying along the platform.

"*Mademoiselle*, I was afraid you had left already." He cupped a hand under her elbow and led her toward the head of the platform. "We will go to the security office." At that moment he noticed Luke walking beside her.

"You are accompanying us, *monsieur*?" He seemed confused. "But I thought you were not traveling with Mademoiselle St. Clair."

"He isn't," Karen said quickly. She addressed her next remark to Luke. "It's really not necessary for you to come with me. I'm sure this gentleman will take good care of me."

"But I insist," Luke said decisively. "I've all the time in the world."

The conductor listened to this exchange looking from one to the other, but said nothing. It was clear he was intrigued. "If you don't mind," he inserted apologetically, "I must hurry. If you could come with me now..."

Karen wasted no more time on Luke. It seemed pointless to argue with him. For whatever reason, he was obviously determined to accompany her, and she was too tired to resist.

They were nearly at the end of the platform, just drawing even with the juice cart, when Karen had a feeling that they were being watched. She let her gaze roam the area. Near the center of the broad walkway that ran perpendicular to the tracks was a large board that listed the schedules for incoming and outgoing trains. Beside the board stood the man Karen had spotted talking to Irene when they stopped in Menton. It was clear to Karen that he was watching them. His stare was too fixed, his pose too studiously casual, for there to be any other explanation. Suppressing a shiver of apprehension, she attempted to convince herself without success that she was merely imagining things.

The conductor led them to a small cluttered office inside the terminal proper. Seated behind the room's lone desk, a man in uniform looked up when they entered. A rapid conversation ensued between the two railroad officials, and after a moment, Karen gave up trying to follow it. At last the conductor turned back to her. "This man says you must go to the police station to make your report. He will call ahead to make a brief accounting of what has happened. But there will be paperwork, you understand. You must go there in person.''

"Can't I just make my report here?" Karen protested wearily. "It seems so pointless, anyway. The attack happened hours ago.''

"Please, Mademoiselle St. Clair. It won't take too much of your time.''

The other man was busy writing something on a piece of scratch paper. He handed it to the conductor, who passed it over to Karen. "This is the address. You must go to the Commissariat Central Foch.'' He gestured to the paper and Karen took it, reading the address.

"One Avenue Maréchal Foch.'' She looked up from the paper. "Must I go there immediately?''

"You must go there sometime today. When you arrive, please ask for Inspector Bouvier. He will take down your report.''

As soon as they were out of the office, Luke grasped her arm. "Let's grab a cab and find that hotel,'' he suggested.

Karen stopped abruptly and turned to look at him. "I think you're taking this promise of yours to Irene a bit too far. I'm a big girl, you know. I can take care of myself very well, thank you.''

Luke assumed an air of injured innocence. "And were you taking care of yourself when that man attacked you on the train?''

"I'm not dead,'' Karen retorted. "And I've still got my wallet. I'm inclined to think I've made rather too much of the whole thing. After I've given my report to Inspector Bouvier, I intend to put the whole thing out of my mind.''

"That might be a little harder than you think,'' Luke replied. "Those bruises are going to hang around for a while.''

"It's hardly your problem, is it?" Karen asked. "Thank you very much for all your help. Now you're free to find your friend and get on with your vacation."

"Since our friends are staying at the same hotel, wouldn't it make sense for us to share a cab?" Luke asked.

Karen was in no mood to be sensible or logical. She was exhausted, grimy and rapidly developing a killer headache. In the past twenty-four hours she'd had no sleep and someone had tried to choke her to death. No matter how handsome or attractive or compassionate Luke Donovan might be, she didn't have time for him. "You don't seem to be getting the message. I'm not in the mood for a casual pickup and you're wasting your time following me about. Look around, there are plenty of beautiful French girls I'm sure would be more than willing to succumb to your obvious charm."

Luke's smile didn't slip, but she noticed that his hazel eyes had darkened considerably. "You admit I have charm, then?" he asked lightly.

Karen carefully readjusted the strap of her shoulder tote. "Goodbye, Mr. Donovan. I'll probably see you around if we're both staying at the same hotel. But I would prefer to make my way there alone." She turned away and walked toward the exit of the terminal building, not turning to see whether he followed.

LUKE WATCHED until Karen had exited through the terminal's busy front doors. Knowing what she had been through in the past few hours, he had to admire her spirit. She had held her head high and looked neither left nor right, displaying no sign of the nervousness that might have been expected in a woman who had only recently come close to being killed. Still, he hadn't missed the signs of strain and tension on her face that morning. He'd had to tread carefully, though. She wasn't a woman who invited expressions of sympathy or concern.

His own interest in her had only been heightened by the past few hours in her company. Up close, she was even prettier than he'd first thought. More than once he'd been tempted to reach out and draw her into his arms. When her smoky, gray-green eyes met his, their warm intensity made him forget everything else. He'd given in once to the urge to touch that cloud of blond hair. It had felt as soft and silky as he thought it would, and his imagination had gone into overdrive, picturing that hair spread on a pillow, those eyes looking up at him....

Luke brought himself back to the present abruptly. His lips lifted in a smile as he laughed inwardly at himself. Anyone would think he'd never felt this way before, and maybe that was true. Karen St. Clair got to him on a different level than any woman had in the past. He wanted to know everything about her.

Instinct prompted him to keep a close eye on her. Every time he thought of those bruises on her throat, he had to quell the rage that boiled up in him.

He abhorred the idea of physical violence against women. It might be old-fashioned, but he liked to think that women should be protected from that side of life. That attitude could be blamed on his upbringing, he supposed. With three younger sisters, he'd spent his earlier years acting the part of an overprotective big brother.

Now it seemed that he had a familiar job to do. Whether she wanted it or not, Karen St. Clair had just enlisted the services of a private investigator.

OUTSIDE THE STATION, Karen made her way to the taxi stand, joining the line of people who were there ahead of her. It wasn't until she reached the head of the line that she remembered she hadn't yet changed any currency. When the cab driver reached over to open the passenger door, she didn't get in. "American dollars?" she asked, a sinking feeling in the pit of her stomach when he shook his head no. "Lira?" she asked, extracting the last of her Italian money from her wallet and holding it out. *"Francs, mademoiselle."* He was adamant.

Muttering with frustration, Karen stepped away from the cab and went back into the terminal building. Will I ever get to that damned hotel, she thought with exasperation. Then she saw that the booth labeled Bureau de Change was tightly closed.

"Having trouble?" a voice murmured smoothly from behind her. She turned reluctantly to face Luke. "No francs?" His voice oozed sympathy. "You could always try one of the hotels around the station. Still, they're usually opposed to changing money for people who aren't registered as guests."

Karen stubbornly refused to answer. "My offer to share a cab is still open," Luke said quietly. "That is, if you don't find my charm too terribly offensive."

Unwillingly Karen started to smile. "I guess I was rude," she said. "If that offer is still open, I'd be very grateful."

Luke grinned with the merest hint of smugness before leading her back out to the cab stand. It wasn't until they were ensconced in the back of a cab and had asked to be taken to the Hotel Azur that he spoke again. "Have you been to this hotel before?"

"I've never even heard of it," Karen admitted. "But that's where Diane is supposed to be staying. I'd hoped to catch up with her in Rome, but she wasn't at her hotel there. They gave me the name of this hotel."

"I've never heard of it, either," Luke said. "But then, this is only my second trip to Nice. The last time I was here, I stayed at a youth hostel."

Karen glanced over at him. She couldn't picture the assured, well-dressed man beside her roughing it at a youth hostel. He'd said he was a detective. Her knowledge of detectives was limited to what she'd gleaned from novels, movies and television shows. The untarnished, unfearing romantic hero going down fanciful mean streets. Well, Luke Donovan certainly looked the part.

She knew it wasn't entirely fair, but she mistrusted overly handsome men. Not that she'd had many opportunities to exercise that mistrust. But, whether it was a rationalization or not, she'd always assumed that they would be arrogant and self-centered, unsuited to her simple, well-ordered life. Well, her life was neither at the moment, and Luke had showed no signs of fitting the stereotype, so she'd just have to play it by ear.

With the arrival of morning, the city was starting to come to life. Their cab turned off the Avenue Thiers, making its way through Nice's maze of one-way streets toward the palm-lined Promenade des Anglais. Traffic moved steadily, but it was nowhere near as heavy as it would get later in the day.

Here and there, merchants were rolling up the heavy steel security doors that fronted their shops. Flower vendors were doing a brisk business, as were the corner grocers, with their stacks of glistening Jaffa oranges and tempting North African bananas. A moped buzzed up beside them as they paused at a stoplight and the boy who was riding it stared appreciatively at Karen. As the light turned green, he flashed her an audacious wink before roaring off ahead of them.

"It seems you're the one with all the charm this morning," Luke observed dryly.

"The Riviera does wonders for a woman's ego." Karen felt some of her tension subside as she warmed to the atmosphere that pervaded Nice. Sun and sea and friendly people were a potent combination. For a moment her mood

lightened and she forgot her worry about Diane and the
horrible events of the night before. More than likely, she
thought, Diane would be safe and happy at the hotel and
would be surprised to see her and they'd laugh together over
Karen's newfound penchant for being a mother hen.

They whizzed out onto the promenade and there was the
sea, a breathtaking hue this morning that reminded Karen
of the pure blue in Matisse's painting *Blue Nude*. Palms
waved overhead, bending in the fresh breeze that blew off
the water.

The cab cut across the promenade sharply as they neared
the eastern end, swerving to make a left down a side street.
The driver swung the car in a U-turn and headed back out
onto the main boulevard again, this time drawing to a stop
in front of a small hotel.

"Here we are," Karen murmured, seeing the name above
the front doors. It was a narrow, white stone building, with
two granite steps leading up to the main entrance. The hotel sported tall shuttered windows that led out onto wrought-
iron balconies on the upper two floors.

From the outside, it didn't appear to be as run-down as
the hotel in Rome. An elderly man was in the process of
unlocking the gate that fronted the hotel's tiny courtyard.
A few cars were parked at the side of the hotel, and Karen
wondered if they belonged to guests.

They got out of the cab, and Karen waited while Luke
paid the driver. She paid careful attention when the driver
named the price, determined to reimburse Luke as soon as
she could.

There was no one in the lobby when they entered. A small
desk faced the front door, and to the left of it was a tiny but
inviting television lounge. So far, it was definitely more reassuring than the hotel in Rome had been.

A woman, her hair swathed in a kerchief, poked her head
out of a door behind the desk and stared at them. She dis-

appeared, but a moment later, a man came out the same door. Short and stocky, he had a genial face with smooth, regular features. *"Bonjour."* He looked at them more closely. *"Parlez-vous français? Anglais?* I speak English *aussi."*

"I'm looking for a friend of mine." Karen walked over to the desk. "She's supposed to be staying here. Her name is Diane Garrett."

The man looked her over carefully and thoughtfully. "You are a relative?" he asked at last.

"No, not exactly. A good friend."

"She is expecting you?"

"Then she is here!" Karen hadn't realized how much she was counting on finding Diane until that very moment. She felt an intense surge of relief. This time her smile was genuine. "If you'll just tell her I'm here. My name is Karen St. Clair. I realize it's very early, but my train has just arrived. I'm sure Diane won't mind."

Again the man appeared to be considering something. When he spoke at last, it was cautiously. "Miss Garrett is not here. In fact, my wife and I have been a little worried about her."

Karen felt as if something had snatched her breath away, making it difficult to speak. When she forced the words from her constricted throat, her voice was strident with concern. "Worried? Why would you be worried? What's happened?"

"Nothing has happened," the hotel manager said soothingly. "I'm sure everything is all right. It's just that Miss Garrett left suddenly and hasn't yet returned."

"When did she leave?"

"She stayed only one night. The next morning, she received a phone call. I myself called her to the phone. A few minutes later, she left the hotel. We have not seen her since."

"She checked out?"

"That is what worried us. She didn't check out and she left her suitcase in her room."

"But surely you informed the police? Perhaps she was in an accident..." Karen's imagination clicked into overdrive.

The manager looked uncomfortable. "We did not want to involve the police."

"But didn't she meet some friends here? A man? A group of students?"

The man regarded her with obvious confusion. "There has been no such group here. Your friend was alone." He scratched his chin for a moment and then added, "She seemed to be very happy after her phone call. She told us she was going out for a while and might not be staying here any longer. When she didn't come back, we thought she had decided not to return." He shrugged. "We held the room for two more days and finally removed her suitcase. It was already packed, sitting ready inside the door."

"But didn't you make some effort to discover what had happened to her?"

"How could we?" The man was defensive now and becoming angry. "It was not our responsibility. Sometimes young women are apt to change their minds. They meet someone, they go to stay with friends." He gestured, as if the vagaries of young tourists had long since ceased to amaze him. "Besides, there was the matter of the bill. Perhaps she did not return to us because she did not want to pay the bill...."

"Diane would never do such a thing," Karen started to protest and then stopped. It would be a waste of time to stand here and defend Diane. "Do you still have the suitcase?" she asked.

"*Oui.*" The man nodded toward the office behind him.

"How much is Diane's bill?" she asked, deciding to remove at least one small obstacle to cooperation.

He named a modest sum.

"I'll pay it," Karen said. "And you can give me the suitcase. I'd like a room for myself for tonight, if you have one."

"But of course, *mademoiselle*," he said, now briskly friendly because Karen was offering to settle her friend's account. "I have a room on the next floor, the first, that faces the sea. It is not yet our busy season, so you are in luck. You may have the room right now."

Karen regarded him with a faintly cynical look. Although this hotel was relatively clean and respectable, it wasn't in the same league as the bigger hotels that lined the promenade. She would bet that they were never filled.

"I'll take it," she said. "Will you accept traveler's checks? Dollars?"

"*Certainement.*" He pointed to a hand-printed card on the counter. "Here is our exchange rate for the day. Do you wish to settle Miss Garrett's bill now?"

"Yes, and if possible, I'd like to change a few dollars above that to see me over until I can get to a bank."

"And you, *monsieur*?" The clerk was looking over Karen's shoulder at Luke, who had remained quiet during this exchange. Karen was aware that he had been listening intently. But then, what else could he have done? The entire lobby was within earshot.

"Are you and the young lady together?" the clerk asked discreetly.

"Unfortunately, no," Luke murmured with a sidelong glance at Karen. She glared at him fiercely. "But if you have another room, I'd like it."

Now what was he up to? Karen thought. He'd said he was coming to the hotel to meet someone, but now he was asking for a room and making no inquiries about his mysterious friend. If he'd really been planning all along to stay here, wouldn't he have a reservation?

The hotel clerk had produced a carefully written bill and was pushing it across the counter toward her. Karen paid him and waited as he counted out her change in francs. "I'd like Miss Garrett's suitcase sent up to my room as soon as possible," she said briskly.

"Of course, of course. Right away." He handed her a key. "The stairs are around the corner. We have no lift," he apologized. "But it is a short climb."

Karen moved aside to allow Luke to approach the desk. As he passed her, she held out a few francs. "For the taxi."

After a brief pause, he took the money. "If you don't mind, I'd like to go with you to the police station," he said.

Although Luke had spoken in a low voice, Karen noticed that the hotel clerk had perked up at the mention of the police. Now he was staring at them. Not wanting to argue in front of him, Karen made an unconvincing effort to demur. "It's not really necessary."

Luke grasped her hand and held it, his gaze compelling her to look at him. "Please."

"All right," she relented, pulling her hand away.

"Meet me here in the lobby. In an hour, say? Will that be long enough?"

"An hour," Karen agreed. She walked around the corner. As soon as she was out of sight of the front desk, she paused. Turnabout is fair play, she thought, and besides, she was determined to hear what Luke said to the hotel clerk.

"I can give you a room on the second floor," she heard the clerk say. "That is, the third level. Directly above Mademoiselle St. Clair's room."

"That would be fine," Luke replied. "Also, I'd like to ask you—"

At that moment, the woman in the kerchief came around the corner. She smiled and gestured toward the steps. "This way, yes, *mademoiselle*." She stopped, patiently waiting for Karen to go up the stairs ahead of her.

Karen forced a smile and began to climb the stairs.

LUKE PAUSED as he reached the first-floor landing. The door to Karen's room was tightly shut. For a moment he debated whether he should check to make sure she was okay. Better not, he decided. He had a feeling she was growing wary of his persistent presence.

The layout of Luke's floor was almost identical to the one below. His room was to the right of the staircase, directly above Karen's. He opened the door and tossed his bag inside. After the unprepossessing lobby downstairs, the room was a pleasant surprise. Although small, it was unexpectedly bright and clean. Sunlight streamed in through the slatted wooden shutters that covered the floor-to-ceiling window on the opposite wall. Luke crossed over and pushed open the shutters, discovering a compact balcony.

There was a round, wrought-iron table on the balcony, flanked by two chairs. He settled down in one of them, extending his legs in front of him and leaning back to rest his head on the wall behind him. Although this hotel was not up to the standard of the fashionable, classy ones that lined the other end of the promenade, he couldn't complain about the view. Before him stretched a glistening vista of limitless sea and sky.

Now that the sun was fully up, the air was rapidly warming. He shrugged out of his jacket and rolled up his sleeves, then glanced at his watch. He'd told Karen he'd meet her in an hour. Allowing for the time he'd wasted trying to get information out of the hotel clerk, that left him about thirty-five minutes to shower and change.

Right now, he needed time to think. He hadn't been surprised to find that Mark Turner wasn't staying at the hotel. When he'd heard that Karen's friend had left unexpectedly, he'd had a feeling he wasn't going to find Mark, either.

Unlike Diane's departure, Mark's seemed to have been routine and orderly. According to the clerk, he'd stayed at the hotel the night of May fifteenth, the day before Diane's arrival. He'd checked out the next day around noon, about the time the Garrett woman must have arrived. This time he hadn't left a forwarding address. So, at least temporarily, Luke was at a dead end.

If it hadn't been for Karen, Luke knew he would probably have given up his search about now. After all, checking up on Mark had been a mere whim, an excuse to spend a few extra days in Europe. He'd expected to touch base with Mark over a few drinks, spend a couple of days soaking up the sun and then head back to Washington. He hadn't seriously considered that Mark might be in trouble. He'd just been curious.

Now he was worried. That instinct he relied on to guide him was telling him something wasn't quite right. Luke tried to organize his thoughts and make sense out of the events so far. Was this Garrett woman somehow connected with Mark? Had he come to Europe to meet her? If so, why were they moving around like this? It seemed odd that Mark was always a day or so ahead of Diane and more than mere coincidence that they were following the same route.

There was also that attack on Karen on the train the night before to consider. As soon as he'd heard her story and examined those marks on her throat, he'd decided it had been no simple robbery attempt. Someone had wanted to frighten her, but why? To stop her search for Diane?

None of it made sense. But Luke knew he wasn't leaving until he found out what was going on. Not only for Mark's sake, but for Karen's. For now, he'd keep an eye on her and wait to see what fate had in store for the two of them. Perhaps there was something to this fate business, after all.

KAREN EYED THE BED in her room longingly. What she really wanted more than anything right this minute was a long nap. But that would have to wait until after she visited the police station.

In the cold light of day, she found it hard to credit the events of the night before. Those bleak, terror-filled moments of struggle in the dark had receded to the dim recesses of her mind. She supposed it was a protective reflex, the mind's way of dealing with anything too difficult to reconcile with reality.

So far, this whole trip was proving to be difficult to reconcile with any reality she knew. Ever since she'd left her father's spacious California home to go off to college, she'd lived an orderly, routine life. Her days had been carefully planned, her goals clearly set.

In college, she'd studied hard and managed to complete her degree in art history in three years. In what little spare time she'd had, she'd worked at developing her own modest artistic talent as a watercolorist. One of her instructors had encouraged her to quit her academic studies and devote all her time to her painting. But that had seemed too risky. Instead she'd opted for a safer, surer course and stayed on at university to obtain her master's degree.

After college, it had seemed natural to return to Virginia, the place where she'd lived until her mother died and she'd gone to live with her father and his new family. The teaching position at Hamilton College had fitted well with the smooth course she'd mapped out for her future.

Over the past few years, she'd felt a quiet satisfaction with the way things were going. She owned a town house and a nice car, she'd been promoted from instructor to assistant professor and in a few more years she'd acquire tenure. Her days were full, predictable and nonthreatening. As for her nights... well, if that area of her life wasn't quite so gratifying, she'd refused to admit it to herself.

For a while, she'd drifted into a relationship with one of her fellow faculty members. The decision to break if off had been hers. When he had started to talk about marriage, she'd realized she wanted more than the stale, comfortable but emotionally limited liaison he offered. Since then, she'd fought against a gradually increasing feeling of restlessness, even boredom.

In the past twenty-four hours she'd run through more emotions than she'd experienced in the previous twenty-four months. Now she needed time to pull herself together.

She inched open the heavy shutters, admitting the cool breeze off the Mediterranean. The room wasn't too bad. It was appealingly decorated, the pattern in the flower-sprigged wallpaper repeated in the drapes and the bedspread. A typical motif for mid-nineteenth-century painters, she thought, falling gratefully into her old habits of categorizing things.

The contents of her tote bag took only a second to sort. She hadn't brought many clothes with her, preferring to travel light. A few knit coordinates, lightweight cotton jeans, a plain ivory silk-blend dress, a red jacket and a pair of low-heeled pumps was the sum total of her packed wardrobe. Once empty, her tote bag had a clever design which enabled it to be put to use as a handbag.

The jumpsuit she was wearing would have to be cleaned and repaired, she realized. Perhaps the hotel could arrange it for her. Her linen jacket was badly wrinkled. She shook it out and hung it up. Next, she sorted quickly through her wallet. As she slipped her passport and traveler's checks back in the side pocket, a photograph fell out.

It was a snapshot of her and Diane, taken over a year ago. At the last minute she had tossed it in her wallet, perhaps as a subconscious response to a premonition that something was very wrong. The two of them posed a dramatic contrast. Whereas Karen was tall and fair, Diane was petite and her straight dark brown hair was cut at an angle around her face, with a soft fringe across her forehead. Karen studied the photo for a moment and, with a sigh, slipped it back into her wallet.

A knock sounded on the door as she was starting to undress. Hastily she refastened the buttons on her jumpsuit and then opened the door. A teenage boy stood in the corridor. He indicated the large canvas suitcase beside him and then pushed past her to deposit it in her room.

Diane's suitcase. From the size of it, Karen assumed Diane must have been planning a long stay in Europe. Or perhaps she had overpacked, the biggest mistake first-time travelers usually made.

Karen waited until the boy left, smiling his thanks for the sizable tip she had given him. As soon as the door closed behind him, she knelt beside the bag. The airline identification label was still stuck on the frame of the bag, the address written in Diane's tiny, angular handwriting.

Karen reached for the nearest catch and then let her hands fall to her sides. Should she open the bag? It seemed wrong, somehow. Normally Karen wasn't one to pry. She guarded her own privacy zealously and gave the same consideration to others. But under the circumstances, perhaps she owed it to Diane to look inside, in case the bag held some clue to her whereabouts.

Before her resolve weakened, she briskly reached for the catch. It was locked. Karen pushed it futilely, frustrated now that she'd made up her mind to have a look inside. The bag was good quality, with a tricky combination lock. After a few more minutes of struggling, she gave up and pushed the suitcase away. Unless she was prepared to cut or break it open, the bag wasn't going to yield any clues.

Karen had five minutes to spare before meeting Luke after she finished dressing. A warm shower had soothed her jangled nerves and eased the stiffness in her muscles. She had chosen to wear an ecru knit skirt and matching cotton sweater. In order to conceal the startling bruises on her throat, she'd tied the red scarf around her neck again. As she checked the effect in the bathroom mirror, she heard a faint tapping at the door.

Glancing at her watch in annoyance, she ran to the door of her room and flung it open, only to find herself face-to-face with Luke.

He had exchanged his corduroy slacks and leather jacket for a pair of light gray denims and a black cotton pullover. For the first time since before the incident on the train, Karen allowed herself to appraise his rugged good looks. When he smiled, his eyes crinkled at the corners and his hazel eyes seemed lighter, friendlier. She noticed that he had shaved and that his hair was slightly damp, as if he'd just emerged from the shower. Her gaze lingered on the tanned skin that showed above the top of his pullover and she wondered what it would feel like beneath her fingers. Karen's pulse raced as she looked at him and she flushed in acknowledgment of his attraction for her.

Karen had been so intent on Luke that it took several seconds for her to realize that he was not alone. An older man stood slightly behind him, clasping the handle of a black bag in one hand. "Guess what?" Luke advanced into her room. "The doctors here still make house calls. I had the desk clerk send over a doctor to look at those bruises."

Karen bit back an exasperated retort, silenced by the presence of a stranger. She would have to wait until later to tell him what she thought of his interference. "Come in," she said stiffly and stepped aside for the doctor to enter the room.

"This is Dr. Gerould. He doesn't seem to speak much English, so I'll leave the communication problem to you," Luke said.

"Thanks," Karen replied curtly.

Luke crossed to the shuttered doorway and disappeared onto the balcony. The doctor was thorough and competent, assuring her after his examination that there seemed to be no permanent damage and recommending warm compresses for the bruises. He rummaged through his bag, then handed her a packet of tablets that she gathered were some sort of painkiller.

Luke rejoined them as the doctor prepared to leave. "Everything okay?"

"He says I'll live."

"Then I'll see you in the lobby in five minutes," Luke said, ushering the doctor out of her room. Karen retied the red scarf around her neck, then shook out two tablets and swallowed them. Without anything to wash them down, they tasted bitter and vile, much like the words she had had to swallow earlier, she thought.

Luke was waiting in the lounge when she rounded the corner into the lobby, frowning attentively at a local television newscast. "Can't understand a word these guys are saying. I knew I shouldn't have slept through French class." He glanced at her. "Ready to go? I had the manager call for a cab. It's here already."

"I'm not looking forward to this, but I'd better get it over with," Karen replied. "You don't have to go with me, Luke. It's not as if any of this is your problem. By the way, I thought I told you I didn't need to see a doctor."

Luke shrugged. "I felt you should."

Karen glared at him. "Wasn't it rather presumptuous of you to call one without asking me?"

"Look, I'm just trying to be helpful. Maybe gratitude is too much to expect, but I didn't expect hostility." He motioned toward the door. "Our cab is waiting."

For a moment Karen debated whether she should insist that Luke leave her alone. From the moment he'd found her in the train compartment, he had tried to take charge of her life. She was going to have to put a stop to his interference. Or was she overreacting? There was no time to sort out her feelings now. Not when a cab was waiting, with its meter running.

Luke cupped his hand under her elbow as they neared the outside doors, reaching ahead with his free hand to swing the door open. By the time they neared the gate, the cab driver had the passenger door open. "Commissariat Central." Karen announced as she got inside. She held out the slip of paper on which the conductor had written the address.

*"Oui, mademoiselle."* The cabby shifted his squat body around and cast a sidelong glance at Luke, waiting for him to close the door after himself. As soon as the door was shut they darted off into the traffic.

Luke sat quietly, looking out the window. Karen felt his nearness with every nerve in her body, registering his strong shoulders, lean torso and powerful thighs on some inner radar screen. She seemed too aware of the unleashed energy smoldering beneath the surface of his streamlined body.

At last Karen could bear the silence no longer. "Is your friend staying at the hotel? What was his name . . . Mark?"

He took a moment to answer. "No," he admitted finally. "Apparently he checked out without leaving a forwarding address."

"Wasn't he expecting you?"

"Not exactly," Luke said. "I haven't seen him in a while and thought I'd look him up."

Karen digested that information, not sure what to make of it. "So what will you do now?"

Luke stared at her without speaking. He appeared to be considering his words carefully. "That depends on you."

Karen withdrew just the slightest bit. "I don't think I understand."

"We'll talk about it after we visit the police station," Luke said. He turned his face away, apparently concentrating on the view out the cab window. Karen stared at him, her eyes narrowed. *We'll talk about it, all right,* she thought.

# Chapter Four

The cab slowed, and the driver sedately maneuvered the car into the one-way street in front of a square stone building. Luke leaned over to pay the fare but Karen stopped him. "I'll take care of this. After all, I'm the one who had to come down here."

Luke looked uncomfortable. "Put your money away, Karen."

"I insist." Karen shoved her money toward the driver. After a minute, Luke slowly stashed the bill he'd been holding back into his wallet with a sidelong glance of irritation that was impossible for her to miss.

A smartly uniformed *gendarme* leaped to open the door as Karen approached the entrance with Luke in tow. The young policeman smiled politely, eyeing Karen approvingly as she spoke to him in French, asking where she could find Inspector Bouvier. He directed them to an office on the second floor.

Karen and Luke climbed the wide steps to the lobby on the second-floor landing. A long hallway led off toward the right, lined with bare wooden benches. Luke followed as Karen walked along the hall reading the signs above the doorways. "This is the inspector's office," Karen said, stopping at a doorway where several other people stood waiting.

The queue dwindled rapidly, and when Karen and Luke drew even with the doorway, they were beckoned inside by a middle-aged man in civilian clothes. *"Bonjour, mademoiselle,* how may I help you?"

Somehow the inspector's appearance fitted the humble office he worked in. His sallow complexion suggested long hours of toil under the bare light bulb that hung overhead. But when he smiled at Karen, his face lit up the way most Frenchmen's did when they were in the presence of a beautiful woman.

"My name is Karen St. Clair, and I'm supposed to see Inspector Bouvier in order to file a report." Karen returned his smile.

"Ah, Mademoiselle St. Clair." Inspector Bouvier extended his hand. "And you are . . . ?" he asked, looking at Luke.

"Luke Donovan," Luke replied firmly. He pulled out his wallet and handed the inspector one of his business cards.

"You are a private investigator?" The inspector eyed the card curiously. "I don't understand . . ."

"Mr. Donovan kindly offered me assistance on the train after the incident," Karen explained. "Since we're staying at the same hotel, he offered to come with me today. But he's not here in any official capacity."

"Oh." The inspector seemed unconvinced. "Well, let's get right to the matter at hand. Come along with me."

He led the way past three or four small interview rooms into a room that was slightly larger than the others. It contained a battered office chair and a wooden desk on which an ancient manual typewriter sat. Two straight-backed chairs were positioned in front of the desk. The inspector settled himself behind the typewriter and then motioned for them to sit down.

It took less than a half hour for Karen to finish her report. The inspector asked questions in a monotone, and Karen answered them as succinctly as possible.

"Please read this over, Mademoiselle St. Clair, and then sign it if you feel it is correct." While Karen read, he continued to speak. "There is probably nothing to be done about this now. All we can do is post extra security on our trains operating in the area and hope that nothing like this happens again."

"That doesn't really help Miss St. Clair," Luke said quietly.

The inspector shrugged. "I can only offer you the apology of my countrymen and myself for this unfortunate incident. It's a pity, but there are—" he paused and searched for a word "—crazy people and bad people everywhere. In your own country you have many such problems. So what can I say, except that I very sincerely regret that this happened to so lovely a guest."

"Then you think it was merely a senseless, random act?" Luke asked.

"What else is there to think?" The inspector glanced first at Karen and then back at Luke, his eyes questioning.

"Well, there is the matter of Miss St. Clair's reason for being in France in the first place."

"And what is that?"

Karen felt a surge of irritation. She had planned to discuss Diane's disappearance with the inspector but hadn't mentioned that to Luke and now here he was, sailing right in where he didn't belong. "I was hoping to meet a friend here in Nice," she explained reluctantly. "But when I arrived at the hotel this morning, I found that she had apparently disappeared."

"She was no longer staying at the hotel?" The inspector picked up a pen off the desk and began tapping it against the side of the typewriter. "But was she expecting you?"

"No, not exactly." Now that she had started the story, she might as well tell all of it. "She came to Europe about three weeks ago, to meet up with a church group that's making a tour of several countries. But when I went to the hotel where she was supposed to have linked up with the group, I learned that she had left the hotel alone and come on to Nice. Then when I got here, the man at the desk said she had left without paying her bill and that there had been no church group staying at that hotel, either."

"Perhaps you misunderstood. Or perhaps your friend wanted to keep private her real plans. Is she a young woman?"

"She's twenty-four." Karen paused. "I must confess that I'm quite worried about her. She's led a very sheltered life and she's scarcely equipped to be wandering about in an unfamiliar country by herself."

"You can't be sure that she is by herself," the inspector suggested delicately. "After all, this is France. Many young women come here alone but most of them soon find friends. Perhaps she has found a boyfriend? It wouldn't be unusual for her to be invited to stay with new friends...."

"And leave her suitcase behind and an unpaid bill at the hotel?" Karen dismissed his suggestion immediately. "Besides, Diane was hoping to further a relationship with the church group's leader, a young minister. And according to both hotels, there hasn't been any such group."

"I'm sure she will turn up, safe and sound," the inspector said reassuringly. "But surely you don't think your friend's absence is somehow related to the attack on yourself on the train?"

"It had entered my mind," Karen admitted.

"Do you have reason to believe your friend is involved in something dangerous? Something illegal, perhaps?" Suddenly the inspector's face looked stern. "Is there something that you are perhaps not telling me?"

"There's nothing specific," Karen said. "At least nothing other than the facts that I've already given you. But I was hoping that perhaps the police could make a search for her. Someone must know where she has gone."

"I'm afraid there's nothing we can do," the inspector said gently. "Until you have some evidence of trouble, we can't pry into your friend's private life."

"I'm not asking you to pry." Karen was getting angry now. "But I should think that the least you could do would be to check the hospitals and your records of recent accidents. Anything could have happened to her. And I don't think Diane would just go off without her suitcase and without formally checking out of the hotel and settling her bill."

"If you would give me your friend's name and her description, or even a photograph if you have one, I would be happy to check our accident records and inquire at the local hospitals and clinics. But I think you will find that your friend is perfectly fine. It's not unusual for young people to be careless or perhaps a little irresponsible. Life is very tempting at that age and one rushes to meet it heedlessly."

"I would appreciate your looking into the matter." Karen pulled out the photograph of Diane and handed it to him. He studied it and then made a few notes before giving it back to her.

"Don't you want to keep it?" Karen held the photograph out to him.

"That won't be necessary. I have written a description of her and we will circulate it as you requested." He stood up and it was obvious they were dismissed.

"We'll do our best," the inspector reassured her, as Karen and Luke prepared to leave. "But don't worry yourself, *mademoiselle*. I feel certain your friend will turn up soon and she'll be most chagrined that she has caused you so much anxiety."

As Karen and Luke walked through the corridor to the door of the station, she spoke without looking at him. "I don't think he took me quite seriously."

"He had a valid point," Luke pointed out.

"He doesn't know Diane. She's a very timid person. It probably took most of her courage to come to Europe in the first place. And the only reason she came was to meet up with this minister and his tour group. There's no way she'd go wandering around on her own, and it's absolutely out of the question that she would take off with some guy she picked up here."

"People aren't always so predictable," Luke said. "That's one thing you learn early on in my line of work. Never think that you can be sure of what anyone is capable of. Most of us are creatures of impulse, and all of us are tempted to act out of character now and then."

"I know Diane," Karen said stubbornly. "Something's happened to her. I won't rest until I find her."

"And how do you propose to do that?"

"I don't know yet," Karen admitted.

"I might have a few suggestions," Luke murmured. "After all, I'm a detective. I've looked for people before."

"You've already given me too much of your time, Luke. Don't think I'm not grateful, but I really don't want to involve you in this any further."

"It looks like I may be involved, anyway," Luke countered.

"What do you mean?"

"You seem to forget that I'm looking for someone myself. So far, he and your Diane seem to have followed the same route."

"You mean both of them being at the Hotel Azur?"

"And both of them stayed at the same hotel in Rome."

"In Rome?" Karen jumped back as a police car narrowly missed her in the crowded parking lot. "You didn't

tell me about this before.'' Suspicion clouded her gaze.
"You were at the Hotel Gran Duca in Rome? I didn't see
you there."

"No, but I saw you." Luke pulled her aside as another
police car honked at them. "Come on, we can't stand here
talking. How about some lunch?"

Karen refused to budge. "I'm not going anywhere until
you tell me what this is all about."

"It's a long story. If you want to hear it, you'll have to
have lunch with me."

"That's blackmail. I don't think I like that. And I'm not
sure I like you very much, either."

"You'll like me better when you've eaten something."
Luke took her arm and tugged her toward the street. "Look,
there's a cab. Come on, we'll talk when we find a restaurant."

IT WASN'T UNTIL they were seated in a busy café on the
Promenade des Anglais that Karen got Luke to tell her anything. She waited until they had given their order before
starting to ask questions.

"Why didn't you say something about that guy you're
looking for when we were at the police station?" Too many
things were not making sense, she thought. She had already let her guard down, but if she couldn't get some
straight answers from Luke over lunch, the defenses she
would throw up would be impenetrable. "You'd better tell
me what this is all about. Do you know something about
Diane?"

Luke poured them both a glass of the cool, bubbly mineral water from the bottle the waiter had brought to the table. He took a long sip, as if bracing himself for a barrage
of relentless questioning. "I'm afraid not. But there seems
to be a similar pattern between what Mark and Diane are
doing. Perhaps I'd better tell you about Mark first."

"He's the man you're looking for?" Karen looked at him over the rim of her glass. "You said he was a friend, but is this somehow related to one of your cases or something?"

"Let me explain." Luke seemed to be choosing his words carefully. "Mark Turner and I have been friends for about five years. He's thirty-five now, two years older than me. At the time we met, he owned a restaurant in Alexandria, right outside D.C. Even though he was only thirty then, he was already making his name in the restaurant business. I met him when he hired me to find out why his restaurant had begun to lose money, despite the high volume of business. It didn't take me long to discover that his manager had his hand in the till, but during that time, I became friendly with Mark and his wife."

"He's married? Didn't his wife come to Europe with him?"

"Alicia died two years ago. She was ill when I met them. She was Mark's whole world, and when she died, he felt like he'd lost everything. He sold the restaurant and his home and moved to Virginia's Eastern Shore. He bought a cabin there—a shack really. In a way, he seemed to want to give up living."

Luke paused as the waiter arrived with their lunch. Although she had been convinced she wasn't hungry, Karen perked up at the sight of the mouthwatering seafood crepes.

*"Crêpes aux fruits de mer,"* the waiter murmured. He placed a steaming plate of delicate crepes in front of each of them. Next to their plates, he set a colorful butter lettuce salad topped by a glistening vinaigrette dressing.

"It smells wonderful." Karen suddenly realized how many hours it had been since she'd last eaten. When the waiter started to pour wine for her, she refused it with a smile. Luke glanced at her questioningly. "I'd better not. Before we left the hotel I took two of those pain tablets the doctor gave me."

"Would you like something else? Coffee? Soda?"

"Water will be fine." Karen waited until the waiter left the table. "You were telling me about Mark?"

Luke ate several bites before he continued. "I got in the habit of spending the odd weekend at Mark's place last summer. D.C. gets crowded in the summer—too many tourists. So every now and then, I'd take off and drive out there. Mark never minded my showing up. We'd spend most of our time fishing. Once or twice I tried to talk to Mark, ask him about what he planned to do with himself. But he wasn't ready to decide that yet. Getting away from things seemed to help him, though. By last fall, he could talk about Alicia without breaking down under the devastating sense of loss that had weighed so heavily on him since she died."

"So how did he end up in Europe?"

"I'm getting to that. Just wait." Luke took a long swallow of his wine. "I got busy this past year, and I didn't see much of Mark. I called him around Christmas time, and he sounded more like himself. He was all enthusiastic about some civic action group he was trying to put together. He was furious because some sort of fish-processing plant was planning to expand its operations on the Eastern Shore."

"Oysters," Karen corrected absently, her eyes slowly opening wide as she realized that she already knew this part of Luke's story.

"I beg your pardon?" Luke stared at her.

"It was an oyster-packing plant," Karen explained. "Diane talked about it all the time. It's a big operation owned by Gilbert Industries. They built the plant despite the protests of local residents. Diane's father was very upset about it. He was dying then, and Diane was worried that his anger was going to cut his time even shorter."

Luke seemed riveted by what she had said. "Diane lived on the Eastern Shore?"

"Yes," Karen said slowly. "Odd, isn't it. I mean, both of them being from the same place and ending up in the same part of Europe." For the first time, Karen almost believed that perhaps Luke was right. There did seem to be more than coincidence linking Diane and Mark.

"More than odd," Luke replied. "Like I said, I've got a feeling that somehow Diane and Mark are connected. But let me tell you the rest of what I know about Mark. Mark's always had this thing about ecology, and I was glad to hear him enthusiastic about something at last."

Karen interrupted. "Do you know if he was involved with the citizen's coalition that Diane's father started? Maybe Diane and Mark knew each other. Diane took over as chairman of the coalition after her father died."

"A citizen's coalition?" Luke looked thoughtful.

"They call themselves Citizens Against Industrial Marine Exploitation. They're an activist group, you know. They write letters and stage protest marches outside the plant. In the past year, they've managed to get some media attention, but so far, the plant has gone on with its plans to expand."

"Now that you mention it, I seem to remember Mark talking about a group of some sort. To tell the truth, I didn't pay a lot of attention to the details. I was more interested in the fact that Mark seemed to be taking an interest in something outside himself at last."

"If he was angry about the oyster-processing plant, he must have been involved with the coalition," Karen said. "But go on and tell me the rest of your story."

Luke took another swallow of wine. "Mark asked me when I was going to get back to visit him, and I told him I'd try to make it soon. But somehow, the right time never came along. Not until a few weeks ago, that is."

"What happened?"

"I found myself with a whole weekend free, so I decided on impulse to visit Mark. I tried calling him before I left, but he wasn't there. But that didn't worry me. Mark had given me a key to his place on one of my previous visits, and I figured if he wasn't there or if he had other plans, I could find another place to stay. But when I reached his cabin, I got the feeling he hadn't been there for a while. The place was dusty and had a deserted feeling. It's not a fancy place. Just a small cabin that sits off by itself. Lots of places like it on the Eastern Shore."

"And then you found out he had come to Europe?"

"Not right away. I spent the night at the cabin. It was late and I knew Mark wouldn't mind. The next morning, I waited around a while and then left. On the way out, I decided to stop at his closest neighbor's house. Mrs. Fanning's place is a couple of miles from Mark's, and they've never been really friendly. But I thought maybe she'd know where he went."

"And did she?"

"She said that Mark had gone to Europe. She knew, because he'd asked her to check on his place every now and then, collect the mail, take a look around. She was quite put out because apparently Mark had given her to understand he'd only be gone a few days. At that time, he'd been gone almost two weeks, and she was tired of having to look out for his place. When she found I had a key to his cabin, she asked me if I'd take the mail back there."

"But what made you come to Europe to check on Mark? That's a pretty big step to take."

"I didn't come to Europe specifically to check on Mark. In fact, I didn't really get the idea right then. After I'd dropped the mail off at his place, I locked up and went back to town. But last week, I had to go to Zurich on business connected with a case I'm working on. On impulse, I called to see if Mark had returned yet. I'd left a note at his place, but he'd never contacted me. When he didn't answer, I called Mrs. Fanning. She said Mark had never returned. That got me to thinking and when I finished my business in Zurich, I decided to check up on Mark."

"But how did you find the hotel in Rome? I thought you had no idea where Mark went?"

Luke looked slightly embarrassed. "I hate to admit it, but I snooped a bit. I still had Mark's file at my office. When I'd handled that case for him, I'd collected quite a bit of personal data about him, including his charge card numbers. I made a few phone calls and found that a charge from Europe had come through on his American Express account. A charge for that hotel in Rome."

"Do you always check so closely on your friends?" Karen savored the last forkful of her crepes.

"Mark seems almost like a member of the family." Luke's eyes took on a distant expression, filled with remembered pain. "It's something I can't explain. But when you watch a friend deal with the death of his wife...you get very close, very fast."

Karen could have kicked herself for pressing the issue. Obviously the experience had been painful for Luke. Already she had seen that he was capable of intense concern and compassion, so it was natural that Mark and Alicia's situation had affected him deeply. She sought to return the conversation to a more businesslike level. "So you went there..."

Luke recovered himself with visible effort. "They told me he'd left. He did leave behind a forwarding address, and it just happened to be the Hotel Azur."

"The same as Diane," Karen breathed.

"Exactly. The clerk told me Mark had been there before Diane."

"You spoke to him about Diane?" Karen pounced on his statement immediately. "What do you know about Diane?"

"Nothing," Luke admitted. "But the clerk seemed to think it was a remarkable coincidence. He said a young American woman had just been asking after a friend of hers. He thought it odd that both Mark and Diane had headed for the same hotel and odd that both of us should be asking after them. I saw you leaving the hotel before I spoke to the clerk."

"This is really strange," Karen said contemplatively.

"It's enough to make me curious," Luke agreed. "Now suppose you tell me about Diane. Who is she?"

Karen took her time before she replied. It seemed she had to make a decision about Luke Donovan. It seemed crazy to trust him, especially since she had legitimate grounds for being wary of almost everyone right now. Crazy as it was, however, she knew suddenly that she had no choice. Strange or not, if divulging something of her personal life would help her find Diane, she would have to do it.

"Diane Garrett is a family friend," she began at last. "My mother was Diane's godmother. Diane's mother died a long time ago, so I've always tried to keep an eye on her. She and her father moved to the Eastern Shore about ten years ago, after her father retired from his teaching position at the University of Virginia. Diane was fourteen at the time, and I think she took the move badly. Professor Garrett was a naturalist, and after he retired, he spent his time writing articles and books about ecological subjects. He leaned too heavily on Diane, expecting her to become his personal assistant after she finished high school. Not a pleasant man."

"But why did Diane continue to stay with him? Surely she was old enough to leave and make her own life."

"Diane was no match for her father. She felt an excessive sense of obligation. And by the time she reached twenty or so, his health had begun to fail. For the next four years, she devoted herself entirely to acting as his nurse. When he died last year, Diane floundered for a while. I think she almost felt relieved that she was free at last, but that feeling turned into unbearable guilt. I tried to keep in touch with her, but I was busy teaching and I didn't get a chance to see much of her after the funeral."

"So what made her come to Europe?"

As quickly as possible, Karen told him what she knew about Diane and the man from the personal ad. Luke remained silent until she had finished, then beckoned the waiter over. He ordered coffee for himself and Karen requested tea. After they were served, Luke said, "So she came to Europe and you're here because you're worried about her?"

Karen sipped her tea. The food and the warm sun were taking their toll, and she was starting to feel drowsy. "Something like that, yes. When she called, Diane told me she was leaving the very next morning, stopping over in D.C. for a day to walk through her passport application. From there, she was flying on to Rome. The only information I could get out of her was the name of that hotel in Rome. She promised she would write as soon as she linked up with the tour group, to let me know everything was fine."

"And did she?"

"Not a word. When my classes ended last week, I decided to fly over and check on her. I usually spend a few weeks in Europe in the summer, leading study workshops for art students. This summer, I'd decided to take off, but then I felt at loose ends. It seemed like a good excuse to come over to Europe, anyway."

"And I think I know the rest of what happened," Luke concluded.

"Not quite all of it," Karen said after a moment. As she explained, she watched Luke closely, observing his reaction. "Just before I was attacked on the train last night, I overheard a strange conversation. I really didn't think much about it at the time, but after I was attacked, I began to wonder..."

"What did you hear?" Luke's expression revealed only natural surprise and curiosity. Karen saw nothing in his eyes to indicate that he had any prior knowledge of the conversation, nothing to tell her whether indeed he had been one of the men involved. Before she could lose her nerve, Karen quickly recounted the fragments of conversation she had overheard. "You don't suppose they were talking about me, do you?"

Luke's face had assumed a grim expression. "At this point, I don't think we can discount any possibility. The more I think about this, the more I'm convinced that Mark and Diane have gotten themselves involved in some sort of trouble."

"Diane, yes," Karen agreed. "But what about Mark? What connection do you think he has with all this?"

"I don't know. It's just an instinct, I guess." Luke paused.

"And you have no idea why he came to Europe?"

"None," Luke replied. "I knew he'd been lonely and a bit restless, but it's not like him to simply take off like this without telling any of his friends where he's going."

The waiter interrupted their conversation at that point, inquiring as to whether they wanted dessert. "Not me," Karen demurred. Luke also declined. Before she could protest, he'd settled the bill.

"And don't say a word," he instructed. "This lunch is my treat."

"Not even thank you?" Karen said quietly. Luke grinned at her.

The café wasn't far from the hotel, so they decided to walk. The promenade wasn't as crowded now. Most of the shops had closed for the lunch break, but a few people still strolled along beside them, window-shopping. There were the usual loungers at café tables here and there, and traffic still hummed steadily on the road itself.

"What do you plan to do now?" Luke asked.

"Wait, I guess. Perhaps Diane will show up in a day or so."

"Or perhaps the police will come up with something."

"I'm hoping they don't, really," Karen explained. "After all, that would probably mean she'd been in an accident or was in some sort of trouble."

"Are you going to try to look for her yourself?"

"I'd like to," Karen stated. "But I haven't a clue where to start."

Luke paused, speaking slowly as if testing the waters with each word. "You might find something in Diane's suitcase."

Karen looked over at him quickly. That hardness had settled in around his mouth, and she thought she sensed an unexpressed intensity in his manner. The next moment he smiled, and she wondered if she had only imagined it. "I thought of that. But it's locked. Anyway, that seems too much of a violation of Diane's privacy."

A brief silence stretched between them. "I think you ought to look inside it," Luke said. "Maybe she left some clue as to where she's gone."

"It's a combination lock. I can't see any way to get inside it without damaging the bag."

"Why don't you let me have a look at it?"

Karen paused beside a bench that faced out toward the sea. She sat down, composing in her mind the speech she wanted to make. "Luke, you seem to be taking it for granted that we're working on this together. But we have no proof that Mark Turner and Diane Garrett are connected to each other in any way.''

"We've already been over that." Luke lounged against the railing that edged the pavement, his hands in his pockets.

"I'm not even sure there's a problem." Karen made a helpless gesture with her hands. "You're a stranger, Luke. I feel uncomfortable now about how much I've told you."

Luke moved swiftly, seating himself beside her. He grasped her left hand between his palms. His next words surprised her. "Do you believe in fate, Karen?"

"That's an odd question." Karen searched his eyes.

Luke grinned sheepishly. "Never mind. Karen, I've got a certain instinct for knowing when something isn't quite right and that instinct is telling me you're headed for trouble. I've got a few days to spend here in Nice. Let me help you find Diane. I've reached a dead end in my search for Mark, but maybe I'll learn something by helping you."

"I'll think about it." Karen refused to give him an answer right then.

"What about Diane's suitcase? I think we should take a look at it today."

After a moment's hesitation, Karen gave in. She was desperate to find out something about Diane. If Luke could help her get in that suitcase, why not let him?

When they reached the hotel, the lobby was empty. Karen waited impatiently at the desk for someone to come out and get her key for her. "Never mind, I'll get it." Luke leaned across the desk and said, "I thought you were in room 4."

"I am."

"Your key's not there. Did you take it with you?"

"No, at least I don't think so." Karen thought back for a moment. "I'm certain I handed it in when I came down to the lobby."

"Maybe the maid's in your room. Let's go on up."

The first-floor landing was deserted. Karen's gaze went immediately to her door. It stood partially ajar. She felt Luke's body go rigid beside her. "What's wrong?" she whispered.

His jaw tightened grimly. "I'm not sure. Stay here." He moved silently across the hall and edged his way along the wall until he reached her door. Karen crept over beside him. He motioned for her to stay back, his gaze riveted on something inside her room.

Straining to see past him, Karen caught a glimpse of a man in her room. He was bent over Diane's suitcase, apparently intent on getting it open. She started to move past Luke but his arm wrapped around her waist, jerking her back. A moment later, he pivoted and barged into the room. There was a muffled shout and then Karen heard the sound of bone crunching against flesh.

# Chapter Five

As Luke darted into Karen's room, he was met by the surprised and desperate glare of a thin, balding man who looked vaguely familiar. In a second, Luke recognized him. It was the man he had seen leave the Hotel Gran Duca in Rome shortly after Karen's departure. The man was wearing the same crumpled jacket, but now his face sported a bruise across the bridge of his nose.

Instantly Luke made a lunge for him and managed to land a glancing blow against his jaw. "Freeze," Luke ordered. But the man ignored him, leaping backward until his back was against the wall. His gaze darted frantically from Luke to the doorway.

Luke turned to see that Karen had followed him into the room. "Get out of here!" he bellowed, not waiting to see whether she obeyed him. The man charged toward him and Luke ducked to miss the force of his fist.

They circled each other warily. Luke made a grab at the man but he parried, pulling the bedside table into Luke's path. Luke's body smashed into the table, his speed and momentum working against him. As he hit the floor, he heard Karen scream.

Out of the corner of his eye, he saw her race to the dresser and grab the heavy porcelain lamp that sat on its corner. She held it aloft, her eyes on the man in the rumpled jacket. As he moved toward her, she hurled the lamp at him but the cord, still firmly plugged into the wall, brought it up short and the lamp smashed to the floor at her feet.

Luke scrambled to his feet and made a flying leap at his opponent. For the next few seconds, the only sounds in the room were the soft thuds of fists making contact with flesh and harsh breathing. One blow sent the intruder staggering back toward Karen, and before she could move away he had grabbed her and pulled her in front of him like a shield.

Luke muttered an oath. Why hadn't she stayed out of it? Karen began to struggle in the man's grip and Luke started toward them. He winced as he saw her take aim with her fist and strike a blow at her captor's jaw. She bit off a cry of pain and Luke saw that her knuckles had taken the brunt of the blow.

"Let go of her," Luke shouted, lunging forward. Too late, he saw the heavy metal base of the smashed lamp in his path. He tripped over it as the balding man connected with a swift uppercut left to his jaw, sending Luke sprawling to the floor.

In less than a moment, the thin man had bolted for the window. He scrambled over the edge of the balcony and Karen raced to follow him, reaching the rail just in time to see him drop to the ground, roll and then leap to his feet. He ran to a beige compact car that was parked at the curb. The engine roared to life and he was gone.

Rushing back inside, Karen reached Luke just as he was pulling himself to his knees. "Are you all right?" She placed her hand softly against the side of his jaw.

"For a skinny man, he had one hell of a punch." Luke shook his head as if he were still slightly dazed.

"Who was he?" Karen looked around the room helplessly. "What was he in here for? He was looking at Diane's suitcase..."

Luke stood up and leaned against the bed. Karen noted the grim set of his mouth and the darkness in his eyes as he struggled to pull himself together. Despite all evidence of his being good-natured and kind, there was a hard side to Luke that she had noticed from the very first. "I don't know what he wanted." Luke spat out the words. "But I intend to find out."

"Right now, we'd better do something about that jaw." Karen hurried into the bathroom and returned with a damp towel. She dabbed his jaw, relieved that at least it did not appear to be broken. "You're going to have a bad bruise." She brushed her fingers against his skin. Only a few hours before she'd wondered what his skin would feel like. She hadn't anticipated finding out quite so soon, and certainly not in this manner.

"Isn't that what I said to you not long ago?" Luke grinned crookedly, and she could see that he was making an attempt to recover his customary sense of humor. "This may prove to be a very dangerous relationship."

Karen eyed him coolly. "Who said anything about a relationship?" She handed him the towel.

Taking it from her, he tossed it onto the bed and strode across to the balcony. "Did you see which direction he went in?"

Karen came to stand beside him. "He had a car. I couldn't see the license number. What was he doing in my room, Luke?"

"Looking for something, apparently." Luke rubbed his jaw gingerly. "Now I'm sure we need to take a look in that suitcase. And the sooner the better." He started back into Karen's room, stepping clear of the smashed lamp on the floor.

"This is crazy. What would he want with Diane's suitcase?" Karen surveyed the damage in her room with a sense of bewilderment.

"We won't know that until we look inside it." Luke reached for the bag.

Karen stopped him. She moved in front of him, putting herself between him and the bag. "This is my problem, Luke. I don't feel you should get involved."

Luke gestured toward his jaw. "I've got a personal score to settle now, Karen."

Once again dark violence masked his expression and Karen noted it, this time with distaste. "You sound almost as if you're looking forward to it." She stepped back. "You seem to be determined to get involved in my problems, whether I like it or not. I'm not sure I want you around, Luke Donovan."

There was a brief silence and then Luke closed the distance between them. He slipped an arm around her waist and leaned down to whisper in her ear. His breath teased gently against her skin. "Lady," he asked, his voice rich with laughter, "don't you know you can't argue with fate?"

BY THE TIME the hotel manager and his wife had viewed the damage to the room and heard their story, it was late afternoon. A maid had managed to produce an ice pack for Luke's jaw, and fortunately it seemed to be stopping the swelling. No one had seen the man or had any idea how he had got into Karen's room. Luke offered the most logical explanation. "He must have taken the key from the desk when the lobby was empty."

The hotel manager agreed. "There's a list of the guests and their room assignments posted beneath the counter." He apologized profusely for leaving the lobby unattended.

Karen used the manager's phone to call Inspector Bouvier. The inspector said little in response to her report of this latest incident, but he sent a young *gendarme* to inspect the hotel room and take down the details.

By the time the room had been restored to order, Karen wanted nothing more than to crawl into bed. She'd lost count of the number of hours she had gone without sleep. But Luke insisted on going through Diane's suitcase.

"Let's have a look inside." Luke pulled it into the middle of Karen's room and knelt beside it. "That man was looking for something."

Karen was too tired to argue with him. "Who was he? How did he know I had Diane's suitcase?"

"I don't know," Luke replied grimly. "But I've seen him before."

Karen dropped to the floor beside him. "Where?"

"In Rome. At the Hotel Gran Duca. He was sitting in the lobby, but as soon as you went out the door, he left."

"He followed me?" Karen regarded Luke with suspicion. "Why didn't you mention this before?"

"Until I saw him here this afternoon, I wasn't sure he'd followed you. But he was there. And he left right after you did." Luke looked the bag over carefully, fiddling with the dials on the combination lock. Apparently they'd caught the man before he'd managed to pry open the lock, for the bag showed no signs of damage.

"Can you open it?" Karen asked eagerly.

"It's a canvas bag," Luke commented. "I could easily cut it open."

"Oh, no," Karen protested. "Surely there's a better way to get it open. Think of something. You're the detective."

Luke studied her in silence. "What's your friend's birth date?" he asked abruptly.

"You think she used her birth date for the combination?"

"You'd be surprised by the number of people who do," Luke replied. "It's simple, easy to remember, personal."

Karen gave him the date. Luke twirled the dials but nothing happened. "Don't worry, she may have used the numbers in a different order." He worked silently for several minutes, trying different combinations of the numbers. At last the bag popped open. "Clever girl, your friend. She'd moved each number over a space, creating her own special little code."

Karen eyed him, noting that he looked rather proud of himself. "I suppose you like the idea that you've outsmarted her."

"Sure do." Luke moved to make room for the open suitcase.

"Not so fast, Luke." Karen grasped the suitcase possessively. "After all, she's my friend. I don't think she'd want a stranger going through her things."

Diane's clothes were as drab as Karen remembered. And painfully neat. They were arranged in careful stacks, but taken as a whole the garments were depressingly alike. Beige, tan, colors that Karen knew did nothing for Diane's brown hair and pale face.

It wasn't until she reached the bottom of the bag that she found the letters. In contrast to the other contents of the suitcase, the red ribbon that bound the letters together stood out vividly. Karen pulled out the stack. There were about fifteen letters in the bundle.

A folded newspaper clipping was on the front of the stack. Karen gingerly extracted it from the bundle and opened it up. "It's the personal ad," she said after a moment.

"Let me see," Luke demanded.

"Here, I'll read it aloud." Karen took a breath.

"Single white minister, thirty-five, six foot one, husky blue-eyed blond, is looking for friendship (maybe more?) with compassionate, warm, single woman, preferably one who lives in the country and is interested in ecology. I'm sincere, financially secure, but shy. Hobbies are reading, travel, meeting interesting people. Not really wife-hunting but not afraid of commitment. Box #4668.''

The ad didn't impress Karen. "A shy, husky, blue-eyed blond? Oh really, Diane. How could you be so stupid? If he's so shy, why did he send a woman he's never seen before a ticket to Rome?''

"The ad's not too bad," Luke protested. "And lots of men are basically shy. We just can't admit it.''

"You're not trying to tell me you think you're shy, are you?" Karen looked at him disbelievingly.

Luke exaggerated a wounded look, then changed the subject. "The ad doesn't really tell us much, but at least we have a box number." Luke reached over and took the bundle of letters. Untying the ribbon, he picked up the first letter and started to open it.

"Hey, what do you think you're doing?" Karen tried to grab the letter away from him.

"We need more information," Luke said.

"They're Diane's private papers, Luke. We can't read them.''

"I don't see why you're so squeamish about reading them," Luke said after a moment. "I think we should do anything that might help us find her.''

"No," Karen said with finality.

"Okay." He shrugged as if it didn't matter, but Karen could tell from his expression that he was disappointed.

"If we have to, we'll read them. But let me think about it first," Karen compromised.

The rest of the suitcase yielded no further clues. There was a small flat jewelry box tucked into the side pocket. Karen opened it, explaining, "Diane has a weakness for earrings. See?" She showed the box to Luke. There were at least a dozen pairs.

Luke picked up a pair of bold bronze and black earrings. "These don't quite go with your friend's clothes, do they?"

"She loves earrings, especially in a butterfly shape or design. Last Christmas I found a fabulous pair for her—tiny antique silver filigree butterflies. They're her favorite pair." Karen sifted through the earrings in the box, but didn't find them. "Perhaps she was wearing them the day she went out."

"Or perhaps she left them at home," Luke suggested. "There doesn't seem to be anything in the suitcase to tell us anything, except the letters." Luke looked at her pointedly.

"Not yet," Karen insisted. She frowningly turned back to the suitcase, taking her time feeling along the sides and looking in all the pockets. "Here's something," she said at last, pulling out a sheaf of papers. "Diane's traveler's check receipts."

"Great." Luke took the papers and flipped through them quickly. "I'm going to call my office in D.C. That is," he added with exaggerated politeness, "if you don't feel I'm being nosy. I can have them check with the newspaper about that box number. And they can find out whether Diane has cashed any more of her traveler's checks. If she has, it might tell us where she's staying."

Karen accepted his offer gracefully. "I'd appreciate it."

"Don't forget. I have a vested interest in finding Diane. She might lead us to Mark."

Karen couldn't suppress a yawn. Her eyes felt gritty and tired, and the rich lunch had added to her fatigue.

"You look exhausted, Karen." Luke's expression softened.

"I've only slept in snatches these past three days."

"Then I'd suggest you stop worrying about Diane right now and catch some sleep. Maybe by the time you wake up, I'll have found something out from my office." He looked around the room broodingly. Crossing to the window, he fastened the latch securely. "As soon as I leave, I want you to lock this door. I don't like the thought, but that man might come back."

"The police did promise to have someone watch the hotel for the next couple of days."

Luke frowned. "If you hear anything suspicious, just scream. I'm right upstairs."

"Don't worry about me, Luke. I can take care of myself."

"Sure." His expression was openly disbelieving. "And by the way, remind me to teach you how to punch."

Karen inspected her tender knuckles, her smile rueful. "I think I'll stick to throwing lamps. But first I'll make sure they're unplugged." Luke's answering laugh mingled with hers.

"Sleep well, Karen," Luke said softly. For the first time since she had met him, he looked unsure of himself. He moved closer, stopped and then took another step toward her.

His kiss caught her by surprise. It was gentle, beginning with a tender brush of his lips against hers. Then, as if he hadn't meant to go further but found himself unable to refrain, he tasted her lips more fully. His hands caressed her back firmly. Once he made up his mind to do something, it appeared that Luke Donovan carried through without hesitation.

When at last he let go of her, Karen felt bemused. It had been a long time since she had been so thoroughly and warmly kissed. There was nothing practiced about Luke's affection. His feelings ran deep and were genuine, and he seemed to have no difficulty expressing them.

"Good night, Karen." He smiled into her eyes. "Don't forget to lock the door."

She stared at the closed door after he left, her thoughts confused. How had she managed to get so involved with Luke in such a short period of time?

Everything was moving too fast for her. She'd always abhorred physical violence, yet twice in the past few hours she'd been at the center of it. And she'd always needed time before moving into any sort of intimacy, yet she and Luke had already exchanged a kiss.

Exhaustion put an end to her confused musings. Until she got some sleep, she wasn't going to be able to figure things out. After she climbed into bed, she remembered Diane's letters. From what she'd seen, they were the only thing in Diane's suitcase of any real interest. Had that been what her intruder had been searching for? If so, it wouldn't hurt to hide them.

Padding across the room in bare feet, she got the letters out of the bag and put them under her pillow. It wasn't much of a hiding place, but it would have to do for now.

SUNLIGHT WAS STREAMING IN between the slats of the shutters the next morning when Karen awoke. She showered and then dressed quickly in a one-piece tank dress. The bruises on her throat stood out clearly this morning, so she was forced to don the red scarf again. She flung her red jacket over her arm in case it was still cool outside and then retrieved Diane's letters, putting them in her tote bag.

Her first stop was at Luke's door. There was no answer from inside when she knocked.

Finally she went down to the lobby. "Has Mr. Donovan left the hotel?" she asked the manager when he emerged from his office at the back.

"Early this morning, *mademoiselle*," he informed her. "You didn't request *petit déjeuner*. Would you like coffee, perhaps?"

"That would be nice."

"If you wish, we will send a tray up to your room. Or you may have it in the lounge if you prefer."

"In my room, please."

Karen went back upstairs to her room. Not long afterward, a maid knocked on the door and in response to Karen's reply, entered the room. She took the tray out to the balcony and set it on the table.

After she'd left, Karen poured the rich black coffee, mixing it with warm milk from the small pitcher. There was a basket of rolls, flaky croissants and buttery brioches.

She had barely swallowed a sip of coffee before another knock sounded on the door. "Luke?" she called and when no one answered, she went to the door.

The teenage boy who had brought up Diane's suitcase the day before was standing in the hall outside her door. "Telephone, *mademoiselle*. In the lobby."

Karen sighed. Turning her back on the coffee and rolls, she followed the boy downstairs. "There is a private booth over there," the hotel manager told her when she reached the lobby.

Karen went into the tiny booth and shut the door. Picking up the receiver, she said, "Hello?" She half-expected to hear Luke's voice.

There was a long silence and then a man's voice spoke. "Mademoiselle St. Clair?" Karen assumed he was French and replied in that language.

*"Oui?"*

"I have information about your friend. Mademoiselle Garrett."

"Who is this?"

"I must talk to you. Not on the telephone. It isn't safe."

"Not safe?" Karen took a deep breath. "Who is this? Is Diane all right? Where is she?"

"Do you know the flower market?"

"Yes."

"I will meet you there. Nine o'clock. There is a stall near the east corner, owned by a family named Vallois. They deal in tea roses and their stand is clearly marked with their name. Look for me there."

"But who are you? How will I know you?"

"I'll be wearing a tan jacket with one of the roses pinned on the lapel. In my hands will be a copy of this week's *L'Express*. I know what you look like."

Before she could demand that he tell her more, he had hung up.

Karen stood there for a moment after the phone went dead, staring blankly at the receiver. A chill of terror crept up her spine. What was Diane involved in?

THE POST OFFICE on the Avenue Thiers was a beehive of activity. Luke Donovan paced the floor near the telephone booths, glancing from time to time at his watch. When he'd placed his call to the States, the clerk had promised a fifteen-minute wait. That was half an hour ago.

He strode over to the counter where the clerk was seated. Pulling a well-thumbed French phrase book out of his jacket pocket, he attempted to make himself understood. She ignored him, speaking into her microphone instead. "Monsieur Donovan. *Numéro trois.*"

Luke glared at her and then stalked abruptly to the booth marked number three. The operator was on the line when he picked up the receiver. Thank God she spoke English. "Your party is on the line. Go ahead."

A moment later, Helen's sleepy voice came over the wire. "Is that you, Luke? The operator said this call is from France. I thought you were in Rome, checking up on Mark."

Luke smiled at his secretary's slightly admonishing tone. Helen Price had started to work for him a week after he'd opened Donovan Investigations. After raising two sons, she'd felt a need to start another career. Luke knew that she liked to picture herself an amateur sleuth, and actually, she'd surprised him more than once with her astute observations. "Sorry to wake you at this hour, Helen. I need you to check on some things for me."

"Haven't you found Mark yet?"

"Not yet. But I may have a lead on his whereabouts. I want you to run a couple of background checks. Two women. Diane Garrett and Karen St. Clair." He could almost see Helen's knowing smile.

"What are you up to, Luke?"

"Never mind that." Luke laughed. "Here, take down this information..."

After he'd given Helen as many details as he knew about Karen and Diane, Luke directed her to check out the personal ad. "Don't tell me you've resorted to getting your dates through a newspaper," Helen teased. "I keep telling you I can fix you up with a real nice girl, Luke. You need to get married. You don't want to wither on the vine, do you?"

Luke grinned. "Hey, I'm not even ripe yet."

Helen ignored him. "You better get back here soon. Vandiver Insurance wants you to check out a claimant. They think someone's padding the hospital charges. And—"

"Have you heard of Gilbert Industries?" Luke interrupted. "They handle oyster packing on the Chesapeake."

"Gilbert Industries..." Helen was silent for a moment. "Want me to have them checked out? I can put Harrison on it."

"Have him see what he can find out about a group that calls itself Citizens Against Industrial Marine Exploitation. I'd like to know if Mark was involved with the group." Luke paused. "Call me back. Tonight, if possible." He gave her the name of his hotel.

"You watch out for that blonde," Helen said as they prepared to end the conversation.

"What are you talking about?"

"Don't try to fool me. I heard your voice when you described her."

"Helen, I swear, one day the FBI is going to steal you away from me." He could still hear Helen laughing as he hung up.

AT EIGHT-FORTY, Luke had still not returned to the hotel. Karen, who had been pacing the lobby anxiously for the past fifteen minutes, gave up and walked over to the desk. "Could you call a taxi for me? I want to go to the flower market."

"Very well." The clerk made the call, and when the taxi arrived, Karen hurried out the gate to meet it. "The flower market," she directed. "And hurry, please."

It was pushing nine when the cab turned into the Cours Saleya. Once the elegant promenade of Nice, the street was now lined with shops and restaurants. The cab drew up at the market and Karen paid the driver, then leaped out of the cab without waiting for her change. She thought she heard the driver calling after her, but she didn't turn back.

The market was a sea of perfumed color. Buyers and sellers hovered over the lanes of roses and banked masses of carnations and anemones. A few stalls proudly offered the season's first fragile, costly sprigs of jasmine while others stocked mignonette and violets from Grasse, spiky, fragrant hyacinths and irises from Toulon and lavender from the hills of Haute-Provence.

Conversation filled the air. There was an urgency to it, as sellers quoted prices and buyers jotted notes, comparing prices and haggling to make deals. There was a sense here that time was precious. Flowers were perishable and they must be put on trains to Paris, Geneva and other European cities without delay.

Karen surveyed the controlled pandemonium with a
sinking feeling. How was she to find one mysterious
Frenchman, unknown to her beyond those brief, hurried
words over the telephone?

She knew that Luke would be angry that she had come
here without him. Against her will she found herself wishing that Luke was beside her. There was something about
him that inspired confidence. He was a man who acted as if
nothing much surprised him. No doubt he'd had meetings
like this one before in the course of his work.

A thousand questions filled her mind. She wanted to
know how the caller had known who she was. How he had
known she was looking for Diane. And most of all, whether
he knew where Diane was at this very minute.

She pushed her way through the crowd, scanning the
room constantly. In vain, she tried to figure out which
direction was east. The direction she finally headed proved
to be wrong. Instead of the Vallois rose stand, she found a
stall stocked with herbs. Pausing to get her bearings, she
inhaled the fragrant air, heavy with the scents of sweet basil,
verbena, sage and peppermint.

Finally she decided to leave the building, hoping that out
on the street she would be able to orient herself according
to the direction in which the sea lay. To the north sat the elegant facade of the former government palace, decorated
with alternate Corinthian and Doric columns and crowned
by a balustrade. On her left was a clock tower—from the
eighteenth century, she surmised.

After determining which direction was east, she went
slowly back inside. If anything, the pandemonium had
worsened. The market was winding up to fever pitch, and
vendors filled the aisles, urging buyers toward their stalls.
She glanced at her watch and gasped. Six minutes past the
hour. He had told her nine sharp. Would he wait?

She had almost given up hope when she spotted a sign bearing the Vallois name. Yes, there were the roses, banks and banks of them. Fighting a growing panic, she looked over the area around the stall, her eyes passing, then moving back to more closely inspect a man who was half hidden by a stack of crates.

His face was in shadow, but the tan jacket, with its May tea rose pinned on the lapel, identified him as the caller. She slipped around the corner of the stall, wanting to get a better look at him before she approached him.

From this angle she could see his face. Deep-set, watchful eyes dominated his sharp, angular face. His light brown hair had started to turn yellowish gray at the temples and it was tousled, as if only recently he had run his fingers through it.

His tension was obvious, even from this distance. She crept closer, dreading the moment when she had to speak. She searched for and saw the magazine he'd promised to be carrying. Yes, this was the man who had called her.

Karen saw that she could delay no longer. He was beginning to fidget, glancing nervously at his watch and then searching the aisles that led to where he stood. She stepped out into view and the moment he saw her, he started in her direction. Glancing warily from left to right, he closed the distance between them. "Mademoiselle St. Clair?" he asked in a low, heavily accented voice.

"Are you the man who called me?"

He ignored her question. "Come with me. We can't talk out in the open like this."

He seemed very agitated, looking over his shoulder several times as he led Karen around behind a bank of flowers.

"What do you know about Diane?" Karen demanded, shaking his grip from her arm. "Who are you? What is this all about?"

"Please keep your voice down," he warned nervously, shifting his focus constantly from her to the area around them. "Your friend is in grave danger. And you are not safe, either."

"What are you trying to tell me? What kind of danger is Diane in? How can I help her?"

The man leaned closer, his voice dropping to an urgent whisper. "You must do as I tell you . . ." He looked up suddenly and his face paled. For a moment he looked as if he wasn't going to be able to speak. His throat worked visibly, and he moistened his lips.

"You must find the Sospel connection," he said hurriedly. "Look for Monsieur Henri. Tell him the dog is barking."

Then he left her, taking off at a dead run. He dodged past startled customers and flower vendors, knocking fragile blossoms to the floor and trampling them heedlessly under his feet. A heavyset woman stepped into his path, shaking her fist and shouting in French. The man pushed her aside with a burst of strength, not breaking his stride.

The air filled with shouted oaths and startled screams. Karen began to run in the direction the man had gone. For a moment she lost sight of him in the noisy confusion. She maneuvered her way around a bank of delicate carnations, looking around cautiously. Then she spotted him. He paused, turning, a look of horror crossing his face as he stared at something off to her right. Then, as if in slow motion, his face changed expression and he crumpled to the floor.

A momentary hush fell over the crowd closest to the man. Then a woman's scream cut through it, unleashing a flurry of movement. The crowd surged toward the spot where Karen had seen him fall and she was swept along with them. When she reached him, she saw that another man was bending over his sprawled body. "He's dead." Karen mentally translated the man's words. "Someone call the police."

Stunned, Karen stood motionless, staring incredulously at the man's body. Closing her eyes, she tried to fight the gagging sensation that convulsed in her throat.

The man was lying facedown on the ground, a crimson stain forming an ever-widening circle on the back of his tan jacket. In the center of that circle was the hole made by the bullet as it had exited his body. Someone stepped into the path of her view, breaking her horrified concentration, and she was able to turn away.

Someone shot him. The thought washed through her mind but she seemed unable to absorb it. She'd heard no shot. Had the noise of the crowded market shielded the sound of the gun being fired? Suddenly the reality of it seized her, and with a rush of panic she realized that whoever had murdered the man was probably close by.

Her heart beating rapidly, she searched the faces of the people around her. She would never forget the look of fear, then horror, that had crossed the man's face. She closed her eyes, trying to blot out the memory but the image lingered stubbornly.

Sickness clawed through her stomach, climbing into her throat. She was chilled through and yet her skin was clammy and sticky. Terror paralyzed her, rooting her to the spot. Whoever had killed the man might still be in the market, might have seen them talking. Might be watching her this very moment.

Willing her legs to move, she skirted the aisles, trying to lose herself in the crowd, hunching her shoulders and cursing her height. Her wavy, blond hair was a distinctive feature, she knew, and she wished she had something to cover it with. Blindly she broke into a run, pushing her way past the curious onlookers.

At last she reached the exit and allowed the flow of pedestrian traffic to carry her out into the street. As she reached the sidewalk, two police cars swept to a halt, lights flashing and sirens blaring. Car doors slammed and *gendarmes* tumbled out, dispersing the crowd immediately in front of the doorway. Karen melted into the shadows along the outside wall, leaning against it for support and willing her breathing to return to normal.

Her first instinct was to flee the scene. Although she knew she should stay and report to the police, since she had been the last person to speak to the dead man, she couldn't risk going back inside. Not now. She had seen how easily and quickly the man had been killed, even in the middle of a crowded marketplace. If, as the man had told her, she was in danger, there would be no safety for her inside.

Her steps faltered as she started to walk away from the area. In the aftermath of the event, she felt weak and drained. Her mind was just now beginning to take in the implications of this incident. Diane was in trouble. In grave danger, the man had said. And moments later he had been killed.

She stumbled along in the crowd. People had gathered in the streets, leaving their shops and apartments and abandoning their cars in the streets around the market, drawn by curiosity to the scene. *I must find a taxi,* she thought. *I'll return to the hotel and find Luke. He'll know what I should do next.*

At first she wasn't fully aware that someone had called her name. But when a deep masculine voice shouted "Karen!" again, she turned, startled to realize he must have been calling her for some time.

"Luke, what are you doing here?" She stared at him distractedly, wondering if he had materialized out of her thoughts.

He shouldered his way over to where she stood. "Are you all right, Karen? What's going on? The police..." He gestured at the street and she saw that more police cars had pulled up.

"That man... He was killed. I saw it, Luke." Karen caught her breath on a sob. "And he said that Diane is in grave danger."

"What are you talking about?" Luke put his arm around her shoulders, shielding her as a group of pedestrians pushed against them. "Let's get out of here."

They made their way as quickly as possible onto a side street, out of the way of the crowds and confusion. Luke slowed to a halt, turning Karen so that she faced him. "Now tell me, what's this all about?"

Karen glanced around the narrow street cautiously. It was deserted, oddly quiet in contrast to the Cours Saleya. The only noise was faint music, probably from a radio inside one of the apartments. Spotting a small courtyard through an open wrought-iron gate, Karen pointed and took Luke's arm. "Let's go over there to talk." She looked down at her red jacket. "I feel conspicuous here. This jacket is so easily recognizable."

Luke withheld comment until they had crossed the street and entered the courtyard. Karen headed over to a bench in one corner and sat down, suddenly aware that her legs were trembling. She huddled on the bench, and then as dizziness overcame her, she leaned over, crossed her arms on her knees and laid her head on top of them.

Luke settled beside her and rubbed her back gently. He didn't press her for an explanation, giving her time to regain control. "Ready to tell me what this is all about?" he said after a while. "What happened back there? You looked scared out of your wits."

"How did you know to find me at the flower market?" Karen raised her head and looked at him.

"The desk clerk told me. He said you'd asked for a taxi so you could go to the flower market. What on earth made you decide to play tourist this morning? I told you to wait for me."

"I didn't go to see the flowers," Karen said. "A man called me this morning. They summoned me to the lobby to take the call. He spoke in French and asked for me by name."

"Who was he?"

"I never found out." Karen wrapped both arms around herself. She still felt weak and shaky. "He told me he had information about Diane. He gave me instructions to meet him at the flower market at nine, and then he hung up."

"You shouldn't have gone without me." Luke's voice was sharp now.

"I didn't have any choice." Karen's eyes narrowed accusingly. "And by the way, where were you? The hotel clerk said you'd gone out early this morning."

Luke didn't answer immediately. His expression grew remote and an impenetrable barrier came down over his eyes. But when he spoke again, his tone was pleasant. "I went to the central post office to call my secretary."

"Couldn't you have called from the hotel?"

"I thought I'd have more privacy somewhere else."

Karen waited for him to elaborate, but he said no more. Finally she continued. "You didn't return, so I had to go to the market by myself. When I got there, it took me a while to find him."

"What did he tell you?"

Karen concentrated for a moment, trying to remember the man's exact words. "'Your friend is in grave danger,' he told me. 'And you are not safe, either.' Then his expression changed suddenly. He looked odd, as if he'd seen something that frightened him. Just before he took off running, he told me that I must find the Sospel connection.'" Karen paused, searching her memory for the man's exact words. "Then he said something about finding a man. Monsieur Henri. I was to tell this Henri that the dog is barking."

Luke looked confused. "The dog is barking? What's that supposed to mean?"

"I have no idea. None of it made any sense."

"What about the police? What's going on back there?"

Karen willed her voice to remain calm, trying to relate the facts as quickly as possible. "He was talking to me. Suddenly he looked up and I could see the fear on his face. That's when he mentioned Henri and the Sospel connection. Then he took off running. I lost sight of him for a moment but when I was able to glimpse him again, he had stopped and turned. A look of horror crossed his face and then he crumpled to the ground. I ran forward with the rest of the crowd, but when I got near him, a man was standing over him and said he was dead."

For a moment Karen stopped speaking, unable to go on as she remembered the sight. "There was a red stain on his jacket. I realized that he'd been shot. But I never heard the gunfire. The noise of the crowd must have masked it. There were lots of people shouting."

"It must have been horrible." Luke's gaze softened. He wrapped his arm around her shoulders and pulled her against him. Karen leaned into his comforting warmth. After a moment, Luke spoke. "Whoever shot him must have used a silencer."

"I hadn't thought of that," Karen murmured. "But after it happened, I was frightened. Whoever shot him must have seen us talking together. I was afraid that..."

"That whoever it was would come after you next," Luke finished grimly.

"In this red jacket, I'd be easy to spot," Karen explained.

"Take it off now," Luke ordered. Karen shrugged out of the jacket. There was a sort of controlled fury in Luke. She felt it in his clipped tone and powerful movements.

He stood up and paced back and forth across the pavement in front of the bench. Suddenly he smacked his fist into his palm and Karen jumped. "I've got to get you out of this," he said abruptly.

"I've got to find Diane, Luke. I've got to find this Monsieur Henri."

"If you aren't careful, you won't live long enough to do either." Luke's voice was solemn.

Karen, remembering the man who had died of a single deadly bullet in the flower market only minutes before, could find no reason to argue.

## Chapter Six

Afternoon shadows were falling over Nice's sheltering amphitheater of hills when Luke and Karen returned to the hotel. A visit to the police station had yielded little new information.

Inspector Bouvier's expression had lost its friendliness when he'd heard that Karen had been involved in the shooting at the flower market. "You know something about this murder? But how, *mademoiselle*?"

According to the inspector, the man with whom Karen had spoken had been killed by a 9 mm round, most likely fired from a silenced automatic pistol. Karen filed another lengthy report under the inspector's careful supervision. He then gave her an update on his investigation into Diane's disappearance.

"I'm sorry, but we haven't found any trace of Mademoiselle Garrett. No woman by that name has been treated at a hospital and our records show no sign of any accident...."

Karen received this information with a mix of emotions—relief that at least Diane was not lying injured in some hospital, and disappointment that there was no word on her whereabouts.

Luke hadn't said much on the ride back to the hotel. Once they got out of the cab, he led her away from the hotel entrance. "I've been thinking about what that man told you at the flower market. I don't think we should go straight back to the hotel." He took her arm. "Why don't we walk along the promenade? I'd like to talk to you."

As they turned onto the path at the edge of the sea, Luke asked, "Do you have any idea what he meant by the Sospel connection?"

Karen thought for a moment. "There's a small town by that name not far from here. I haven't been there, but some of my students went there when we were here last summer."

"That must be it." Luke's gaze darkened with triumph. "How far away is it?"

"I'm not sure, exactly. An hour, maybe a bit more." Karen glanced in both directions along the sidewalk and then pointed ahead to a tiny kiosk. "Perhaps we can purchase a map over there."

The kiosk offered a limited but adequate selection of maps. "Here it is." Karen studied a map of southeastern France. "There, in the mountains. Above Menton."

"That must have been what he meant." Luke handed the attendant some money and as he waited for his change, picked up a guidebook, studied it for a moment and then purchased it, as well.

"This Henri person must be there." Karen refolded the map. "We'll have to go there right away."

Luke didn't reply immediately. They left the kiosk and walked in silence along the sidewalk. From time to time Luke glanced behind them, attentively scanning the area. After a while, he stopped beside a bench and motioned for her to sit down. "Don't be so eager, Karen. I don't like the sound of this. Maybe it's a trap."

"But the man told me—"

"Who was he?" Luke interrupted. "Why should you believe anything he told you?"

"He was trying to warn me," Karen said. "He knew something about Diane, but he was killed before he could tell me what's happened to her." She put her hand on Luke's arm when she saw that his mouth was still stubbornly set. "He told me about Sospel because he wanted to help me find Diane. So I've got to go there."

Luke shook his head. "No, Karen. It's obvious your friend is mixed up in something dangerous. You can't risk going to Sospel on your own."

Karen shifted as far away as the narrow bench would allow. "Diane's my friend. I think the best way to find her is to go to Sospel and look for this Henri. I am going, alone if need be. You've already done enough."

Luke stood up abruptly and shoved his hands in his pockets. "Dammit, Karen, listen to me. Have you already forgotten what happened on the train? Do you want to get yourself killed?"

Karen jumped up and faced him, her face warming with anger. "Of course not, Luke. But I do want to find Diane. I can't just sit here and do nothing when she may be in danger."

Luke's expression softened. He touched her shoulder gently. "I know you want to help your friend, Karen. But why don't you let me go to Sospel by myself?"

"I'm going to Sospel," Karen said firmly.

"I'm a detective, Karen. Let me check out this Henri for you. If there's danger, I can take care of myself."

"Really?" Karen said coolly. "Like you did when we found that man in my room yesterday?"

Luke's mouth flattened into a thin line, and a muscle twitched in his jaw. Finally he spoke. "If you won't let me go by myself, then why don't we go to Sospel together? You may not think I'm the best detective in the world, but I do know my business."

For a moment, Karen considered refusing. Then she thought better of it. Why shouldn't she accept his offer? His experience would be an asset, and besides, she wasn't all that eager to head off on her own right now. "All right," she said finally.

"Good," Luke said briskly. He motioned for her to sit down. With the map spread out between them, they studied the route to Sospel. "It looks like a pretty rough trip." Luke's finger tapped the winding route indicated on the map. "I think we should rent a car. Maybe drive up there first thing in the morning."

"Do you think we'll be able to get a car at such short notice?"

"I'll try the rental places at the airport. One of them should have something." Luke gathered up the map and guidebook. "I don't think you should go back to the hotel, Karen."

"Do you want to go to Sospel tonight?"

"From the way the road looks on this map, we'd better wait until morning." He glanced at his watch and she saw him frown. "It's getting late, so I'd better get out to the airport." He studied her for a moment. "I'm going to find someplace for you to wait while I go get the car."

"Why? I can go with you, Luke."

He shook his head. "After I get the car, I want to go back to the hotel alone. That'll give me a chance to find out whether we've got anyone keeping an eye on us. It'll be better if you stay out of the way."

Karen opened her mouth to protest, but Luke stopped her. "Trust me, Karen." He looked at her searchingly. "Like I said, I know what I'm doing. If we've got anyone on our trail, I want to lose them before we head toward Sospel. You're pretty conspicuous, with that blond hair of yours. It'll be easier for me to keep a low profile if I'm alone."

"If you insist," Karen said grudgingly.

Luke didn't give her a chance to change her mind. "Now where would be a good place for you to wait?"

Karen glanced across the street. They had walked quite a distance down the Promenade and now were near the Hotel Negresco, with its distinctive Baroque exterior. "The Hotel Negresco?" she asked.

Luke frowned. "Maybe..." He hesitated and glanced along the street.

Karen studied the area around them. From here it would take only a few minutes to reach the Massena Museum. "Why don't I wait for you at the Massena Museum? It's not far from here, at the corner of the Promenade and the Rue de France."

"Seems like a good place to hide a professor of art history." A slight smile eased the worried lines on Luke's face. He thought for a moment. "You should be safe there. I don't think we're being followed now. If someone is keeping an eye on us, he's probably waiting for us back at the Hotel Azur."

"Then I'll wait for you at the museum," Karen said. She pointed to his watch. "We'd better hurry."

Luke folded the map, then rose to his feet and held out his hand. "I'll take you over to the museum." He waited until she was standing beside him before reaching out and grasping her shoulders. His dark gaze sought and held her own. "Promise me you'll wait there, Karen. Don't go off on your own. I don't want anything to happen to you."

"I'll wait," Karen promised. "But don't take too long, Luke. Otherwise, I might start worrying about you."

THE MUSEUM was pleasantly cool and dim. Constructed at the end of the nineteenth century in the style of an Italian villa, it housed an eclectic collection of art, as well as some significant historical items. Karen strolled through the

rooms on the ground floor, soothed by a world that was reassuringly familiar to her. Luke had left her just inside the
front entrance, promising to pick her up at five. "Be careful, Karen. If you see anyone suspicious or anything fright-
ens you, go straight to the museum office and have them call
Inspector Bouvier."

Karen knew the museum well enough to act as a guide.
Indeed, on past trips to Europe with her students, she had
frequently performed that function. On this Wednesday
afternoon the building was virtually deserted and she took
the opportunity to enjoy a leisurely look at her favorite
works.

When she finally glanced at her watch, she realized that
it was nearing four-thirty. She climbed the staircase to the
second level, passing Flameng's portraits of the Massena
family. Once there she passed a group of ten or fifteen
schoolchildren who were being guided into the left wing to
examine the museum's collection of religious objects.

Karen headed in the opposite direction, into the room that
housed paintings of the early Nice school. She had the room
to herself. Moving from painting to painting, she let the
peaceful visual images slowly supplant the all-too-real horrors she had witnessed that morning. Here, in this quiet
setting, it was easier to allay her worry about Diane.

She tried to mentally piece together the past few days, to
find some meaning in the seemingly unconnected chain of
events. There were so few facts, really. She knew that Diane had answered an ad in a personal column and struck up
an ongoing correspondence with a young minister. In ad-
dition, she now knew that Diane's trip to Europe had not
gone the way she had thought it would. But where was the
tour group Diane had come to Europe to join? It was beginning to look more and more as if Diane had been tricked.
But if so, for what purpose?

Someone had known the answers to some of her questions about Diane. But now that man was dead.

Karen shivered, suddenly anxious not to be alone with her thoughts. She hurried back out to the landing. There was just enough time for a quick visit to her very favorite works. A series of watercolors lined the staircase to the second floor. The delicate reproductions of frescoes that adorned the many country chapels around Nice were the work of Mossa.

On previous visits the watercolors had commanded her total concentration, but today, she found herself glancing over her shoulder from time to time. There was nothing to indicate that anyone was nearby, but Karen felt unable to relax. Her heels clicked lightly on the staircase as she made her way back down.

On the ground floor, she decided she had time to stop at the rest room before Luke arrived to pick her up. The main area of the ladies' room appeared to be empty. Karen went into the last stall.

A minute later, she heard someone enter the rest room. Footsteps moved slowly along in front of the stalls. She held her breath, willing whoever it was to go into one of the other stalls. Instead, the sound of the footsteps receded as the person went to the opposite end, then got louder as the path was retraced.

For a moment Karen was afraid her heart had permanently stopped. It lurched inside her chest and then resumed beating so loudly that she felt as if it must be audible to whoever was outside the stall.

Finally the footsteps stopped in front of the door to her stall and Karen froze. In her worst nightmare she could never have visualized a scene like this.

A masculine hand grasped the top of the door and then two shoes moved into view beneath its edge. The narrow black loafers were heavily scuffed.

"Don't move, Mademoiselle St. Clair." The words were spoken in English, but the accent was unmistakably French.

She opened her mouth, but not a sound would come out. He didn't have to worry that she was going to move. She felt as though she would never move again. It shocked her that this man knew who she was. She could see nothing of him aside from the shoes and the hand that was holding the door of her stall firmly shut.

When he spoke again, his words came in a harsh staccato. "The man at the flower market. You must repeat to me every word he said to you."

Karen struggled to find her voice. "Who are you?" she managed to whisper at last.

"Do as I tell you." He shook the door to the stall as if to emphasize his point.

Karen shrank back from the door. Her mouth felt dry and cottony. "I don't remember exactly," she said, trying to buy time. "He said something about Diane Garrett. That she was in danger."

When she said nothing more he shook the door again. "What else? You must repeat to me every word."

"I don't remember anything else," Karen lied.

There was a shuffling sound outside the stall and Karen saw the loafers move back abruptly. She caught a glimpse of movement and then watched in horror as the barrel of a black pistol was shoved under the stall door. The man spoke again, his voice low and menacing. "You will tell me everything he said to you. Now, or I won't hesitate to shoot you." The pistol was withdrawn and a second later, he shook the door of the stall again.

Karen's throat worked convulsively, but for a moment, no sound would come out. "He told me to find the Sospel connection. To tell Henri that the dog is barking."

There was a long silence on the other side of the door. "Is this everything?"

"Yes. Who are you? What's happened to Diane?"

"You must stay away from Sospel. If you and Donovan persist in trying to find her, things will only go worse for her."

Suddenly Karen heard the outer door to the rest room swing open. A moment later, a woman screamed and the door slammed shut. The black shoes disappeared and the door slammed again.

It was a moment before Karen could unlock the door. She pushed it open cautiously, peering out into the larger room. It was empty. As she reached the outer door, it swung open and a uniformed guard entered, followed by a frowning woman who was gesturing and speaking angrily in French. Karen tried to get past them but they stopped her, firing questions at her in rapid French.

Fifteen minutes passed before the furor died down. No one had seen the man leave the rest room. The woman who had screamed could give only a sketchy description of him— dark-haired, she remembered, but since she had seen only his back, she couldn't be of much help.

The security guard seemed inclined to view the incident humorously. He made a cursory search of the museum, with Karen and the other woman behind him, but there was no sign of the man. There were only a few people left in the museum this near closing time. Karen looked at every pair of shoes she passed, certain that she would never forget that particular pair. As they returned to the lobby, Karen saw that Luke was waiting.

"ALARD MUST HAVE BEEN afraid they knew who he was." The man who spoke the words turned away from the window and faced the other occupant of the office. Before he spoke again, he took off his wire-rimmed glasses and polished them carefully. "Otherwise, why would he have risked contacting Karen St. Clair? Or had he found out that she was mixed up in this?'' He frowned and pushed his glasses back onto his nose, then reached for a cigarette.

"She said he told her to contact Henri. She was to tell him that the dog is barking." Pierre Benoit waited for the other man to offer him a cigarette. When one wasn't offered, he helped himself.

"The dog is barking...." The man at the window touched a lighter to his cigarette and then tossed the lighter to Benoit. "He must have been referring to the East German. But what did he mean? That they'd found him out or that the whole plan is in jeopardy?"

Benoit didn't answer immediately. When he did, his voice was heavy with bitterness. "Alard was a good man. I knew something was wrong when he didn't show up for our meeting this morning."

"But why contact the St. Clair woman?"

"To protect us," Benoit said simply. "If he knew that they were on to him, he'd have wanted to avoid making any direct contact with us."

The other man didn't appear to be listening. He took off his glasses and began polishing them again. Benoit said nothing, merely watched him and waited. He had worked for this man on other operations and knew it was best to wait quietly for his orders. His patience was rewarded when the other man spoke again. "We'll have to put Miller in Alard's place. I want someone to watch the East German all the time."

"And if he suspects?" Benoit exhaled a cloud of smoke.

"Henri must make sure he does not suspect." The other man slammed his fist down on the windowsill, causing Benoit to sit up abruptly. "I have arranged to meet with Henri two days from now to arrange the final details. Until then, he will continue to play his part."

"He'll be here in Nice?"

"Tomorrow night. But stay away from him. You keep an eye on Donovan and St. Clair."

Benoit shifted uncomfortably in his chair. "It may take some time to locate them."

"What?" The other man advanced a step toward him.

Benoit stood up and stubbed out his cigarette. "I had to leave the museum in a hurry. I tried to pick up their trail at the Hotel Azur, but it seems they've checked out."

"Find them." The sharp command sliced the momentary silence. "They mustn't get in the way of our plan."

"And if they do?"

"Do whatever you must to stop them."

LUKE LISTENED QUIETLY while Karen described what had happened at the museum. Then he led her out to a cream-colored compact Renault and helped her into the passenger's seat.

A muscle twitched in his jaw as he heard out her story. "Damn, Karen. I shouldn't have left you alone."

Karen tiredly pushed her hair away from her face. "I'm beginning to feel like maybe I'm going crazy, Luke. I don't know what to make of all this."

Luke's eyes darkened as he looked at her. "You're exhausted, Karen." He pointed to a large shopping bag on the back seat. "I've got your clothes. After I got the car, I circled back by the hotel and checked us both out." His mouth tightened into a grim line. "As far as I could tell, no one followed me after I left the hotel. Apparently no one needed to. At least one person had already found you."

Karen shivered and glanced out the car window, looking for invisible watchers in the deserted street. "Where are we going now?"

"I've booked you a room at a hotel near the airport." This time it was Luke who studied the area outside the car. "We won't drive straight there. I think we'll take a round-

about route, just to make sure we're not being followed."
He started the engine and put the car in gear. Once they were
out on the promenade, joining the steady stream of traffic,
he spoke again. "You'd better check to make sure I got all
your things."

"The manager let you into my room?"

Luke smiled wryly. "He was so eager to see me leave that
he provided the shopping bag himself." Luke's smile faded.
"Karen, maybe you'd better stay here in Nice while I go to
Sospel. After what happened at the museum..."

"No way," Karen said stubbornly. "I'm going to Sospel. And besides, look how much trouble I get into when
I'm by myself. I should think you wouldn't want to leave me
alone."

Neither of them spoke until they were stopped in front of
the hotel where he'd booked them rooms. "I didn't see
anyone behind us," he commented. "There's no way I can
be sure, though." He switched off the engine and turned to
face her. "Karen, I'm worried that we may be walking right
into a trap. We're going to have to be very careful."

"I'm going with you." Karen got out of the car and
started toward the hotel.

Luke came after her. "The car rental clerk told me the
roads are dangerous that direction."

"You discussed Sospel with the rental clerk?" Karen
halted abruptly. "That doesn't seem very smart to me. That
may make it easy for someone to follow our trail."

"I'm a good detective, Karen."

"Unless you're prepared to treat me like an equal part-
ner, I'm going to rent my own car and go to Sospel by myself." Karen took a couple more quick steps and stopped
again. "I have no intention of sitting here in a hotel room
while you go look for Diane."

Luke stared broodingly at her. "You're a stubborn
woman, Karen. And you've got a nasty temper."

"You haven't seen anything yet," Karen warned. She reached to open the door, but Luke was there ahead of her, blocking her way.

"What about dinner?"

"I think I'll make an early night of it, Luke."

"You'll have to eat something," Luke pointed out. "Besides, it'll save time if we make our plans over dinner."

"All right," Karen conceded after a moment. "By the way, how much do I owe you for all this? You'll have to let me know what you paid to check me out of the Hotel Azur. I also insist on paying at least half of the car rental."

"We'll settle all that after dinner. Meet me here in the lobby in half an hour."

LUKE WAITED until they were seated at a corner table on the terrace of a cosy bistro before he told her his latest news. The maître d' lit a covered candle on the table between them and then withdrew. "I got a call from my secretary while I was collecting our things at the Hotel Azur."

Karen was immediately alert. "Has she found out anything about Diane or Mark?"

"She's still checking with the newspaper about the person who placed that personal ad. But she was able to check on those traveler's checks of Diane's. The last check she cashed was issued on May 15. Apparently Diane exchanged it for francs at the rail station when she arrived in Nice."

Candlelight flickered softly over the white tablecloth between them. Karen searched Luke's face hopefully, then, realizing that he was not going to say more, asked quietly, "And there hasn't been anything else since then?"

"Nothing else has come through back in the States. But by now there could have been other checks cashed."

For a moment Karen couldn't speak. She picked up a fork and drummed it absently against the tablecloth before setting it back down. Until this very minute she hadn't realized how strongly she'd been hoping that she was wrong about Diane's disappearance. But now she could no longer rationalize. It seemed unlikely that Diane would go this long without needing money under ordinary circumstances. Still... "She could have used a charge card, Luke. We have no way of checking that. I haven't any idea whether Diane has any accounts."

"That's true." Luke leaned forward and placed his hands on the table. "Don't worry about this too much, Karen. It doesn't mean something has happened to Diane. But at least for now, the traveler's checks aren't going to help us find her."

"I don't know what to make of all this, Luke. From the moment Diane called me, I've had a bad feeling about this trip of hers. But I never seriously considered that she might be in danger."

"You're going to have to consider that possibility now, Karen. That man you talked to at the flower market today told you Diane is in danger. And we can't discount that attack on you on the train."

Karen looked down at the tablecloth, not meeting his gaze. "Why are you so interested, Luke?"

"I've told you. I've got a feeling Mark Turner is involved in this thing somehow. It can't be just coincidence that he and Diane followed the same route, stayed at the same hotels."

Karen thought hard for a moment. Then, before she could change her mind, she looked up quickly and spoke. "I want to hire you, Luke. You're a detective and you told me you've handled missing persons cases before. So I want to pay you to find Diane."

"I thought you understood that I've already offered to help find Diane."

"That's not what I meant. I want to offer you a business proposition. I'm willing to pay your usual rates for this sort of work."

She had made him angry. There was no doubt of that. A muscle tightened and tensed in his jaw and his eyes clouded. Karen felt a momentary surge of satisfaction. At last she had managed to wipe that amused, patient smile off his face. When he spoke, his voice was thin with fury. "What's this hang-up you've got about money, Karen? Every time I turn around you've got your damned purse open."

"I just want to clarify our relationship. If we both go to Sospel tomorrow, we'll be spending a lot of time together. So far, we don't have any proof that your friend is connected with Diane. Until we discover evidence of that, I won't feel comfortable accepting your help."

Luke was beginning to recover himself. His body grew dangerously motionless and only the glitter of his eyes revealed that he was still angry. "Afraid I might presume to be a friend?"

"That's not what I meant, and you know it."

"On the contrary. From the moment we met, I've been trying to offer my friendship. But you haven't missed a single opportunity to put me in my place. Is it just me personally that you don't like or is it men in general?"

"I think that remark was uncalled for." Karen managed to keep her voice calm even though she was seething inside. "And I didn't mean to imply that I don't like you."

Luke leaned back in his chair and regarded her with a speculative gleam in his eyes. "Does that mean you *do* like me?"

Flustered now, Karen fidgeted with the silverware and tried to avoid meeting his gaze. "This is what I don't like, Luke. The way you try to make everything mean something personal. I was trying to talk to you about Diane. Does it really matter whether I like you or not?"

At least a full minute passed before Luke answered. "It matters," he said bluntly. "Because you see, Karen, I'm beginning to like you quite a lot."

Before she could say anything, the waiter arrived to take their order. They both studied their menus, made a selection, and Luke chose a bottle of wine.

After the waiter had gone away, Luke was the first to speak. "You'll accept my help?" he asked. "With no more talk about payment? I don't want to work *for* you, Karen, I want to work with you, as a friend."

"Okay," Karen agreed. "Partners?"

He nodded. "Good. Then we need to make a few plans. First of all, let's try to put together what we know so far."

"It's not much," Karen admitted. "We don't know what's happened to Diane or Mark, only that there may be a connection between them."

"My secretary researched the background of that citizens' coalition. She was able to confirm that Mark was a member."

"Then Mark and Diane must have known each other."

"It seems likely." He waited while the waiter poured the wine—a ruby, full-bodied red from the southern slopes of the Maures. Their first course, a delicate concoction of flaky pastry and savory cheese, was set before them. "That doesn't explain why both of them came to Europe at the same time. And it doesn't explain Diane's friend from the personal ad."

Karen took a sip of her wine and then looked at Luke over the rim of her glass, her eyes thoughtful. "None of this makes any sense. Diane is not the type to be mixed up in anything dangerous. And it doesn't sound like your friend Mark is, either."

"That citizens' group is the only link we've got between the two of them." Luke paused. "Mark never mentioned Diane to me."

"And I've never heard Diane mention Mark's name. She doesn't have that many friends."

"When was the last time you saw Diane?"

"At Christmas," Karen replied promptly. "My father and his wife live in California. I get along with my stepmother but I don't really fit in at home. They have children of their own now, my two half brothers. So this year I spent the holidays with Diane instead of going home."

"You said that your mother was Diane's godmother?"

"Yes, but both my mother and Diane's died when we were quite young. We didn't see that much of each other until I came back to Virginia to teach. Since then, I've visited her several times and we try to keep in touch by phone. Luke, Diane's just not the type to do anything the least bit underhanded. You'd have to know her to understand what I mean, but she's very timid."

"Not like you, then?" Luke regarded her teasingly.

Karen chose to ignore the remark. They were on their second course now, a hearty saffron-scented bouillabaisse poured over thick crusty slices of bread. A cool breeze had begun to waft across the terrace, making her appreciate the steaming concoction of local Mediterranean fish. "What about Mark? Could he be mixed up in something dangerous, do you think?"

Luke shook his head. "It's unlikely. You can never be sure you know someone, but Mark has been almost as close as a brother to me. My own family lives in Ohio. Until I met Mark and Alicia I hadn't really realized what I was missing by not living near my family."

"How did you end up in Washington?"

"I served in the Marine Corps for a while after I left college. At the time, it seemed like a good way to get away from home. My family's great, but looking after three sisters and a mother, sometimes against their wishes, can become a bit wearing after a while. My father passed away years ago."

"An ex-Marine. I should have guessed." Karen smiled.

Luke raised his eyebrows. "Oh?"

"The way you rush in and take charge of things. That must be left over from the Marines."

"Sorry to disappoint you," Luke said. "But I'm afraid that's the legacy of having three younger sisters."

"So you left the Marines," Karen prompted.

"I was working at the Pentagon when I decided to leave the corps. There are plenty of jobs available in D.C. for ex-Marine officers, especially those with a background in investigative work. So I stayed in the area. It seemed a natural step to go into business for myself."

"And that's when you met Mark and Alicia?"

"Yes." Luke paused. "And I think I know Mark well enough to be fairly certain he wouldn't knowingly get involved in anything underhanded, either."

"So if he is somehow connected with whatever's happened to Diane, it's probably by accident," Karen concluded.

"I can't think of any other explanation." Luke offered her cheese and fruit from the selection that had been put on their table. "That brings us back to Sospel. Our next step is to check out this Henri, whoever he is."

"And if we can't find him?"

"Let's not worry about that until it happens, Karen." Luke looked grim. "For now, he's our only lead."

As they prepared to leave the café, Luke asked her if she would like a drive. Karen didn't need much persuasion. The night was cool and bright with stars, the Mediterranean a gleaming wash of midnight blue. Luke guided the car into the stream of traffic heading down the promenade. Before long, they reached the old harbor area, circled it and headed onto the Lower Corniche, the road that followed the coast to Monte Carlo.

Luke pulled the car over onto a wide graveled verge that overlooked the sea. Before cutting the engine, he looked back the way they had come. "Just making sure we weren't followed," he said lightly.

Karen sat up abruptly. "You really think someone might?"

"Until we know more about what's going on, we might as well be prepared." Satisfied that the road behind them was clear, Luke turned off the engine. In the distance, the lights of Villefranche curved like a necklace of gleaming diamonds. Luke rolled down his windows, letting the sounds of the sea provide their own natural music.

Luke took her hand after they had sat for a few minutes. His fingers wrapped around hers and his thumb rubbed against the base of her fingers. "No rings," he observed quietly. "You're not married, are you, Karen?"

"I'd hardly be holding hands with you if I were," Karen retorted. Her words sounded sharper than she had intended, but she didn't quite know how to respond to Luke. He was almost frighteningly blunt at times.

"Does that mean you're unattached?"

"If you're asking whether I'm seriously involved with anyone, then the answer is no." When he didn't say anything, she decided she had a right to ask a few questions of her own.

"What about you, Luke?"

"Well, what can I say, Karen?" His tone was bantering. "A man with my charm, as you pointed out, obviously has to fight off female attention."

"You're impossible." Karen stopped and turned to face him.

"But not married," he said lightly. "And not seriously involved. At least not yet...."

THE WARM MOOD lasted until they reached the hotel. They had to wait at the gate until the night clerk came and opened it, then Luke found a parking space and they got out of the car. As they went toward the hotel, Luke slipped his arm around her waist. "Are you sure you ought to come with me to Sospel tomorrow, Karen? I'm worried about what we may run into. If that man was right and you are in danger..."

Karen's mellow mood evaporated rapidly. A tiny dart of pain pierced her happiness. Had Luke's friendliness been just a ploy to get his own way? From the first he'd wanted to go to Sospel without her. Had the dinner been simply a maneuver to manipulate her into changing her mind? When she spoke, her voice was cold. "I'm going to Sospel, Luke."

His arm dropped away from her waist. "I don't think that's wise."

Karen waited until they reached the door. As he leaned to open it, she looked him fully in the face. "If that's what this has all been about, then I'm afraid you've wasted your time. I have no intention of changing my mind. And I'd appreciate it if you'd give me the car keys. I'm not sure I trust you."

Luke dropped the keys into his pocket and folded his arms. "And what makes you so sure I trust you? I'm keeping the keys. Otherwise I'm apt to come down in the morning and find that you've taken a notion to go to Sospel by yourself."

For a moment Karen savored the thought of punching him. His complacent arrogance set her teeth on edge. "Then maybe we should compromise," she said at last. "We'll leave the keys with the desk clerk."

"That's ridiculous. I won't leave without you, Karen."

"Nevertheless, I'll sleep better knowing the keys are safely down at the desk."

Inside the lobby, the night clerk eyed them strangely when they made their request. "*Oui, mademoiselle,* I will give the keys only to the two of you together." Although he didn't say anything else, Karen could see the amusement in his eyes.

Without waiting for Luke, Karen hurried up the stairs. She wasn't yet ready to admit that anger wasn't the only emotion she was feeling. She was disappointed, but she didn't want to admit that to herself.

A KNOCK AT THE DOOR woke Karen. Slowly she forced herself back to consciousness and switched on the lamp beside the bed to glance at her watch. After midnight. She groaned and lay back down. But after a moment the knocking began again, more insistent this time.

She threw back the quilts and climbed out of bed. She didn't travel with a robe, so she wrapped one of the quilts around herself, and after glancing in the mirror to make sure it covered the silk teddy that doubled as her pajamas, she padded across to the door. "Who's there?" she called and then repeated the phrase in French.

"Luke."

"It's after midnight," she whispered back heatedly. "And I'm quite happy spending the night alone, thank you."

"Sorry to disappoint you," he whispered back, "but it's not sex I'm after, it's conversation. I've found out something."

Karen unlatched the door and swung it open. Luke was still wearing the clothes he'd had on earlier. His gaze openly took in the quilt and her disheveled hair. "May I change my mind?" he asked playfully. "About preferring conversation, that is?"

Karen rolled her eyes in reply. "Did you find out something about Diane?"

Luke sauntered into the room and after a quick look around, he sat down on the edge of the bed. He moved over to make room for her to join him but Karen stayed where she was. She looked quickly up and down the hall and breathed a sigh of relief when she realized it was empty. At least no one had watched Luke come to her door.

"Aren't you a little warm?" Luke eyed the quilt.

"Get to the point, Luke. You'd better not be here under false pretenses."

"I don't know, Karen." Luke lounged back. "Now that I see you, I realize any pretense to get in here would be justified."

"Don't make yourself too comfortable," Karen warned him. She tried to tug the quilt more firmly about herself but only succeeded in making things worse. "Either start talking or get out."

Luke sighed and made a show of sitting up straighter. "I called my secretary again. She's come up with more information about that personal ad."

Karen forgot her irritation and hurried over to stand beside him. "Did she find out who placed the ad?"

"A man named Ron Ferguson. He placed it through the mail and asked that all replies be sent to him at an address in Washington, D.C."

"Did your secretary check out the address?"

Luke nodded. "She drove out there immediately. It was a box-rental facility in a neighborhood shopping center. The manager remembered only that a man rented the box, paying in cash."

"But what about this man, Ferguson. Did your secretary find out whether there's any minister by that name in D.C.?"

"Helen checked the phone book herself and then put two of my investigators to work checking out every lead they could think of. As far as they can ascertain, there's no minister by that name anywhere in the D.C. area."

"But what about the box? Couldn't someone watch that?"

"Helen says the manager of the facility finally admitted that the box has been inactive for a couple of weeks now. The box holder is behind in his rent, and there's been no mail since the first part of May."

"It doesn't make sense," Karen protested. "Diane was so sure this man was a minister. And someone sent her that ticket to Rome. Why would anyone go to so much trouble?"

"It looks to me like your friend had been set up for something, Karen. But what?"

"And why Diane?"

"Helen checked out that Gilbert Industries you mentioned."

"The oyster-packing plant?"

Luke nodded. "Seems that the Chesapeake Bay is the largest oyster-producing area in the world. Gilbert Industries packs a lot of those oysters and ships them to the country that just happens to have the largest per capita consumption of oysters in the world."

"France?" Karen hazarded a guess.

"You guessed it." Luke drummed his fingers on the pillow.

"Are you saying you think Diane's disappearance has something to do with oysters?"

"It seems farfetched, I agree. But Diane and Mark both opposed that plant. And they've both ended up in France." Luke was silent for a moment. "Well, it doesn't add up to much. I think it's time we looked at those letters." He stood up and glanced around as if searching for Diane's suitcase. When he spotted it, he went over and opened it.

"I guess you're right." Karen hesitated. She hated the thought of prying into Diane's affairs, but what choice did they have?

When the letters were spread out on the floor, Karen felt worse. "Don't start reading them yet, Luke. I'm going to put some clothes on first.'' She retrieved a pair of cotton jeans and the knit top she'd been wearing earlier and went into the bathroom.

When she came out, Luke handed her the first letter. "We'll read them in order," he directed. "Why don't you read them out loud."

The letters, written in a pleasant masculine scrawl, seemed innocuous enough. From the very first, this "Ron" seemed friendly and pleasantly interested in Diane. He asked questions about Diane's life and apparently she answered him, for each letter grew more personal and knowledgeable. He told Diane a little about his own life and his work as a minister, and in the most recent letters, he described his upcoming trip to Europe. But mostly he showed interest in Diane herself. "I guess it's easy to see why Diane liked this man," Karen said as she read the last of the letters.

"You mean it's easy to see how he fooled her," Luke pointed out. His expression was serious, mirroring some of the anxiety Karen was feeling.

"You really think this guy tricked her?"

"There's not much else to think right now. I'm afraid Diane is mixed up in something way over her head. Let's hope we can find her before it's too late."

"There's nothing in these letters that tells us anything new." Karen regarded the pile of letters in frustration.

"Maybe we've missed something." Luke picked up a letter and began reading it silently, and after a moment Karen followed suit. Slowly and more carefully this time, they examined the letters.

"He sure seemed interested in the Eastern Shore," Karen commented after a few minutes.

"And the oyster plant." Luke tapped the letter he was holding against his palm. "Have you noticed how often he asks Diane about Gilbert Industries? He asked about the citizens' coalition, as well."

"She probably wrote a lot about both those subjects. I told you, she helped her father with his work. It was really Diane's only interest. And Mr. Garrett was violently opposed to the building of that new oyster-packing plant. He claimed the Chesapeake Bay would be destroyed. He didn't think the oyster population could survive such massive exploitation."

"Mark shared that viewpoint. He talked about it constantly last year." Luke seemed lost in thought.

"You don't think their disappearance has something to do with that?"

"It doesn't seem like much," Luke admitted after a moment. "But for now, it's all we've got to work with."

"I don't see how it's going to help us."

"Neither do I." Luke glanced up at her and smiled grimly. "I'd hoped the letter would tell us more. I guess we're right back where we started."

"Except for the Sospel connection."

"And Monsieur Henri," Luke added.

Luke watched as Karen sorted Diane's letters and replaced them in her tote bag. *Too bad she's changed into those jeans. I liked the quilt better,* he thought.

Helen's telephone call had confirmed the information Karen had already given him about herself. Karen St. Clair was exactly who she'd said she was—an art history professor. Although she hadn't mentioned it, apparently she had a fair amount of artistic talent herself. According to Helen, some of Karen's work turned up now and then in a gallery near the college.

Luke wondered why she'd chosen to teach instead of painting full-time. That was just one among many of the things he wanted to learn about Karen. Personal details that didn't show up in a routine background investigation. Did she want to marry? Was she interested in having a family of her own? It didn't sound as if she'd had much family life as a child.

Luke was basically a loner himself. That's why he'd left the Corps. He hadn't liked the feeling of being confined and regimented, and he supposed that partially explained why he'd never married. Once he had come close to settling down, when he was in his early twenties. But, until lately, he hadn't minded being single. A woman like Karen St. Clair could make him reconsider his views on the subject.

She turned to find him watching her. "You'd better leave now, Luke." Her eyes, darkened now to a deep gray green, contradicted her words.

Luke reached for her, pulling her down onto the bed beside him before she could protest. He shifted until their bodies were facing each other, then stroked the curve of her cheek, his fingertips memorizing the smooth texture of her skin. He wrapped a strand of her hair around his thumb, then gave in to the urge to tangle his hand in the silky waves.

"Luke, I think . . ." Her voice was soft, slightly husky.

"Shh," he whispered. "Don't think." He lowered his head slowly until he found her lips. The moment he felt her lips move beneath his, he was lost. He gathered her close, kissing her slowly and with infinite care. She responded, hesitantly at first and then with an answering passion.

He felt the soft swell of her breasts against his chest and slipped his hands beneath her sweater. A sigh escaped her as his fingers found the delicate, velvety underside of her breast. With a whispered moan, Luke succumbed to the fire that was burning slowly out of control inside him. He crushed her against him, deepening their kiss, exulting in her immediate response. "Karen," he murmured. "This feels so right. . . ."

Then, from somewhere he found the strength to pull away. He wanted to stay here with her forever. But he knew it wasn't yet the right time. She didn't stop him when he stood up. He leaned over and dropped a kiss lightly on her temple. Then he left, waiting in the hall until he heard her lock the door behind him.

# Chapter Seven

Through the plate-glass windows that fronted the coffee bar, Karen glanced out at the Mediterranean. Pale and smooth, it glowed softly iridescent at this early morning hour. Luke sat across from her at a small wrought-iron table, his attention focused on a map of southern France.

"It shouldn't take us more than an hour to reach Sospel." He folded the map and laid it to one side of the table. "Why don't I do the driving?"

Karen met his quizzical hazel gaze with cool remoteness. Events of the previous night had given her second thoughts about her relationship with Luke. They'd met under unusual circumstances, but as far as she was concerned, things were moving too fast. She was partly to blame, she knew, but she'd been overwhelmed by her immediate and uncharacteristic response to him. After he'd left her room last night, she'd come to the conclusion, a bit reluctantly, that she needed to put some distance between them. And she needed to make it clear that she was quite capable of making her own decisions.

"I think it would be best if we take shifts behind the wheel, don't you?" She reached for her cup and slowly took a sip of coffee.

"What do you suggest? Fifteen-minute shifts? If we don't watch out, we'll be running circles around the car, playing musical chairs." Luke leaned back in his chair, grinning lazily.

"Why don't you drive as far as Menton. We can switch there."

Luke leaned forward abruptly, the front legs of his chair hitting the floor with a bang. "You can't be serious, Karen? Don't you think you're carrying this thing a bit far?"

"We're partners, Luke. That means we share equally in the responsibility, right?"

He drummed his fingers on the table and then looked away from her. When his gaze rested on her face again, the hardness had returned to his features. "Right. And since we're partners and we're sharing equally in everything, I believe it's your turn to buy the coffee. How about seeing if you can get us two coffees to go. We should be hitting the road." After he spoke, he pushed his chair back and stood up. A tiny smirk of male satisfaction played at the corners of his mouth as he took in her reaction to his statement.

"All right," Karen said coolly after a moment of silence. "Café au lait? Or do you prefer it black?"

"Black will be fine."

Karen managed a distant smile as she headed for the counter at the back. She'd gotten what she wanted, hadn't she? Then why did she suddenly have the feeling that she'd just been outmaneuvered?

UNDER OTHER CIRCUMSTANCES, Karen would have enjoyed the drive along the scenic Lower Corniche to Menton. The road wound along the coast, following the curve of the sapphire sea that glowed under the brilliant morning sun. It was no wonder that Renoir had been inspired here to paint his many impressionistic landscapes, Karen mused.

For a moment she allowed herself to imagine making this trip with Luke under normal circumstances. Their days would be spent exploring the area's artistic and historical riches, their nights— She brought her daydreams to an abrupt halt. It didn't seem to matter that she was determined to keep her feelings for Luke under tight rein while they searched for Diane. That resolve melted swiftly when she was with him.

She glanced over at Luke. He drove competently, his grasp loose on the wheel, yet maintaining firm control over the small car. She stared at his hands and she felt her mouth go dry. It was as if he were touching her, controlling her response with that same effortless ease. A sharp twist of desire uncurled deep inside her, and she looked away sharply, feeling heat rush to her cheeks. *Concentrate on how you're going to find Henri once you get to Sospel,* she told herself. *Don't think about what it would be like to make love with Luke Donovan. You don't even know the man.*

A sign indicating that they were nearing Menton came into view as they rounded a curve. Karen forced herself to reach for the map. "Once we get into Menton, we'll have to start looking for the turnoff to Sospel." She was surprised, and grateful, that her voice sounded normal.

Menton was starting to wake up as they drove into it a little later. The wave of progress that had run roughshod over the other towns along the Riviera had somehow bypassed Menton. It retained its winding cobbled streets and tall, narrow buildings, all overlooked by the ornate, stone tower of the cathedral. Luke slowed the car as a woman darted across the street ahead of them, a basket over her arm from which peeked the tips of crusty loaves of bread, most likely still warm from the baker's oven. Through open gateways, Karen caught glimpses of cool, flower-smothered courtyards and mysterious narrow alleyways whose flights of steps disappeared into dark shadows.

Near the market area, Luke maneuvered the car into a skinny space between two buildings and stopped. "Your turn to drive," he announced.

Karen was out of the car by the time he came around to the passenger side. She took the keys from him, circled the car and climbed in on the driver's side. Luke didn't say anything, but she was uneasily aware that he was watching her. She switched on the engine and then reached for the gearshift, praying it would mesh smoothly into reverse.

Luckily the car cooperated. Before long they were leaving the city center behind. Now that she was behind the wheel, she noticed that the car seemed slightly sluggish. She revved the engine once they were out on the open road and frowned when she detected a slight misfire.

"Something wrong?" Luke glanced at her.

"The engine feels a little sluggish."

"It felt fine to me," Luke murmured. "I wouldn't worry about it."

Karen refrained from arguing, but as they continued down the road, she was sure she felt the car misfire again. With a sinking feeling, she realized that something was not quite right about the engine.

She kept her own car in perfect running order. She'd taken a class in automotive mechanics on a dare, but had ended up enjoying it immensely. Now whenever she needed an escape from the orderly, placid routine of her teaching job, she would retire to the garage behind her town house, wearing old blue jeans and carrying her tool box. It was the one private quirk in an otherwise predictable life.

Luke didn't seem to be noticing anything amiss with the engine so she dropped the subject. "The turnoff should be up ahead soon. Could you look at the map, Luke?"

"We need the Castillon Pass road." Luke bent over the map briefly and then began watching the road ahead of them. "There it is!" He pointed to a turnoff just ahead, and Karen had to slam on the brakes to stop in time.

"According to the map the road from here on is pretty winding," Luke warned.

"It's twenty-two kilometers to Sospel." Karen nodded toward a sign as they passed it.

The road began to climb quickly as they left the coast behind. Although the road was well surfaced, at times it was barely wide enough to hold the Renault. Karen's grasp tightened on the steering wheel and her shoulders tensed.

"Want me to drive?" Luke asked.

"Thanks, but no," Karen returned hastily. She made a conscious effort to appear relaxed, even managing a slight smile. The driving required all her concentration as they embarked on a ribbon-wide course of steep hairpin bends, seemingly layered one on top of the other.

As they rounded one bend the road smoothed out and widened. A stony promontory had been paved to provide a parking spot for viewing the scenery. "There's the Mediterranean," Karen pointed out. Behind them, there was a clear view all the way to the sea. At this distance it had a surreal quality, as if it floated at the same level as the clouds.

Luke was looking at the road. "Sure you don't want me to drive?"

Exasperation edged Karen's voice. "I'm a good driver, Luke. You don't have to hold on to the dash like that."

The terrain had changed drastically since they'd left the coast behind. Up ahead, snowcapped mountain peaks melted into a purple haze. The mountainsides themselves were patterned with weathered stone terraces and above those, gnarled stands of spruce and juniper ringed the peaks.

Karen eased the car on around the curve but as the road began to climb again, she felt the engine slowly lose speed. She gave it more gas but instead of responding, the engine sputtered and died. "I told you something was wrong," she said. She guided the car toward the side of the road as they coasted to a halt.

Luke reached for the door handle. "Unlatch the hood and I'll take a look." He got out, and as an afterthought, leaned his head back in the car. "The hood latch is right over there, under the dash."

Karen eyed him coolly. "I think I just might be able to find it." Her sarcasm was lost on him. He was already heading around to lift the hood.

After she released the hood latch, Karen put on the emergency brake and got out of the car. Luke had removed the air filter and was examining the carburetor when she reached the front of the car. "It's got gas," he said, sounding puzzled. "Why don't you take a look at the scenery. I'll have this engine running again in no time."

Karen quelled an urge to have a look under the hood herself. She strolled back to the promontory and stared out at the Mediterranean. They had already climbed well above the coastal plain. On one side lay the sea, with its beaches and candy-colored buildings. Ahead of them loomed the Maritime Alps, still capped with snow, their tops poking into purplish, hazy clouds.

Karen glanced down into the ravine that etched its way along the road and fought a sensation of dizziness. Far below, tangled in an encroaching bed of scrub and brush, lay the rusted remains of a car. Apparently other drivers had not been so skilled at negotiating the hairpin turns. Stepping quickly away from the edge, she turned her attention back to the sea.

At last she could take the waiting no longer. She went back to the car. "Any luck?" she asked hopefully. "Have you checked the distributor cap?"

Luke looked around from behind the hood, frustration evident in every line of his face. "I know what I'm doing, Karen."

"Then why isn't the car running yet?" she asked sweetly.

"If you think it's so easy, why don't you have a look yourself?" Luke replied with barely restrained impatience.

"Thank you," Karen exclaimed, smiling brightly. "I've just been waiting for you to ask me." She reached down and unsnapped the distributor cap with ease, removing it from its housing. "Just what I thought—the contacts need to be cleaned. Do you have a pocket knife? Or even a key would do."

"What the..." Without commenting further, Luke went around to the car and got the keys out of the ignition.

"This is the one that's been causing the misfire." Karen showed him the cap when he returned with the keys. Without further explanation, she cleaned off the contact and replaced the cap.

"Where did you learn to do that?" Luke spoke quietly.

"A woman is allowed a few secrets," Karen replied. "They add to her mystique." She looked down and grimaced when she saw the black grease smeared on her hands. "Do you have a handkerchief?"

"Here." Luke thrust a clean handkerchief at her. "I have to admit, I'm impressed, Karen. You look more like an art history professor than an auto mechanic. It's one surprise after another with you."

"But, Luke," Karen raised her eyebrows in mock ingenuousness. "You told me not to be surprised by what people do. Besides, you don't really know me that well, do you?"

"Apparently not," Luke commented, slamming the hood shut and heading for the driver's seat.

THE SMALL CAR had been running perfectly ever since Karen had made the necessary repairs, but the conversation with Luke had definitely stalled. She had made several attempts to break the silence, but each time his replies were brief and monosyllabic. At last she could take it no longer.

"Look, I'm sorry about the car back there. We both know that if I hadn't helped we would still be stranded. Or worse yet, you might have damaged the car to the point that we would have had to have a tow truck pick us up."

"You don't have to sound so smug about it," Luke said tightly. She hadn't dared to comment when he'd taken over the driving, and now he was concentrating intently on managing the steep, twisting climb.

"Don't tell me you're angry." Karen sat back and regarded Luke with disappointment. "Surely you wouldn't let this threaten your male ego."

"I'm sorry," Luke said after a moment. "It's just that I think I'm the one who is supposed to do the rescuing."

"Isn't that a bit chauvinistic?"

"I prefer to think of myself as a romantic." Luke grinned at her sheepishly. "I felt pretty stupid back there."

"Next time, I promise I'll let you do the rescuing." Karen smiled back, relieved that they were talking again.

"And do you always keep your promises?" he teased, echoing the question she had asked him soon after they met.

"Almost always," she admitted, and they both laughed.

As they approached Sospel, Karen noticed that the area retained the vestiges of what had once been a rough and precarious way of life. The valley sides and hill slopes were crisscrossed with terraces and stone walls. Numerous olive groves dotted the hillsides, their domed tops a shimmering silvery green.

The road squeezed its way through a tunnel and entered Sospel. Ahead of them was a river, and Karen saw from the map that it was called the Bévéra. A medieval bridge, complete with twin arches and a watchtower in between, bisected the river. On either side, tall narrow houses with wrought-iron balconies crowded the banks.

Clotheslines loaded with laundry provided a splash of color throughout. As they passed narrow alleyways, Karen could hear the echoing cries of children at play.

There was a map of Sospel in the guidebook Luke had purchased. The police station was located in a small square known as St. Michel's. It was surrounded by houses with heavy Gothic arches, some of them still bearing scars from the air and artillery beating this area of France had taken during the Second World War.

At midmorning, the square was alive with activity. On the opposite side a grocer was doing a bustling business, and as they looked for somewhere to park, two women crossed the square, carrying baskets over their arms and staring at Luke and Karen with obvious curiosity.

Luke parked the car in a narrow slot to one side of the square and they got out. The Romanesque belfry of a church towered above them. Despite the bright sunlight, the air was still slightly chilly, and Karen reached for the jacket she had brought along.

"We'll have a word with the local inspector first," Luke suggested.

The police station was crosshatched with light, its windows shuttered against the sun. Luke and Karen crossed the red tile floor and she asked a young *gendarme* seated behind the reception desk if the inspector would see them. "Wait here, *s'il vous plaît*." He hurried away.

A few minutes later, he returned and led them to a pleasant office. The man who awaited them rose as they entered and explained that he was temporarily in charge. "Our chief inspector is on holiday. I'm Inspector Ronet, the acting chief inspector for this jurisdiction."

"I'm Karen St. Clair." Karen held out her hand. "And this is Luke Donovan. Do you speak English?"

"Americans?" The inspector motioned them to chairs, switching to slightly halting English. "May I offer you a drink? Some coffee, perhaps? And then you can tell me how I may help you.''

"No coffee, thank you." Now that they were finally in Sospel, Karen couldn't contain her anxiety any longer.

"We're looking for someone, Inspector. A man known as Monsieur Henri."

The inspector looked confused. "But is that his full name, *mademoiselle*? Henri is usually a first name, is it not?"

"I don't know." Karen paused and drew a deep breath. "I was told to look for a Monsieur Henri in Sospel. I'm hoping that he will help me find a friend of mine, Diane Garrett."

"Garrett," the inspector murmured. "No, I do not recognize that name, either. But why would your friend be in Sospel? Is she a tourist?"

As quickly as possible, Karen explained about Diane's disappearance, leaving out nothing. When she finished the story of the man in the flower market, the inspector's eyes had widened and he was leaning forward over his desk.

"But this is a strange story," he said. "What does this Diane Garrett look like?"

Karen opened her purse and took out the snapshot of Diane. For several minutes, the only sound in the room came from outside the windows, while the inspector studied the photograph. At last he looked up, a rueful expression on his face. "*Je suis désolé, mademoiselle.* But I am afraid I can tell you nothing. I have never seen this woman in Sospel."

"And this Henri? Do you have any idea who this man might be?" Luke asked.

The inspector thought for a moment. "No, I'm afraid not. Perhaps if you had more information about him, something that would give me a clue as to who he could be..."

"Could you ask around, perhaps find out if anyone else has ever heard of this man..." Luke suggested.

"But of course." The inspector seemed to be relieved that at last he could be of some service. "I will start an investigation at once. Are you staying in Sospel?"

Karen and Luke looked at each other. "We've only just arrived," Karen began.

"If you think it might be helpful, we could probably arrange to stay the night here," Luke added.

"Yes," the inspector said. "Stay here in Sospel. And I will see what I can find out for you." He reached for a pad of paper and made some notes. "Here, this is the name of a small inn, an *auberge*. It's a quiet place and I'm sure they would have room for you tonight. I will stop by and see you there if I find out anything."

As Karen and Luke left the police station, she turned to him. "Do you think we ought to stay?"

"Right now, this is the only clue we have," Luke responded. "We can stay here and have a look around. We might stumble on something or the inspector might come up with some information for us. We have nothing to lose by staying here. I hope."

THE AUBERGE SOSPEL was on a hill at the eastern edge of the town. It was a long, two-story terra-cotta building with a pantiled roof and boxes of flowers at every window. Karen followed Luke up the stairs to the side door.

The entrance opened into a small lobby. To the right was a spacious dining room with floor-to-ceiling windows. A narrow staircase led up to the second floor on their left side, and a tiny counter with a wall of boxes for keys above it served as the inn's desk. An elderly woman sat in a rocking chair in a small room off to the side, a crocheted coverlet over her legs. She smiled as they entered and called out for someone in French.

A young woman hurried out to the desk. "You must be the Americans. The police inspector called and told me you were on your way."

"I hope we aren't inconveniencing you, arriving without a reservation." Luke introduced first Karen and then himself.

"I'm Yvonne Perret." The other woman spoke English with a lilting accent. "I have a room for you."

"Two rooms," Karen said quickly and firmly.

"Two." Yvonne looked up from the register she was consulting and then nodded. "Yes, I have two. They're on the second floor."

Yvonne handed them both keys and turned an old-fashioned registry book around for them to sign, handing it first to Luke. He wrote his name quickly and then asked about the car.

"You can park it around to the side. Here, I'll show you." Yvonne led the way out the door and after a quick look at Karen, Luke followed.

Left alone in the lobby, Karen reached for the book and then realized that Luke had taken the pen with him. She was trying to fish a pen out of her purse when she knocked the register with her elbow and it fell to the floor. The old woman in the rocker looked up sharply but then went back to her knitting when she saw that nothing serious had happened.

Karen found her pen and then leaned over to pick up the book. It had landed upside down, and when she picked it up, it was opened to another page. She was just about to flip back to the correct page when one of the names caught her attention.

She studied it carefully, feeling a growing sense of shock. "Irene Miller," she read aloud softly. She glanced at the date and saw that the book had been signed on May 17. For a moment she couldn't quite take it in. Irene Miller had stayed at this *auberge* on the seventeenth of May? But that was the day Diane had disappeared from the hotel in Nice. And that completely contradicted the story Irene had told Karen. She'd claimed this was her first trip to France. Added to the obvious lie Irene had told her about her whereabouts in Italy, the implications were overwhelming.

Karen heard Yvonne's quick footsteps outside the door, followed by a comment in Luke's distinctive tones. Hastily she turned to the correct page of the register and signed her name below Luke's. By the time the two of them entered the lobby, Karen had managed to assume her customary poise.

But as soon as she and Luke had climbed the stairs to the second floor, she grabbed his arm. "I've got to tell you something. Not here." She looked up and down the narrow hallway.

Luke started down the hall, looking at the room numbers and comparing them with his key. "Here's my room," he said suddenly. "We'll talk in here."

Karen scarcely paid attention to the room they entered. "Irene stayed here. On May seventeenth."

"What?" Luke's eyes narrowed. She had his full attention now.

"Her signature was in the register. She had a room here on the seventeenth and checked out the next day. But that isn't the story she told me. She lied. She told me on the train that this was her first trip to France. But she'd been here before and on the day that Diane disappeared from her hotel in Nice."

"Are you sure it was the same Irene Miller?"

Karen didn't reply immediately. "I can't be sure it's the same Irene Miller," she said finally. "But don't you see how this would all tie in, Luke? She lied to me about coming from Venice when she had actually been in Rome. And after I was attacked on the train that night, she acted strangely. At the time, I thought she was upset and worried, but now

I'm not so sure. Maybe she had something to do with what happened. Maybe she set me up. She knew when she left me that I was all alone in the train compartment.''

"Hey, slow down.'' Luke looked dazed. "You can't be sure it was the same Irene Miller. The name isn't that unusual. We could be talking about two different women.''

"That's possible. But I have a feeling the woman I met on the train is the same woman whose name I just saw in the register. Doesn't it strike you as a strange coincidence that a woman with that name stayed here the very same day that Diane disappeared?''

"I admit it's intriguing.'' Luke narrowed his eyes and pushed his hair back impatiently. "Still, it's not much to go on.''

"It must have some connection with whatever's happened to Diane.'' Karen's voice took on an imploring note. "Remember that conversation I overheard on the train? I couldn't hear what the other person said. I assumed the other person was a man, but what if it was a woman? I was in the bathroom when the train stopped. I'd left my compartment several minutes before, plenty of time for Irene to enter that other compartment. Those people were speaking in English, maybe because that's the language Irene speaks. They could have been talking about me.''

"Okay, Karen. Let's assume for the sake of argument that it was Irene.'' Luke started pacing the room. "That still doesn't explain what's going on or what's happened to Diane.''

"If Irene was here on the day Diane disappeared, it could mean that Diane is here.''

"Here at the *auberge*?'' Luke stopped abruptly and turned to face her. "I think your imagination is working overtime, Karen.''

"Maybe Yvonne is in on it, too," Karen speculated, ignoring Luke's expression of disbelief. "And maybe even the police inspector. After all, he sent us here."

"He sent us here because Yvonne is his niece and this is the best place to stay in Sospel," Luke said dryly. "Yvonne told me about her uncle while she was showing me the car park. Her husband's family has run this inn for a number of years. Her husband was killed in a car accident on that road we drove this morning. Now she owns the inn. Apart from a few smaller guesthouses, this is the nicest accommodation in the area."

"So maybe Yvonne isn't involved. But I think it's more than mere coincidence that Irene Miller's name is in that register down there."

"There's only one way to find out if we're talking about the same woman. We'll have to find out what this Irene Miller looked like. But even if it does sound like the same woman, I don't see how that information is going to help us. Right now, I think we should concentrate on looking for a man named Henri."

"You're the detective, Luke," Karen said. "Where do we start?"

"There obviously isn't a whole lot to Sospel," Luke replied. "We'll have to be careful. I'm still not convinced this isn't a trap of some sort."

"We've got to start somewhere, Luke."

Luke went over to the window and pulled the drapes open. Karen studied him, noting the taut muscles in his neck and the hunched set to his shoulders. He finally turned back to her, his words coming quickly as if he had made up his mind about something and was eager to put a plan in to action. "I suggest we start in the town square. It seems as though everyone passes through there sooner or later."

Locking the door behind them they proceeded down the windowless staircase and exited past the front desk. Yvonne called out as Luke reached for the door. "Dinner is served at six. Will you be eating with us?" Looking at her watch, Karen nodded and followed Luke out the door.

The shops around the cobblestoned square probably looked much the same as they had for the past seven hundred years. Their quiet, peaceful courtyards and flower-decked balconies did much to describe the leisurely life-style of the townspeople.

As the afternoon wore on, the maze of alleys and pathways began to make sense. "It looks like all roads lead to the central square." Luke took out a pair of dark sunglasses and slipped them on, then leaned against the small fountain they had stopped beside. "All the shops are closing up for the afternoon and we haven't gotten a single clue as to where Diane or Mark or this Monsieur Henri could be."

They had found nothing, but it was not from lack of looking. All afternoon, they had driven up and down the narrow, crowded streets, getting out at times to explore the shadowed alleyways behind the buildings.

"What now?" Karen fought back a rising sense of frustration.

"How about that old church? We could ask a few questions about this Henri up there."

Karen turned to look at the building he indicated. She checked Luke's guidebook. "St. Michel's. The belfry is Romanesque, and the rest of the church is Classical baroque."

"Right now, it's easy to believe you're a professor." Luke flashed a smile at her.

Karen walked toward the ancient cathedral, and Luke followed her into the dim interior. Their footsteps broke the silence, echoing hollowly off the aged walls. Near the front, a woman finished praying and rose quickly, moving silently past them as she left the church.

Shadows played on the altar, reflections from a bank of flickering candles. For a moment the only sound was the gentle sizzle and hiss of melting wax. The huge altarpieces and various frescoes were pure baroque. A denticulated cornice, barely visible in the faint light, ran the entire length of the nave walls.

"I'll tell you what." Luke leaned close and whispered. "You go ahead and check out the art and I'll have a look around."

Karen wandered into the apse on the left. A landscape of the Annunciation, the work of François Bréa, captured her attention and she studied it in solitude. Suddenly, her concentration was broken by what sounded like a muffled thud. Karen whirled around, looking for Luke. A second later, she heard another noise. Somewhere, footsteps hurried away in the darkness.

"Luke?" Karen called out his name in a low voice. "Luke, where are you?"

Fear was becoming familiar to her. The sensation once again surfaced as she consciously fought to remain calm. She ran lightly through the central chamber, pausing every few feet to listen. The third time she stopped, she heard a man groan. "Luke?" Her whisper was barely audible, even to her own ears.

An entrance into the side transcept was open. Karen's heart pounded painfully as she paused, searching the darkness, looking for Luke. Then she saw him. He was leaning against the wall, his hands clutching his chest.

"Luke, what's wrong?" She ran to his side. "Are you all right?"

"That seems to be our main topic of conversation these days, doesn't it?" His voice was weak, but at least he was able to speak.

"What happened?"

"I've got to catch him." Luke looked past her. "Stay close to me but don't get in the way." Without waiting for her to reply, he headed for the door. She could hear his breathing, harsh and irregular.

The sunlight blinded them momentarily as they stepped into the side courtyard. There was only one person in sight, an old man who was busy locking his bakery shop. He looked up at them and then glanced away.

"He's gone." Luke spat out the words. "Damn." He looked all around the area, his gaze sharp and searching.

"Who are you talking about?"

Luke rubbed his chest, drawing in a deep breath. "It happened when I turned into the passageway there. I must have surprised him. Before I knew what was happening, he landed a punch square in my chest. The next thing I knew, he pushed past me and took off. By the time I got my breath back, you were in there."

"Did you see him?"

"It happened too fast." Luke shook his head. "He must have been following us. Maybe he was afraid I'd see his face. I think we'd better pay that inspector another visit."

IT WAS AFTER SIX when Luke and Karen returned to the *auberge*. Their meeting with the inspector had at least erased Karen's suspicion that he and Yvonne might be involved in Diane's disappearance. The inspector had checked with Yvonne as soon as they'd quizzed him about Irene Miller. Over the telephone, he had elicited a description of the woman who had stayed at the *auberge* on the night of May 17. There was no doubt it was the same woman. Yvonne could tell them nothing about Irene's reason for being in Sospel. As far as she had known, the older woman had been an ordinary tourist.

When he heard about Luke's encounter at the church, the inspector had reprimanded them sharply. "Go back to the *auberge*. Don't try to investigate on your own. If I don't find out anything, I'll enlist the help of Inspector Bouvier at the Nice prefecture.''

Dinner was about to be served when they entered the inn. Yvonne wore a harassed expression as she greeted them. "Sit at any table where there are empty seats," she directed.

Karen looked around the dining room. There were three large tables set for dinner. At one of them, a couple and their three children had already taken over. The second of the tables was occupied by an older couple and two teenage girls. Karen and Luke made their way to the third table where a man was seated. As they approached, he looked up from the book he was reading.

He was about fifty, with the tanned, leathery appearance of someone who had spent much of his life exposed to harsh weather. Deep creases etched the corners of his eyes and heavy eyebrows dominated his forehead. His hair was dark and coarse, seeming to match his broad shoulders and heavy frame. A brown cardigan sweater, worn and stretched at the pockets, hung open over his tan shirt.

Karen noticed the title of the book he was reading. It was a guidebook, in English, of the Alpes Maritimes district.

Yvonne appeared behind them, carrying a large tray loaded with soup bowls. "This is Gunther Werrmann," she explained. "Monsieur Werrmann is Austrian. But he speaks English." She smiled at Gunther and introduced Karen and Luke. "Sit down, sit down. Your soup will grow cold."

Gunther acknowledged the introduction, but he didn't speak again until Yvonne had served the soup and departed for another table. "You are Americans? What brings you to Sospel?"

Before Karen could reply, Luke said, "Karen is an art historian. We're touring the area."

"Art history?" Gunther nodded at Karen approvingly. "There is much to see here. Have you visited the Chapelle des Penitents Blancs? There is a fine sixteenth-century *pietà*.''

"We've just arrived today," Karen murmured. She cast a surreptitious glance at Luke.

"You will like Sospel. It's a quiet place."

Gunther spooned some of his soup and then spoke again. "I, myself, prefer the artistic beauty of nature. I spend my time walking over the hills."

"You're a hiker, then," Luke remarked. He nodded at the guidebook. "Are you familiar with the area?"

"Somewhat." Gunther smiled deprecatingly.

"Don't let him be modest." Yvonne's voice carried over to their table as she approached with their main course. "Gunther is a true Austrian. He leaves early each morning and doesn't return until night, roaming our hills. In fact, he sometimes hikes to other towns in the area and stays overnight. We never know when to expect him. He knows more about Sospel than I do."

"You've been here before, then?" Karen smiled at him.

"Years ago. That was soon after the war. This area was badly hit. The bridge, the church . . ."

Yvonne brought wine to their table. "Has he told you about his project?"

"Project?" Luke poured some wine into Karen's glass and then offered it to Gunther.

Gunther looked embarrassed. "It's nothing, really. Only a small booklet that I am writing."

"You're a writer?" Karen leaned forward.

"No, no. I merely hope to organize a hiking guide for the area. I've worked on such projects before, in Austria."

"Don't let him fool you," Yvonne interrupted. "He's absolutely dedicated to his work. Sometimes he walks the hills all night, not returning until late the next afternoon. If you wish to learn about Sospel, you must listen to Gunther."

The evening passed quickly, with Gunther entrancing them with his knowledge of the area. Yvonne joined them after dinner and shared dessert and coffee. When Gunther pulled out his pipe after the coffee was served, she protested. "This is the only thing I do not like about you, Gunther. This pipe. It is terrible."

Gunther laughed warmly. He tamped down his pipe and lit it. "I won't smoke long, Yvonne. But my dinner is not complete without my pipe."

Secretly Karen had to agree with Yvonne about the pipe. The tobacco Gunther used was unpleasantly pungent, some variety of Turkish tobacco, she surmised. Soon after he lit it, she felt ready to leave the table.

"I'm going up to bed," she announced. "But thank you so much for sharing your knowledge of the area, Gunther. It's been a pleasure to meet you."

"And you, Miss St. Clair." For a moment his eyes held an odd glint, but then his smile warmed again.

Luke accompanied Karen upstairs. "The tobacco drove you away, I guess."

"Yes, I hated to say anything." Karen wrinkled her nose. "But it was awful."

Luke laughed. "I'll take that as a warning not to take up pipe smoking."

Karen reached the second-floor landing and started toward her room. "Oh, I don't know, Luke. A pipe might suit you and I can't see how it matters whether it suits me."

"Can't you?" he said, roughly. His grasp was gentle and tender when he reached for her. His mouth descended on hers. "Everything about you matters to me, Karen," he whispered just before their lips met.

Although she hadn't been aware of it before, she had been waiting all day for his kiss. Never mind that she had resolved to concentrate only on finding Diane. For this moment she could think only of herself and Luke and this warm, sweet acknowledgment of their mutual attraction.

She sensed that he was no longer in such control of himself. His mouth tasted of wine as it moved over hers, and his tongue demanded her unqualified response, teasing her lips open with exquisite gentleness before beginning a leisurely, tormenting exploration. He molded her hips against his body, letting her feel the extent of his need.

Karen wrapped her arms around his back and pressed closer against him. His mouth lifted slightly from hers as he rained light kisses over her eyelids and forehead before returning even more urgently to her lips. With heated urgency, his hands sought and found the swell of her breasts. Everywhere he touched, her body burned with answering fire. Under his tender stroking, her nipples hardened, straining against the thin fabric that separated them from his warm palms.

Luke's fingers found, then slipped beneath, the hem of her cotton sweater. As he lifted it, she felt cool air brush her spine and then the hot, fiery touch of his hands against her bare skin. "Oh, Karen..." he whispered against her lips. His mouth brushed her cheek and then she felt his breath caress her ear. "Karen, I..."

She knew what he was asking, and suddenly she wasn't at all sure how to answer. It would be all too easy to give in to her increasing desire for him, but was that what she really wanted? She had never been a person who gave herself easily. For her, lovemaking involved an emotional commitment, something more than physical response. Her feelings for Luke were still confused, overwhelmingly new and intense. No matter how much she hated to say no, she needed more time.... "Luke." She pushed against him with just enough pressure to put a little space between them. His hands still rested on her waist, and when she looked up to find his searching gaze, she met it unflinchingly.

"Not yet." She said the words quietly, aware that they carried a promise.

It was a long time before he released her. His hands reluctantly left her waist, and she noted that his breathing was rapid, as if he were struggling to regain his usual composure.

When Luke spoke again, his words were matter-of-fact. "I think we'd better head back to Nice tomorrow if the inspector hasn't found out anything."

"I guess you're right," Karen replied in a low voice. Luke's manner was faultlessly correct, yet she felt unexpectedly let down. What had she expected him to do? Argue?

"If we leave early enough, we can go to the American consulate in Nice tomorrow. I think it's time we get someone from our country involved in looking for Diane. That seems as good a place as any to start." Luke straightened his shoulders and smiled, a wry grin that didn't quite reach his eyes. "It's late. I'd better not keep you out here in the hall."

Karen fumbled for her key and then turned to unlock her door. Luke waited until she had stepped inside. He made no move to follow her. "We'll leave right after breakfast. Okay?"

"Okay." Karen nodded and tried to smile.

With a brisk good-night, Luke headed for his own room. Karen watched him for a moment before starting to close her door. A sudden shuffling at the top of the stairs caught her attention. She looked that direction and saw Gunther Werrmann.

"You look startled, Miss St. Clair." Gunther watched her closely. "Did I frighten you?" He motioned to a door across the hall from hers. "My room is just here. I'm sorry if I've disturbed you."

Karen stared at him for a moment, not quite sure why she felt vaguely uneasy. "No, no. It's just that I didn't hear you come up the stairs."

Gunther's lips lifted in a slight smile, but his eyes seemed cool and unrevealing. "I walk quietly."

Karen grasped the handle of her door. Gunther shifted his weight from one foot to the other, and her gaze went automatically to his shoes. She wasn't quite sure what type of shoes she'd expected Gunther to be wearing, but the ones on his feet surprised her. Made of flimsy, cheap black leather, they scarcely seemed suited to hiking or walking. Perhaps he'd changed to these before coming down to dinner. A small hole had begun to wear in the toe of his right shoe.

Karen realized that she was staring rudely. "Good night, Gunther."

He moved abruptly, taking a step toward her. "If you'd like, I could show you and your American boyfriend the chapel tomorrow."

"Why, thank you. But we'll be leaving early in the morning."

"So soon?" Gunther's smile seemed forced. "What a pity." He was silent for a long moment before he added, "Good night, then."

Once inside her room, Karen shut the door and leaned against it. Her reaction to Gunther proved how unsettling these past few days had been. She wasn't the type to frighten easily, yet for a moment, he'd made her uneasy. Gunther was probably just lonely. Look at how eager he had been to talk over dinner. Still, how long had he been standing there before she'd seen him? When had he come up the stairs? Had he overheard her conversation with Luke?

With an effort, she forced herself to move away from the door and start getting ready for bed. What she needed now was a peaceful night's sleep. She couldn't afford to fall prey to nervous imaginings now. But that realization didn't keep her from checking to make sure her door was firmly bolted before she climbed into bed.

## Chapter Eight

By eleven the next morning they were seated in an office at the American consulate on the Rue Maréchal Joffre in Nice. The man who sat behind the room's large, cluttered desk had listened patiently while Karen supplied details of her search for Diane. The wire-rimmed glasses he wore concealed the expression in his eyes from her, but when she recounted the episode in the flower market, he took off the glasses and she could see that his blue eyes were cold.

"You say that you've gone to the local police about this?" Oliver Young, who had introduced himself as an assistant consular affairs officer, tipped back his chair as he asked the question. He pulled a handkerchief from his pocket and polished the lenses of his glasses. He appeared to be about forty, with touches of gray threaded through his ash-brown hair and a network of fine wrinkles radiating from the corners of his eyes. An impeccably tailored gray suit jacket hung over the back of his chair. His crisp dove-gray dress shirt was topped with a vest that strained to conceal the evidence of his penchant for high living.

"We've spoken to Inspector Bouvier here in Nice and Inspector Ronet in Sospel." Karen glanced at Luke as she answered Oliver's question. He had remained quiet while she'd explained the story of Diane's disappearance.

Oliver picked up a pen and rolled it between his palms. "They've found no sign of your friend?"

"Nothing." Whatever she had been hoping for, this cool response on the part of the consular officer was not it. She wanted action, concern, anything but the blatant lack of interest in Oliver Young's eyes.

Oliver sat forward abruptly, tossing the pen onto a pile of papers in the center of his desk. "What do you want us to do about this?"

Karen bit back an angry retort. A seething rage welled inside her. Before she could reply, Luke stood up abruptly. Shoving his hands in his pockets, he paced around to stand beside Oliver, glaring down at him.

When Luke finally spoke, his voice was sharp with anger. "Surely there must be something you can do to help. Diane Garrett has disappeared, and apparently is in some sort of danger, as well."

"All I can do as far as Miss Garrett is concerned is to circulate a missing persons' report to some of our other agencies." Oliver tugged at his tie as if it suddenly felt too tight.

"What about Interpol?" Luke glanced at Karen as he asked the question, his gaze warm with concern. "Perhaps they could at least tell us whether any young American woman fitting Diane's description has turned up in a hospital or..."

Luke didn't finish the sentence but Karen was pretty sure she knew what he was thinking. She supplied the final word in her own mind...morgue.

Oliver cleared his throat. "I'll contact Interpol if you wish. As for your safety, Miss St. Clair, I suggest that you consider going back to the United States. If you are in danger, as you believe, then home would be the safest place for you."

"I'm not leaving France until I locate Diane," Karen said hotly.

Oliver ignored her. "Go home," he urged. "There's nothing more you can do. Your friend will probably turn up in a day or so. Most likely you've magnified these events into something they're not. It never pays to play amateur detective." He broke off as the door to his office opened and a woman stuck her head inside.

"You're due at the planning meeting in ten minutes," the woman reminded Oliver. An attractive brunette in her mid-thirties, she had brought Karen and Luke back to Oliver's office when they arrived.

He flashed a harassed frown in her direction. "Yes, yes. Bring us some coffee, would you, Renée?" After she left, Oliver made a show of glancing at his watch. "If I can be of any assistance in helping arrange your flight back to the States, let me know. Renée has copies of all the flight schedules out of Nice."

"I think Miss St. Clair made it clear she's not leaving," Luke interjected quietly. Karen smiled at him, grateful for his defense.

"What about this Monsieur Henri?" Karen felt she had to elicit some sort of information from Oliver Young. So far, her trip to the consulate appeared to have been a wasted effort.

The office door opened again and Renée entered, bearing a tray arranged with cups and a pot of coffee. Luke strode over and took the tray from her, placing it on Oliver's desk. For a moment the only sounds in the room were those made by Renée as she poured coffee for each of them. "You'd better drink yours in a hurry," she said as she handed Oliver a steaming cup.

"I know nothing of any Monsieur Henri." Oliver finally replied to Karen's question.

"What do you know about the oyster business in France?" Luke's abrupt inquiry took Karen by surprise. She lowered her coffee cup and tried to catch his eye, but he didn't look at her.

Oliver set his cup down carefully on the desk. "Oysters? That's an odd question, Donovan."

"I think it's got something to do with Miss Garrett's disappearance." Luke's expression hardened. "I think there's a connection of some sort between Diane Garrett and this fellow she was corresponding with and an outfit on the Eastern Shore known as Gilbert Industries."

"Gilbert Industries? Never heard of them." Oliver laughed slightly. "That's not surprising. You say they're on the Eastern Shore. That's in Virginia, isn't it? I've never been there."

"Yes, Virginia." Luke nodded. "They pack oysters, mainly for shipment to France. Diane Garrett opposed the whole operation. Those letters she received from her pen pal boyfriend were filled with questions about Gilbert Industries. Doesn't it strike you as odd that she's now disappeared in France, the company's biggest export customer?"

"Are you suggesting that Gilbert Industries has something to do with her disappearance?" Oliver shook his head. "That's the craziest idea I've ever heard."

Karen had been silent throughout this exchange. Until Oliver had asked the question, she hadn't been sure what Luke was getting at. Was it possible that Diane's disappearance had been engineered to silence her opposition to Gilbert Industries? If that was true, couldn't that explain Mark Turner's disappearance, as well? Up until now, she and Luke had focused only on finding Diane, believing that that would lead them to Mark. They had said nothing about Mark Turner to any of the officials they had spoken with, but perhaps now it was time to change that. Before she could say anything, Oliver stood up and reached for his jacket.

"This business about Gilbert Industries makes no sense." When he turned to face them, his expression was harsh. "I'll do what I can to find your friend, Miss St. Clair. Meanwhile, try not to worry yourself. Please don't take matters into your own hands. Give some thought to my suggestion that you go home." He bundled up a stack of papers from his desk and shoved them into a leather portfolio. Extending his hand to Luke, he said a brief goodbye and left. Renée followed him out of the room.

Luke came around the desk and sat back down beside Karen.

"He wasn't much help, was he?" Karen whispered.

"Not much." Luke sighed heavily, about to say something else when Renée returned.

"Anything else we can do for you?" Renée asked brightly. She began collecting coffee cups, stacking them on the tray.

"Here, let me help." Luke was on his feet immediately.

"Thanks." Renée's laugh sounded flustered.

Karen went over by the door and waited. She wasn't quite sure what Luke's display of charm was all about, but he seemed to be laying it on thick.

"Where are you from, Renée?" Luke smiled at her lazily.

"My family's in Florida now." Renée glanced over at Karen nervously, as if not quite sure how to respond to Luke. "Actually I've lived in France for years. My father worked for a shipping company here until he retired, but I decided to stay on."

"Then you must be quite familiar with the area." Luke was flatteringly attentive. Karen fought back a stab of irritation.

"I'm pretty much at home here," Renée agreed.

"Ever heard of any man who goes by the name Monsieur Henri?"

Renée's expression clouded. "Monsieur Henri?" She shook her head slowly. "No, I don't think so..." After a moment, she brightened. "I've got a stack of clippings in my desk. We keep a file of society photos and clips that mention people in this area. It comes in handy if we have to attend an official function and want to brush up on who's who. You're welcome to look at it if it would help."

Luke frowned. "I don't know if he's got any association with this area. We were told that we could find him in Sospel."

"Sospel?" Renée bit her lip. "That's north of here. No, my file probably won't help. You can look through it, though."

"Why not?" Luke picked up the tray. "All right with you, Karen?" He glanced at her, as if suddenly realizing that she was still in the room.

"Sure. I'm ready to try anything at this stage."

Two HOURS LATER, they threw down the last of Renée's clippings. "Nothing." Karen rubbed her temples, attempting to relieve the tension that had been building since their conversation with Oliver. Since they didn't know what this Henri was supposed to look like, Karen had been forced to read the captions under every clipping, searching for anything that resembled the name Monsieur Henri.

Luke's fingers slid beneath the silky strands of her hair. He massaged the muscles of her neck and Karen closed her eyes. "We had to give it a try."

"I guess so," Karen agreed. At this point, discouragement threatened to overwhelm her.

"Find anything?" Renée entered the cubbyhole she had turned over to them for their search. She took in their expressions with one glance. "Nothing, right?" There were several folded newspapers in her hands. "These are the papers from the past two weeks. I haven't had a chance to get to them yet. Want to have a look?"

Luke looked at Karen. "Think it's worth a try?"

"Might as well take a look." Karen tensed and then relaxed her shoulder muscles, trying to ease their tightness. She took the papers from Renée, almost giving up when she saw the tiny print in French. "You sort through this batch," she said, handing half the papers to Luke. "When you come to a photograph, tell me and I'll read the caption."

It was relatively quiet in the room for the next fifteen minutes. From time to time, Luke pointed out a photograph of someone named Henri, but none of the men in the photographs seemed like possibilities. One was a local businessman, but in the article beneath the photograph it said that he was elderly, ill and in hospital. Another pictured a film star, holidaying on the Riviera. A closer look at the caption beneath the photo revealed that the star was now in South America working on a film.

Karen was almost ready to give up the search in frustration when her gaze fell on a small cluster of photographs on the next to the last page of the bottom paper in her stack. At first, she almost missed the name Henri, skimming over the page in hurried exhaustion. But some instinct prompted her to go back over the page more carefully. There were four photographs, all shots of sumptuously dressed young women and their escorts, apparently taken at a dinner party held at Nice's Hotel Westminster-Concorde. One name caught her attention.

"Luke, look at this." Karen thrust the paper toward him. "'Mademoiselle Suzette Devries with her escort, the American, Monsieur Henri Verna.'" Karen pointed to the face in the picture above the caption. "Do you think this could be him? It says he's an American."

Luke was silent as he examined the picture. The man in the photo was in his thirties, with a lean face and fair hair. "It's a long shot, Karen. Yes, the guy's American and his name is Henri, but..." He looked up at her. "I'm doubtful, Karen."

"It's the first Henri who's seemed remotely possible. The fact that he's American sounds interesting." Karen's voice took on a pleading note. "Maybe we should check into this."

"There's no connection with Sospel, Karen."

"I think we should go to this hotel and see what we can find out about him. They might be able to tell us who he is." Karen stood up decisively. "Let's find Renée and ask her if we can borrow this paper."

LUKE SAID NOTHING as they walked to the car. Once they were inside it, he turned to her and cautioned gently, "Don't get your hopes up, Karen."

"I'm not," Karen said in a small voice. "But at least I feel like I'm doing something. Oliver Young infuriated me. He's not going to do a thing to find Diane. He doesn't even really believe our story."

Suddenly the weight of frustration and worry of the past few days had grown too much for her. She leaned back against the seat, turning her face toward the window so Luke couldn't see the tears that had risen to her eyes.

Luke started the engine and then put his arm along the seat behind her to steady himself as he backed the car out of its parking slot. After a moment, she felt the car stop moving. Luke downshifted into neutral and the engine fell to a smooth idle.

"Karen?" His soft utterance of her name was a question.

Karen didn't answer. She curled her fists, wishing she could grope in her purse for a tissue but unwilling to do so in front of Luke. She didn't want him to see her cry. Tears were an indulgence she seldom allowed herself.

The seat creaked as Luke shifted nearer. He slid his arm around her and pulled her toward him. "It's okay, Karen."

"Let go of me." Karen tried to pull away from him but his grasp was too firm. "I'm fine."

"Then why are you crying?"

Karen recognized the note of patient tenderness in Luke's voice. It was a characteristic she hadn't encountered in any other man. He possessed a seemingly limitless capacity for patience and caring. But if she broke down and cried in front of him, he might think she was weak and that thought was intolerable. "I'm not crying," she said stubbornly, willing the tears to disappear from her eyes.

"Of course you're crying," Luke said quietly. "I don't blame you. You're worried sick about Diane."

His words proved to be her undoing. She let him pull her against him, and once she released the tears, she couldn't seem to stop them. By the time her sobs had finally slowed, she could feel the damp patch she had made on the front of his shirt.

"I'm sorry." She drew away from him slightly and tried to steady her voice. "I've made a mess of your shirt."

"Don't worry about it." Luke smoothed her hair back from her forehead and then cupped his fingers under her chin, forcing her to look up at him. "You're not ashamed that you cried, are you?"

Karen tried to look away from him. She reached for her purse and hunted for a tissue.

"Here." A large handkerchief was extended in her direction.

"Thanks." Karen dabbed her eyes. "I seem to be making a habit of borrowing your handkerchiefs."

"Feeling better?" Luke asked matter-of-factly.

Karen was surprised to find that she did. Her headache had abated slightly and some of the tension had melted from her neck and shoulders. "Yes, I do," she murmured.

"Sometimes crying is the best thing to do."

Karen forgot about what a mess she must look. She lifted her gaze to Luke's face. "You're not telling me that you've cried like that?"

Luke shrugged his shoulders and grinned at her. "Why not? I'm human, aren't I?"

Karen laughed shakily. "I can't quite picture a man like you crying, Luke."

"Now who's being chauvinistic?" Luke reached across and laid his palm against her cheek. His hand was warm and slightly roughened, as if he wasn't a stranger to manual work. As he continued to look at her, he lifted a strand of her hair and played with it.

"Your hair was the first thing I noticed about you, Karen." His fingers caressed the nape of her neck and then tangled once more in her hair. "All I could think about was how soft it must feel. The color is beautiful and the waves... I love a woman's hair to be naturally wavy."

Karen drew back slightly. Her conscience twinged uncomfortably. "Luke..." She stopped and then forced herself to go on. "It's not... naturally wavy. I mean, I had it permed."

"Oh."

"Is that all you can say?"

Luke started to laugh, and Karen pulled away from him and leaned against the door on her side of the car.

"Don't get upset, Karen. I'm not laughing at you. It's me. I have a way of saying the wrong thing at the wrong time."

"You can't imagine what a pain this perm has been," Karen admitted.

"I can't wait to see what your hair looks like after the perm's grown out. But, Karen, about the color...?"

She glared at him for a moment and then relented. "Don't worry, Luke. At least the color is natural."

Luke shifted the car into first and once more began to maneuver out of the parking slot. Karen glanced across at the building they had just left, and her attention was caught by a familiar figure emerging from it. Oliver Young hurried out onto the sidewalk, followed by a young Marine guard. They exchanged a few words, then Oliver got into a dark blue sedan and drove off. The Marine went back into the consulate. Karen gazed after him until her attention was drawn to a man standing near the entrance to the building.

"Luke, stop." Karen leaned forward in her seat, straining to keep the man in sight between the pedestrians on the sidewalk. He stood motionless, a man of medium height, with weathered skin and a pencil-thin moustache. As if aware of her scrutiny, he turned away, seeming to be looking at something on the other side of the street.

Karen wasn't fooled. She had seen the man talking to Irene at the Menton railway station, and was sure he had been watching her when she arrived in Nice. Without stopping to consider what she was doing, she wrenched open the car door and scrambled out.

"Karen, wait!" Luke yelled at her, and she heard him open his own door. "Karen, what the hell are you doing?"

"We've got to catch that man." Urgency raised Karen's voice as she saw that the man had spotted her. He quickly looked both ways and then took off, walking rapidly down the street, staying close to the buildings and not looking back. "Hurry, Luke. If we can stop him, maybe we can find out why he's been following us. He's involved in this somehow. I know it."

Karen ran after the man without waiting for Luke. She wasn't quite sure what she intended to do if she caught up with him. All that mattered at the moment was to stop him before he could disappear.

Sensing that she was behind him, he threw a startled glance at her over his shoulder and then speeded up to a trot. Karen quickened her pace, weaving between pedestrians. Footsteps pounded on the pavement behind her, and then

Luke was beside her, grasping her arm in an attempt to slow her down. She tried to fling him away, but he only tightened his grip.

"He's getting away," Karen gasped. She watched as the man paused to look back at them before slipping into a crowd of shoppers.

Luke followed her gaze. "You stay here," he ordered. "I'll follow him." He let go of her and set off at a fast run, shouldering his way past two old men who shook their fists and shouted after him. Ignoring his order to stay behind, Karen followed as quickly as she could.

Through a break in the crowd ahead of them, she saw the man duck into a narrow alleyway. A moment later, she saw Luke dart into the alley after him.

When she reached the entrance to the alley, Karen paused, trying to catch her breath. The narrow passageway was dark and littered with debris. Garbage cans, overflowing with refuse, emitted the foul stench of decay. Karen drew back in disgust.

"Luke?" She called his name but there was no response. The tall buildings on either side of the alley blocked the sunlight, making it difficult for her to see past the entrance. "Luke, are you there?" Again there was no answer. She took a few tentative steps into the alley.

Somewhere ahead, there was a muffled thud, followed by a loud clang. Her breathing grew shallow and her pulse accelerated. A moment later, there was another thud. Fighting her paralyzing fear, Karen forced herself to move farther into the alley. Gradually her eyes adjusted to the dimmer light and she saw that the passage twisted sharply to the right.

Karen inched herself around the turn and stopped abruptly. Ahead of her, two men were locked in a deadly struggle. Luke had his arms tightly interlocked in a vicelike grip around the man's head. "Who are you? Why were you following us?" she heard him demand.

Hugging the stone wall, Karen moved closer. There was no doubt that this was the man she had seen talking to Irene Miller. Neither man seemed aware of her presence, but Karen was able to see them clearer now that she drew near. Suddenly she inhaled sharply.

"The shoes," she murmured almost inaudibly. She had seen those narrow, scuffed black loafers before. For a moment she relived the scene in the bathroom at the museum, remembering the sight of those shoes beneath the door of the stall.

"Who are you?" she heard Luke demand again. The man's reply came in the form of a sharp uppercut to Luke's temple. The force of the blow broke Luke's hold, and with lightning speed, the man took advantage of his momentary victory. He shoved Luke backward, throwing him against a trash can with enormous force. Luke lay facedown on the ground, unmoving.

For a long moment it was absolutely silent in the alley. Karen stopped breathing. Her gaze shuttled back and forth between Luke's motionless form and his attacker. Then the man spotted her and started toward her. Karen backed away. Her blood turned cold as she felt the rough stone wall against her back.

The man's voice quavered as he spoke. "I have warned you to stay away. Go home. Stay out of this. You're only making things worse for your friend."

With those words, he turned and ran back in the direction they had come. Karen wanted to go after him, but her legs refused to cooperate. Besides, there was Luke to consider. She couldn't leave him lying here in this filthy alley.

She knelt beside him and grasped his shoulder. "Luke," she whispered urgently. "Luke, can you hear me?"

Luke groaned. He made an attempt to lift his head and then paused before rolling over. Karen leaned over him, wincing as she saw a streak of blood on his cheek. "You're bleeding."

Luke put a hand up to his cheek. "I'll be all right in a second. He just stunned me. Did he get away?"

"He told me to go home. He said I'm making things worse by looking for Diane."

Luke sat up gingerly, pulling his knees up and leaning his head against them. "I think we've heard that line a few too many times lately."

"Let me have your handkerchief." Karen tentatively explored the damage to his face. She traced the flow of blood to a cut on his temple, and began to clean it gently with the handkerchief. "It doesn't look too bad. The cut's not deep. But you're going to have another bruise."

"Who'll notice it among all our other bruises?" Luke's familiar grin appeared. He managed to get to his feet but the white lines around his mouth belied his lighthearted words. He looked around the alley and then back at her. "Let's get out of here. We'll check out the Henri in that photograph. If he isn't the man we're looking for, then we're going back to Sospel. I'm not quitting until we find out what this is all about."

BY FOUR O'CLOCK that afternoon, Karen felt she'd taken a crash course in detective work. After a brief stop at a small café, where Luke managed to clean himself up in the rest room and they bolted down a quick lunch, they headed for the Hotel Westminster-Concorde on the Promenade des Anglais.

A pale rosy stone building with imposing glass doors and impeccably uniformed doormen, the Hotel Westminster-Concorde at first revealed no clues. Karen was all for going straight to the desk and asking questions, but Luke forestalled her. "If you want information, you find a maid. A talkative maid." He then outlined a plan that he guaranteed was foolproof. An hour later, Karen had to agree that he'd been right. Her first stop was at the desk to inquire about a room.

The disdainful clerk behind the desk looked her up and down. "You have no reservation?"

Karen glared at him indignantly. "But of course I have a reservation. Check your records again." It took her almost twenty minutes to settle the issue. By refusing to capitulate, she finally managed to convince them that perhaps the error was theirs. They didn't buy her story, she knew that, but they did believe that she was perfectly willing to make a very loud scene if they didn't do something about it. A few moments later she was shown by the desk clerk himself to a small single room on the second floor.

The moment the door closed behind his back, she hurried to the phone and placed a call to the housekeeping department. "Have more towels brought to my room," she directed.

The towels arrived fifteen minutes later. By that time, Karen had managed to give the room a lived-in look and had hidden the supply of towels that were already in the bathroom. When the maid arrived, Karen pretended to be indignant and then switched to a display of grateful friendliness for the towels.

"I apologize for the inconvenience." The maid looked puzzled. "I don't know how we missed placing towels in this room."

"Never mind." Karen gave her a soothing smile. "I'm sorry if I was impatient. It's just that I've had such a grueling trip."

The maid's expression softened sympathetically. Karen pressed her advantage. "You see, I'm looking for a friend.

An American, like myself. I thought he would be here at the hotel but I can't find him.''

"Who is this friend? If he is a guest…'' The maid's voice trailed off.

"His name is Henri Verna.'' When the maid's expression went blank, Karen pulled out the newspaper that had his picture. "Here's a picture of him.''

The maid studied the photograph. "Oh, but yes,'' she exclaimed. "I've seen this man at the hotel. He has a suite here. But *mademoiselle*—'' she paused as if reluctant to go on "—this man is your friend?''

"Actually, I don't know him very well,'' Karen said artlessly. "A woman I work with back in the States recommended that I contact him. She said he could show me around Nice.''

"You should be careful.'' The maid's eyes darkened worriedly. She paused as if looking for the right words. "There are things said about this man…''

Karen widened her eyes. "Oh? What sort of things?''

The maid looked around and then lowered her voice. "It's nothing, perhaps. But they say he keeps company with some very dangerous men.'' She would say nothing further, and after another apology for the towels, she left.

Dangerous men. Karen pondered her words. Perhaps this was the right Henri, after all. If so, she'd best not waste any time before putting the next stage of the plan into operation.

Luke was waiting in the car, parked in a side street, when Karen left the hotel. "He's staying at the hotel,'' Karen announced as she opened the door and slid in beside him.

"Did you find out which room?''

"Not yet.''

"Okay.'' Luke switched on the engine. "We have some shopping to do.''

"Shopping?'' Karen glanced over at him.

Luke slanted her a grin. "You're about to learn the fine art of disguise."

"Why can't I just go find his room and question him?"

"Just barge in and ask him where Diane is?" Luke shook his head. "Not good. He's hardly likely to admit to anything. No, our best bet is to follow him."

"And hope that he'll lead us to Diane?"

"That's the general idea."

KAREN GLANCED at her watch. Six-thirty. Over an hour since she had handed the desk clerk a letter addressed to Henri Verna. She had asked for her own room key and then, making a pretense of searching through her tote bag for a tissue, she had surreptitiously watched to see what box he put the letter in. That accomplished, she'd headed up to her own room and donned the disguise Luke had insisted she purchase.

Actually, it wasn't really a disguise. A sleek turban to cover her distinctive blond hair and a pair of lightly tinted sunglasses to mute the color of her eyes complemented the new cream knit slacks and matching tunic Luke had insisted she buy. "You don't have that many clothes with you, Karen," he had warned. "I'd rather you didn't wear anything that someone might recognize. That includes the tote bag," he'd said as an afterthought, adding a slim beige shoulder bag to their purchases.

After checking to make sure that no one was in the hall, Karen had taken the stairs to another floor and then descended to the lobby in the elevator. Such subterfuge had seemed excessive, but Luke had insisted she follow his instructions, explaining, rather cryptically in the language of the trade, that doing so would shake off a tail. While she waited inside for Henri Verna, Luke watched the cars arriving and departing from the hotel.

When she reached the lobby, Karen had headed for a seat in the lounge that would provide her with a view of the front desk. After about an hour of furtive glances each time a guest appeared she was starting to get impatient. What if Henri Verna didn't come back to the hotel tonight? What if this whole exercise proved to be a dead end?

One of the doormen had been eyeing her for the past half hour. Now he walked toward the lounge area and glanced pointedly in her direction. Karen made a show of checking her watch with an annoyed frown. Then she picked up a magazine from the table beside her and pretended to be absorbed in its contents. After a moment, she risked a quick glance up and saw that the doorman had gone back to his post.

She kept the magazine in front of her, now and then turning a page in case anyone was watching her. The main desk was growing busier as guests drifted in at the close of the day and asked for their room keys. Karen fumbled in her shoulder bag for the photograph of Henri Verna, worried in case she missed him.

Squinting behind the unfamiliar glasses, she tried to see whether her envelope was still in his box. She could just make out the outline of a letter. She and Luke had engaged in a heated debate about what to put inside the envelope. A blank page might alert Henri to the fact that someone was following him. In the end, they'd settled for a fictitious request from a reporter for an interview.

Karen shifted uncomfortably in her chair. Her legs were getting stiff from sitting still so long. She glanced down at the magazine and actually read a paragraph, something about the latest romance of a film star, if her translation was correct. When she looked at the desk again, he was there.

At first she wasn't positive it was him. The photograph had shown only his face and that had been in profile. This man was about six feet tall, with a slender yet muscular build. His close-cropped blond hair contrasted sharply with his darkly tanned skin. His casual white jeans and soft blue oversize sweater appeared expensive even from this distance.

Apparently he wasn't alone. A man and a woman waited while he asked for his key. The other man was older, probably in his fifties, tanned and gray haired. He was dressed similar to Henri. The woman was another matter. She couldn't have been more than twenty-four or so, with long straight auburn hair and a face that seemed weighed down by too much makeup. She was wearing a skimpy, strapless sundress.

It took Karen a moment to realize that the three of them were drunk. Henri made some comment to the other two, and they all laughed loudly and boisterously. The woman stumbled, and Henri reached out to steady her, pulling her against him for a quick hug. The desk clerk eyed them with distaste before presenting the key and Karen's letter to Henri.

Henri gave the letter a cursory glance and then shoved it in his pocket. He led the way as the three of them headed for the bank of elevators. As soon as the elevator doors closed behind them, Karen made a quick survey of the room over the top of her magazine. The desk clerk had his back to the room as he answered a phone. The doorman who had been watching her earlier was now busy helping an elderly woman with a heavy shopping bag.

As casually as she could manage with her heart threatening to thump out of her chest, Karen put down the magazine and stood up. She strolled out of the lobby and paused for a moment on the front step before heading in the opposite direction from where she knew Luke had parked the car. This was another of his instructions. She was to walk around to the opposite side of the building and then duck into some bushes, waiting to see if she was being followed.

Then, if the coast was clear, she could safely meet him around on the side street where he waited with the car.

As far as she could tell, no one was following her. Still, she stayed behind the bushes for five minutes before hurrying to find Luke. The cream-colored Renault was barely visible, hidden by a large van. As soon as she opened the door and slid inside, Luke spoke. "I saw him go into the hotel."

Karen took a moment to catch her breath. She whipped off the sunglasses and then rubbed her pinched nose. "Did he arrive in a taxi?"

"No." Luke's voice was quietly satisfied. Karen glanced at him quickly. "Apparently Henri likes to bypass the hotel parking valet. That's his Mercedes parked right over there."

Karen followed his line of sight. On the other side of the street, near the back of the hotel, there was a small parking lot, apparently for the use of hotel employees. A dark green Mercedes was parked between two battered compact cars. "Seems like an odd place to leave one's car."

"Not if you're the type of person who likes to leave in a hurry. This way, he doesn't have to wait while the valet retrieves his car."

"Did you see the couple with him? They all looked drunk to me." Karen took off the turban and shook her head until her hair tumbled down around her shoulders.

"What are you doing?" There was irritation in his voice. "Put that thing back on. You're supposed to look as inconspicuous as possible."

"In the car?" Karen regarded him disbelievingly. "Who's going to see me here? Anyway, if you're afraid someone might be following us, isn't the car itself conspicuous enough?"

"Of course," Luke conceded. "But we might need to get out of the car in a hurry. If so, you'd better be prepared."

"Oh, all right." Karen grumbled as she stuffed her hair back under the turban. "Do you have any idea how hot and uncomfortable this thing is?"

"With luck, you won't be in it for long," Luke said. His expression was grim. "We're going to have to sit here and watch his car until he decides to go somewhere."

"Luke, I still don't see what good all this is going to do. Wouldn't it be better if we just went up there and spoke to him right now? I got his room number when the desk clerk put the letter in his box." Karen leaned closer to Luke and put one hand on his arm. "Why don't we go see him? After all, we've got an excuse. I can pass along that message from the man at the flower market."

Luke covered her hand with his own. "Karen, we can't even be sure we've got the right Henri. If he is the man we're looking for, we still don't know if this is a trap. It could be dangerous to confront him. I'd rather follow him, see what he's up to."

He let go of her hand and leaned back against his seat, his eyes darkening thoughtfully. "I've been thinking about this all afternoon, trying to put together some of the pieces. Who are all these people? What are they after?"

"And what do they want with Diane?" Karen added. "I'd like to know whether Irene Miller is involved in this. And what about that man she talked to in Menton at the railway station? The man who's been following us."

Luke rubbed his temple, gingerly feeling the place where that man's blow had cut him earlier in the afternoon. "We know he's involved, because you recognized him from his shoes as being the man who talked to you in the rest room at the museum."

"Don't forget the man who was in my room at the Hotel Azur. We don't know who he is, but you said you saw him in Rome." Karen reached over and touched his jaw. "You've still got the bruise where he hit you."

"Don't remind me," Luke groaned. "How come I seem to be the one taking the brunt of this?"

"Do you always get into this much trouble?" Karen couldn't keep the teasing note out of her voice. "What kind of detective are you, anyway?"

"Hey," Luke said. His tanned skin reddened and his eyes regarded her uncertainly.

"I'm sorry," Karen said after a moment. "I didn't mean to sound critical."

Luke looked away. The silence between them stretched into minutes. When Luke spoke again, his voice sounded normal and friendly. "Let's hope we're on the right track. I'd like to help you find Diane and not just to prove that I'm a good detective."

"Luke, we've got to find something soon. I feel like we're running in circles and we're not getting any closer to finding Diane."

"All we can do now is to follow this Henri Verna."

"But for how long, Luke? If he isn't the right Henri, we're just wasting time."

Luke turned to face her, pulling her closer until her head rested against his shoulder. "I've got a hunch we're on the right track. But if this doesn't lead anywhere, we're going back to Sospel. Someone has the key to this puzzle and we're going to find that person, and soon."

## Chapter Nine

"This detective work isn't nearly as exciting as I thought it would be." Karen shifted her seat back as far as it would go, which wasn't nearly far enough for someone of her height. The muscles in her legs screamed in protest against their enforced inactivity. Karen and Luke had been sitting in the car for nearly four hours now. Night had fallen in earnest. Much of the traffic had cleared off the road, and the van that had been parked ahead of them had long since driven away.

"I told you it's just routine work." Luke smiled at her, his face barely visible in the dim interior of the car. "Hungry?"

"Thirsty," Karen moaned. "I could use a tall, cold drink about now."

"Nothing to drink," Luke advised. "That's one of the first rules of surveillance work. In case you haven't noticed, we don't have many of the comforts of home here in the car with us."

"I hadn't thought of that." Karen frowned, her expression so downcast that Luke laughed.

"Here." He reached into the back seat and grasped a plastic sack. "There's a shop down at the corner." He nodded toward the street ahead of them. "I managed to pick up a supply of snacks while you were busy getting a hotel room.''

Karen grabbed the sack. ''Cheese. Crackers.'' She looked up. ''I just may survive, after all.''

''You're not doing too bad as a detective.'' Luke spoke a few minutes later, after they had devoured the wedges of Port Salut and brie he had selected. ''Maybe you're in the wrong line of work, Karen.'' Luke smiled at her. ''Art history sounds awfully dull.''

''It's not,'' Karen defended. ''The history of art is a concise, composite profile of mankind. It's man's recorded expression of everything that was important throughout time—war, famine, death, love . . .''

''Wait a minute.'' Luke sounded skeptical. ''Now you sound like a professor. But I bet you have guys signing up for your classes just to look at the work of art behind the lectern.''

Karen looked at him reprovingly, not deigning to reply. After a moment, she sighed. ''One thing is certain. This isn't at all like my usual summer trip to Europe. I'm not sure the college would approve of my playing amateur detective.''

''Maybe your fellow professors wouldn't approve,'' Luke commented, ''but I think it suits you. Maybe you should think about making a career change.''

''I don't know, Luke. This part of the job isn't so great.''

''How'd you end up being a professor, anyway? What is it they say—'Those who can, do. Those who can't, teach?'''

''If that's a roundabout way of asking why I'm not an artist myself,'' Karen replied dryly, ''you might be interested to know that I do like to eat occasionally. A professor's pay is a lot more regular than an artist's.''

''So you're doing it for the money?'' Luke sounded disappointed. ''That's not a good reason for doing anything.''

''Why are you a detective?'' Karen countered.

"Detective? Lady, I'm a private investigator. And I do the job because I'm nosy. I like to know what's going on in other people's private lives."

"Now *that* I can believe." Karen was silent for a moment. Now that they had finished the snack, the night stretched endlessly ahead of them. "Do you think he's ever going to leave?"

Luke squinted into the darkness. "He must have decided to have dinner at the hotel tonight. I haven't seen those people who were with him come out, either."

"Maybe I should go back inside and see if they're in the dining room or any of the public rooms."

Luke considered her idea for a moment and then rejected it. "Better not. As long as that car is here, we know he hasn't gone far. Let's watch it awhile longer."

"Isn't there something we can do to make the time pass quicker?" Karen shifted in her seat. *This is how claustrophobics feel,* she thought. *If I don't stand up soon they'll have to winch me out of here through the roof.*

She could hear the amusement in Luke's voice when he spoke. "This car *is* a little small. We could always cozy up a bit...."

Karen glared at him, catching a clear glimpse of his face in the reflected glare from the headlights of a passing car. "I thought we were supposed to keep our eyes peeled for the suspect."

Luke slanted a mocking grin at her. "Ah, a lady who keeps her mind on business. Well, in that case, why don't I teach you how to punch? It's one of those little skills that comes in handy in detective work."

"Yes, I've noticed," Karen murmured dryly. "Are you sure you're the best teacher? From what I've seen, the best punches have been scored by the other side."

"Ouch." Luke pretended to wince, but she could tell her sarcasm had been wasted on him. "You haven't done too well, yourself. Haven't you ever taken a course in self-defense?''

"I had some friends in college who took some sort of judo class but I could never see the point. I always figured they learned just enough to get themselves into trouble.''

"To some extent, I guess that can be true,'' Luke replied seriously. "But if you're going to run around throwing punches, you'd better learn how not to do it.''

"What could there possibly be to learn about punching someone?'' Karen stared at him blankly.

Luke reached over and grasped her right hand. "Are your knuckles still sore?'' He rubbed his thumb over the back of her hand, his touch warm and comforting.

"A little,'' Karen conceded.

"I saw the way you punched that guy in your room the other day. If you wrap your fingers tight around your thumb and then punch someone, you're likely to break your thumb and bruise your knuckles.'' He gathered her unresisting fingers into a fist to demonstrate his point. "This way, your thumb takes the full force of the blow.''

Karen found it hard to keep her mind on what he was saying. He had leaned closer, shifting his body partly onto the console between them. "You must keep your hand and wrist straight, making a straight line up your arm.'' Luke manipulated her fingers into the correct position and then trailed his fingers up her forearm to indicate what he meant.

"I see,'' Karen murmured.

"One more thing.'' Luke's voice lowered, and Karen detected a faint huskiness in it. "Don't be tense. You must relax and learn not to tighten your fist and muscles until the moment of impact. You snap the punch and allow all your speed and power to be concentrated at the point of impact.''

"Mmm.''

"Are you paying attention?" Luke let go of her hand abruptly. "Here, practice a few times." He held up his palm and indicated that she was to try punching it.

Karen reluctantly eyed his palm. "Really, Luke. I don't approve of violence."

"Then, like I said, you'd better quit punching people." Luke waited a moment and then urged, "Go ahead. Try it once."

"Oh, all right." Karen lined up her fist and arm as he had shown her and made a halfhearted pass at Luke's palm. She was about to try again when she glanced over at the hotel entrance. "Luke, look."

He turned his head immediately, the lesson forgotten. Beneath the bright lights at the hotel's front doors, several people were silhouetted. Henri Verna led the couple who had arrived at the hotel earlier with him out to a taxi. The older man and the woman got inside, and as they drove off, Henri turned back to enter the hotel.

"Do you think he'll leave now?" Karen sat forward eagerly.

"Maybe," Luke muttered. "Then again, he may be headed up to bed. If so, this could be a long night."

Karen didn't answer. The prospect of several more cramped hours in the car didn't bear thinking about.

AT SOME POINT in the night she must have fallen asleep. She was awakened by Luke's triumphant exclamation. "Wake up, Karen! We're about to move."

Karen shook herself, trying to clear the last vestiges of sleep from her mind. She'd fallen asleep in an awkward position, her neck twisted sideways against the cold glass of the car window. Stretching, she tried to work the kink out. "Sorry I fell asleep," she muttered. Her whole body ached, and she was distinctly aware of how disheveled she must look.

Luke, however, looked none the worse for a night without sleep. His gaze was keen and alert as he switched on the engine and watched the dark green Mercedes across the street.

"Henri is leaving?" Karen's mouth felt as if it was stuffed with cotton when she tried to speak.

"He came out of the hotel a moment ago and he's headed for his car. See, he's unlocking the door now."

Karen winced at the bright sunlight that reflected off their car hood. She peeked at her watch and saw that it was after eight. As her eyes adjusted to the light, she was able to see Henri. He was in the car now, and as she watched, the dark green Mercedes began to back out of its parking slot. A moment later, it turned out onto their street and headed for the Promenade des Anglais.

Luke waited a moment and then whipped out of their parking spot, making a U-turn and following the Mercedes. "We'll have to stay back. No need to let him know he's being followed."

"What about us? Are we being followed?" Karen craned her neck and tried to see behind them. As they turned out onto the promenade, they entered a steady stream of traffic.

"No way to tell yet." Luke's voice sounded grim. "I'm keeping my eyes open, though."

"Where do you think he's going?" Karen sat up straighter and adjusted the turban, which had come askew while she slept.

"I wish I knew, Karen."

Henri handled the Mercedes deftly. Luke wove in and out of the traffic, maintaining a safe distance between their car and Henri's. When they neared the harbor area, Karen navigated, trying to help Luke keep the other car in sight. "He's taking the Lower Corniche road." She pointed ahead. "See, there he goes now."

This morning, Karen had no opportunity to enjoy the passing scenery. Once they'd left Nice behind, it became harder to conceal their presence from the driver of the Mercedes. At this hour, there was very little traffic either direction. As they neared Menton, she asked, "Do you think anyone is following us?"

"There don't appear to be any other cars back there," Luke said, glancing in the rearview mirror. "What do you bet we're headed for Sospel?" he added, flashing a grim smile at her and then turning his attention back to the road.

Karen felt a rising sense of excitement. Perhaps at long last they were about to make some headway in finding Diane.

Menton passed in a blur. The Mercedes barely slowed, narrowly missing two women who stepped into the road as it passed. Luke had to slow down and wait for the women to cross the road. "Damn." He revved the engine, and Karen strained to keep the Mercedes in sight.

They caught up with the Mercedes just as it slowed to make the turn onto the Castillon Pass road. "He's going to Sospel, all right." Karen couldn't keep the excitement out of her voice.

Henri drove dangerously fast. At times Karen almost imagined she could hear the tires of the Mercedes squeal as it rounded one of the hairpin bends. Luke's jaw was rigid, his hazel eyes dark with anger, as he pushed the Renault to its limit in order to keep up with the Mercedes.

As they started the descent into Sospel itself, they lost sight of Henri around a curve. Luke trod hard on the gas pedal and the Renault responded after a moment, whisking them at a dizzying speed in pursuit of Henri. Suddenly Luke slammed on the brakes. Karen threw out her hands, bracing herself against the dashboard. It took her a moment to understand why Luke had slowed so abruptly. There, ahead of them, was the Mercedes. It had slowed to a crawl, and as they watched, it turned into what appeared to be little more than a track that led off the main road. Within seconds it was out of sight.

"Damn, he may know we're following him." Luke's body radiated tension as he stared at the road ahead of them.

"Now what?" Karen fought back her growing frustration.

Luke swung the Renault over to the side of the road and shifted into neutral. He frowned and squinted into the sun, staring in the direction the Mercedes had driven.

"Aren't we going to follow him?" Karen's voice was strident now.

"Without knowing what's down that road?" Luke shook his head. "No way, Karen. We'll walk from here." Without saying more, he eased the car back onto the road and drew even with the turnoff. From this angle, Karen could see that the road was wider than she had first thought. Here and there, clouds of brick-red dust settled slowly back to the hard-packed dirt surface.

Luke pulled the car forward slightly and then backed into the dirt side road, maneuvering the car off to one side until they came to a stop behind a clump of bushy, dark green junipers. "Hurry," he urged. "There's no telling how far this road goes."

He jerked open his own door and got out, motioning for her to follow. Karen scrambled out, clawing a prickly branch that tangled in the weave of her sweater. Luke was already ahead of her, aiming for a ridge that lay several yards beyond. By the time she caught up with him, he was near the top, stretched full length on the ground. "There. That must be where he's headed."

"Where?" Karen tried to see what he was looking at.

"There's a building of some sort just off to the right." Luke grasped her wrist and pulled her down beside him. "Stay down." Luke pointed to a cloud of dust that hovered in the air midway between them and the building in the distance. "Come on."

They made their way toward the building, trying to stay within sight of the road but taking shortcuts whenever they could. The terrain was rough, with large bare stretches of rock interspersed with thick carpets of scrub and brush rooted in sandy soil. The sun beat down relentlessly, and Karen could feel rivulets of perspiration between her breasts and trickling down her back.

Suddenly Luke stopped. They had come to a grove of tall, conical cypresses that were bordered on one side by a thicket of gorse and bushy kermes oak. Luke put a finger to his lips, motioning for her to stay behind him. Karen crept close to him, and when he dropped to his knees, she crawled behind him, following him to a hiding spot behind a broad, sheltering boulder.

At first she was aware only of her discomfort. A thorn had scraped her face when she crawled and her hands were grimy and sweaty, heavy with thick, embedded dust. Gradually her breathing slowed, and she was able to look around. Behind them, nothing moved except a lone bird, circling high in the sky above them.

Luke inched his way around the boulder, and Karen followed. From this position, they had a view directly into the center of the clump of cypresses. Off to one side, concealed from the road by the stand of trees, sat the dark green Mercedes. Henri was leaning against its side. He glanced at his watch impatiently, scanning the area with a searching gaze.

A few moments later, noise caught Karen's attention. she gripped Luke's arm, and he closed his hand reassuringly around hers. They crept closer to the boulder. The noise sounded again, a quick shuffling movement followed by the sounds of pebbles striking against rock. "Look." Luke mouthed the word against her ear.

A man's crouched figure hurried toward the stand of cypresses. He came from approximately the same direction they had come from, and Karen's breathing halted abruptly as he neared their hiding place. Luke's arm slipped around her and he pulled her tightly against him, flattening them both against the boulder. The man passed within three feet of the boulder behind which they hid.

Luke waited a moment and then peered around the boulder again, staring into the grove of cypresses. Karen tried to see past him. For a moment, she doubted her vision. She was almost sure she recognized the man who was now talking to Henri Verna. The clothes were different. This time, the man was wearing a pair of faded jeans, a dark shirt and a pair of dark tennis shoes. But the gray-streaked hair was the same.

Frantically she turned to Luke and saw that he too had recognized the man. He leaned close to her ear and whispered. "Now what the hell is Oliver Young doing here, talking to our Monsieur Henri?"

They were unable to hear the conversation from where they hid. Henri and Oliver talked animatedly for about ten minutes, then Oliver hurried back the way he had come. Once Oliver had disappeared from view, they waited. A few moments later, the door of the Mercedes opened and then the engine surged to life.

"Now what?" Luke asked, as he looked around the boulder again. "He's heading for that building we saw earlier. Let's go have a look."

It took them seven or eight minutes to reach a position that allowed them a view of the large front gates that guarded the entrance. From this vantage, the building was much bigger than Karen had originally thought.

A stone wall, about eight feet in height, surrounded the building, which seemed to be a private estate of some sort. The heavy, wrought-iron gates were shut tight and the surveillance camera and speaker box attached to the right post showed that the gates were electronically controlled.

Through the gates, Karen caught a glimpse of the building itself. Made of a light-colored natural stone, it was long and consisted of a main structure connected by a covered porch to what seemed to be some sort of garage or service quarters. The main structure was two stories high, with a large wooden central door. The roof was of tile, a rich, deep terra-cotta color. A tall, bushy lotus tree spread its distinctive branches over the courtyard. Beneath that tree sat the dark green Mercedes.

Karen glanced at Luke and saw that he was scowling. She started to speak, but he stopped her, placing a finger lightly against her lips and shaking his head. "Later," he mouthed.

They watched the building in silence for nearly twenty minutes. There was no sign of human life inside the courtyard. The front door never opened. Finally, when Karen felt as if she couldn't stay there another second without moving, Luke indicated that he was ready to leave.

She followed him back the way they had come. His pale blue cotton T-shirt clung damply to his back, and as they walked, she found herself noticing the way he moved. He had an easy stride, athletic and unstrained, his lean hips and powerful thighs accented by his snug jeans.

*How does he do it? I'm a mess,* she mused. Her knit tunic and pants were dusty and sweaty. The fabric over her right knee sported a tear, the result of crawling through the brush. Beneath her turban, her hair was damp with sweat. Her face didn't bear thinking about.

If she ever caught up with Diane, she'd have a few words to say to her about the trouble she'd caused. As soon as she gave rein to the thought, guilt brought her up short. At this moment, Diane might be a prisoner in that estate back there. If she was lucky, that is. At that thought, Karen quickened her pace, relieved to see that they were almost back to where Luke had hidden the car.

Luke stopped several hundred yards away from the car. He slid his arm around her, pulling her against his chest. She felt his heart pounding and felt the warmth of his breath as he leaned over to speak to her. "Stay here. I'm going to have a look around and make sure no one has discovered the car." He released her, then took her by the shoulders and brought her face close to his. "I mean it. Stay right here. Don't move," he ordered.

"All right," Karen whispered.

A few minutes later he came back. "Everything's clear. As far as I can tell, there's no one around."

Once in the car, he paused before starting the engine. "I'd sure like to know where Oliver came from. He had to park his car somewhere near here."

"Why was he meeting secretly with Henri?" Karen voiced the concern that had been in both their minds since they had witnessed the meeting. "He told us he'd never heard of anyone by that name."

"Obviously, he lied," Luke said. His eyes narrowed and for a moment, Karen thought he was going to say something else. Instead, he backed the car out onto the main road and headed for Sospel. When they reached the tunnel that led into the town, he spoke. "I think we should pay a visit to Inspector Ronet."

INSPECTOR RONET looked them over carefully when they entered his office. "*Bonjour.* I thought you had returned to Nice." He eyed Karen's disheveled clothing and dusty hands. "Has something else happened?"

Luke explained briefly about following Henri to the estate. When he described Henri's meeting with the consular officer, Inspector Ronet couldn't hide his surprise.

"That estate is owned by a woman who lives much of the year in Paris." The inspector picked up a pen and jotted some notes onto the blotter on his desk. "As far as I know, she never goes there herself. But she does lease it to others occasionally."

"Couldn't you search the building?" Anxiety colored Karen's voice. "Diane might be there."

The inspector threw up his hands. "Without proof of any wrongdoing, I have no authority to search the estate." He paused and then seemed to reach a decision. "I will call Inspector Bouvier in Nice and have him approach the American consulate about the matter."

"That will take time," Karen objected.

"I'm sorry, *mademoiselle*. That is all I can do. If you wish to wait at the *auberge*, I promise I will let you know as soon as I find out any information."

No amount of persuasion would change the inspector's position. At last Karen and Luke left.

"Back to the *auberge*?" Karen asked as they got into the car.

"For now." Luke seemed disinclined to talk on the drive to the *auberge*, and Karen didn't press it.

The parking area beside the small inn was almost deserted when they pulled in a few minutes later. Yvonne Perret was in the front hall, sorting through a stack of receipts. She looked up when Luke and Karen entered, a smile creasing her face. "Back already? I didn't expect to see you again so soon." She came around the desk and took a closer look at Karen. "What has happened to you? You have had an accident?"

Karen glanced down at herself and grimaced. "We were exploring the hills, as you suggested," she said, with a sidelong glance at Luke.

"You wish to stay here tonight?" Yvonne glanced at the register. "The room you occupied is open, Karen, and I can give Monsieur Donovan the one across the hall from yours."

"That would be fine." Luke put his hand on Karen's elbow, and she looked at him. "Okay with you, Karen?"

"Right now I'd settle for anything," she said fervently. Already she could imagine the welcome relief of a shower. Then a thought registered. "But my clothes. I left my tote back at the hotel in Nice."

Yvonne looked first at Karen and then at Luke. "I could do laundry for you, if you wish."

By the time Karen headed upstairs, it was all arranged. Yvonne had promised to stop by her room in a few minutes to pick up her clothes, and Luke had talked the innkeeper into bringing a lunch tray to Karen's room, as well.

After the upheaval of these past few days, it was reassuring to come back to a familiar room. Karen stripped off her clothes and tore off the offending turban, before making a beeline for the shower. She was just preparing to dive under the warm spray when she heard a key in the lock and then the sound of her door opening.

"It's just me," Yvonne called. "I'll bring your clothes back in an hour."

Karen poked her head out the bathroom door. "Thanks, Yvonne."

The other woman nodded over the bundle of clothes in her arms. "Your lunch is on the tray on the dresser. I've put Mr. Donovan's there, as well. He said he'd join you in a minute." She closed the door behind her, leaving Karen glaring after her back. So Mr. Donovan planned to lunch in her room, did he? And what was she supposed to wear? A towel?

Luke knocked on the door just as she finished her shower. She turned off the taps and stepped out, wrapping a towel around her wet hair. With the other bath towel wrapped around her, she went to the door. "Who's there?"

"It's me. Luke."

Karen opened the door a crack. Luke had changed into his gray denims and a white T-shirt. His hair was damp, indicating that he too had just gotten out of the shower. But he hadn't shaved. Karen had to concede that the shadow lining his jaw only added to his attractiveness.

He eyed the towel around her head and her bare, damp shoulders. "Finished with your shower? I hope so. I'm starved."

Karen's eyes narrowed.

"For lunch, I mean," he added hastily, a mocking gleam of amusement in his eyes.

"You'll have to wait until Yvonne returns with my clothes. I'm not dining in a towel."

"I can lend you a shirt." Luke put out his hand and pushed against the door. His expression grew serious. "We need to talk."

Karen eyed him consideringly. "How big is the shirt?"

"Short enough that I'll get a great view of those fabulous legs of yours," Luke teased. He turned his back and went into his own room, emerging a moment later with a light blue pin-striped shirt. Karen accepted it gingerly, moving away from the door and going into the bathroom.

When she came out, Luke turned to face her. He had removed the white linen napkins Yvonne had used to cover their trays and Karen could see a tantalizing array of cheese, salad, fruit and bread.

For a long moment, Luke was silent. His gaze drifted over her bare legs, moving upward to her tangled wet hair and then down, coming to rest on the soft, smooth skin outlined by the V-shaped opening at the neckline of the shirt. Karen endured his scrutiny, only the wash of color in her cheeks betraying the flush it created in her.

Finally, Luke turned away from her, reaching for a tray.
When he spoke, his voice was husky. "Here's your lunch."
He brought her tray around and set it on the table beside the
bed. "You can sit here."

Karen sat down carefully on the edge of the bed. Luke
took the room's only armchair, beside the window, and
balanced his tray on his lap. They ate in silence. Luke finally glanced up. "I've decided to have a look inside that
estate tonight, Karen."

Karen put down her fork. "What makes you think they'll
let you inside?"

"I'm not going to ask their permission, Karen," Luke
said dryly. "I'm planning to sneak in."

"I'm going with you." Karen spoke decisively, then
waited for an argument.

Luke surprised her by appealing to reason. "Look, I
know you want to help. But I'll need someone to stay outside, in case I don't make it back out."

"Are you sure it's wise to break in, Luke?"

He set his tray aside, stood up, and turned to face her.
"We can't waste any more time, Karen. If we wait for Ronet to go through channels, we may never find Diane."

Karen stood up and went over to stand beside Luke. She
put her hand on his arm. "Luke, you shouldn't do this for
me. It's too dangerous. At the very least, you could be arrested for breaking into the estate. And that's no small thing
in a foreign country. Think of the legal entanglements. . . ."

"I'll be fine, Karen." Luke's hazel gaze locked warmly
with hers. "Whether you like it or not, I'm going to see you
through this."

Karen let her hand fall from his arm, and Luke stepped
closer. "Karen, I . . ." He paused. Under his warm, intense
gaze a delicious lassitude began to steal over her. Suddenly,
she realized that she could deny her response to him no
longer.

"Luke?"

"Don't do this to me, Karen," he said huskily. "You know I can't resist you. I've wanted you almost from the first moment I saw you in Rome. And when I found out that you were headed to the same place in Nice, I felt almost as if we were fated to meet."

Karen looked at him, her lips curving in a soft smile. Luke took a step away from her. "Not like this, though. Karen, I don't want to take advantage of you. I know you're worried and upset about your friend. It's not fair for me to ask you to sort out your feelings about me."

Karen looked at him tenderly. Until now, she hadn't been sure of her feelings. But how could she not admit that in these past few days, she had come to care for him in a way that was strangely new and precious to her. His brash manner and supremely male arrogance annoyed her immeasurably at times. He wasn't at all the sort of man she'd thought would be best for her. Yet he'd made her rethink her passive acceptance of the staid, unchallenging world she'd created for herself.

She loved him, she admitted. She wasn't sure what kind of love it was, whether it could last, what sort of future they could have together. But for once in her life, she was determined to live in the present. Now was what mattered. And right now, she wanted Luke Donovan with an intensity that shook her.

"Stay with me this afternoon," she said quietly.

Luke looked at her probingly. "Are you sure that's what you want?"

Her reply was to move over to him and slip her arms around him. He hesitated for a moment and then wrapped his arms around her almost convulsively. For a prolonged and tender moment, he looked into her eyes, then he was kissing her cheeks and her throat, his murmured whisper barely coherent. "I've been crazy with wanting you. I've never met anyone like you, Karen."

"You're pretty special yourself," she whispered. She trembled in his arms and he pulled her closer, stroking her hair and then covering her mouth with his. His mouth was warm and insistent, his tongue tracing the outline of her lips and then demanding admittance to the warm, secret recesses of her mouth.

He stroked her back, and she felt the heat of his fingers through the thin cotton of the shirt. Her body curved into his as if it had been specially designed to fit. She sighed, melting against him. The strength of his arousal kindled an answering fire in her. He lifted her in his arms and carried her to the bed, gently placing her against the pillows.

Luke sat down on the edge of the bed, maddeningly close but not touching her. Looking deeply into her eyes, he whispered, "I don't want to rush you, Karen. You can still change your mind."

Karen's answer was a slow smile. Luke's breathing quickened, grew shallow. Then, he stood up and, with a swift tug, stripped the T-shirt off over his head.

Her eyes soft with love, Karen drank in the sight of his smooth, tanned chest. A tangle of curls arrowed beneath the waistband of his gray denim jeans. Under her scrutiny, Luke's hands fumbled as he reached for his zipper.

Then he was beside her on the bed. His fingers sought and found the buttons on the shirt, brushing her skin and sparking her need as he slowly pushed it from her shoulders. "So beautiful," he murmured huskily. "You're so beautiful, Karen." His hands framed her face and then he leaned to kiss her.

A passion unlike anything she'd ever imagined surged through her. Her kiss described the wild need he was creating inside her. With a will of their own, her hands roamed the smooth muscles of his back. His body hardened against hers, pressing into her stomach as she caressed his narrow hips.

He groaned and pulled away from her, trembling slightly. "Do you have any idea what you do to me...how I want you?"

His lips explored the velvety underside of her breasts and Karen gasped, arching herself against him. Then Luke sought and found the soft warmth between her thighs. She opened herself to him, murmuring his name as he pulled her hips firmly beneath his and entered her.

For a moment they lay still, savoring each other's warmth and exchanging tender kisses. Then Luke's control began to slip, and Karen felt his need growing inside her. He began to move, and she moved with him in that inexorable rhythm known to lovers since the beginning of time.

Karen cried out, clasping him to her, as he brought her to the crest of exquisite pleasure and then took her with him, over the edge, into a world of peace and satisfaction and wonder.

THE SKY OUTSIDE the window had begun to take on the haze of dusk. Karen was nestled against Luke's chest, her legs entwined with his. Luke rubbed his jaw against the soft silk of her hair. "It's almost time for us to head to the estate, Karen." He trailed his fingers against the base of her spine.

Karen lifted her head, searching his eyes for a sign that he could be deterred. "Maybe you ought to wait, Luke."

Instead of answering, Luke cupped his fingers around her cheek and pulled her toward him until his lips brushed hers. "I have to get inside, Karen. It's the only way we can find out if that's where Diane and Mark are."

"I know," Karen whispered softly. "But..."

He kissed her lingeringly, then pulled back and smiled. "Don't worry. I'll be careful, especially since I know you'll be waiting for me."

"I wish it didn't have to be this way." Karen's arms tightened around him. "If only we had more time."

She felt the heat of Luke's hand on her back, his fingers caressing her smooth skin. "We will have more time, Karen. I promise you that. Now that I've found you, I'm not about to let you go." His hold on her loosened and he sighed deeply. "Maybe you should stay here at the *auberge* while I go explore the estate."

Karen shook her head. "No, Luke. I couldn't. Besides, you might need me. So far, you haven't done too well on your own."

Luke winced. "I'm going to have to get used to that blunt honesty of yours, Karen. It's bad for my ego."

Karen relaxed against him, her smile teasing. "Maybe you'll just have to admit you need me, Luke. We're partners, remember?"

Luke shifted abruptly, rolling onto his side and pulling her with him until she was beneath him. For a moment, his gaze drank in the sight of her pale blond hair spread against the pillow.

When he lowered his mouth to cover hers, his breathing was uneven. "Partners," he agreed. "I think we make a great team," he whispered before his lips claimed hers.

## Chapter Ten

A brisk breeze had begun to blow as Karen and Luke approached the estate. It was nearly nine o'clock, and darkness had settled suddenly over the hills around Sospel. Karen hunched her shoulders and followed Luke over the rough stones, grateful now for the sweater he'd insisted she wear.

She was clad in his blue denims and black cotton sweater. The jeans were a tight fit, making no concessions for her feminine curves, and she'd had to leave the button at the waistband unfastened. But even she had to concede that these clothes were more suited to the night's work than her cream slacks and tunic.

Luke wore his gray denims and a dark gray cotton T-shirt. They'd made a quick run into Sospel before dinner to buy the rubber-soled shoes they were both wearing and the dark scarf Karen had tied over her pinned-up hair.

They'd left the car in the clump of cypresses where Henri and Oliver had met earlier in the day. Under cover of darkness, Luke had felt he could risk running the car closer to the estate. Now they were standing at a point slightly southeast of the front gate, well back in the shadows. "This is as far as you go." Luke's whispered comment was barely audible. He waited until she was beside him and then dropped a light kiss on her forehead.

"I'll move up along the outside of the wall and make my way in." Luke scanned the perimeter of the wall before swinging back to her. "If I can't get into the house within a half hour, I'll return. Otherwise, I might be gone as long as two hours. You'd best wait for me at the car."

Now that it was actually time for Luke to go, Karen hung back. She didn't want him to go without her. More than anything she didn't want to stay out here alone, worrying about what might be happening inside the estate. "Let me go with you."

Luke's voice was firm, brooking no argument. "We've settled that, Karen. I need you out here. If I don't come back by morning, you must go for help."

"Inspector Ronet might not cooperate if he knew you'd entered the estate illegally," Karen pointed out.

"That's a risk I'll have to take," Luke replied grimly.

They stayed where they were for twenty minutes longer, both of them watching the estate closely. "There's no sign of movement," Luke said finally. "I'm going now." He pointed to his watch. "Does the time on yours match this?"

Karen adjusted her watch by five minutes. At last she could delay him no longer. With a swift, hard kiss, Luke left her.

At first she could see him, darting several yards and then pausing before taking off again. He made his way stealthily around the side of the estate until he was no longer in view. Karen found that in spite of the warmth of the sweater, she was shivering. Except for the occasional whine of the wind, the night was strangely quiet.

From this distance, the house seemed quite dark. A spotlight lit up the area directly in front of the locked gate, but behind it, the courtyard was in blackness. She could dimly make out the shadow of a car. Was that Henri's Mercedes? Was he still inside the estate?

Time dragged by. Every time she glanced at her watch she was shocked to find that only a few minutes had passed since the last time she checked. Finally she began to make a game of it, testing herself to see how long she could go without looking and then trying to beat that record the next time. Nothing seemed to make the time go more swiftly.

A half hour passed, with no sounds of any disturbance. No barking dogs, no shouts...and no shots. Luke must have found a way inside the house, she concluded. She felt the ground around her for a smooth spot, then eased herself down to sit.

At the end of two hours, worry got the best of her. Standing up, she paced in a small circle until the blood flowed freely in her legs. The breeze had picked up, cutting through her sweater and causing her to shiver in earnest now. She peered through the darkness, her senses attuned for some sign of Luke. Surely he would appear any moment now.

Sometime near the end of three hours she became aware of a new sound. She had grown used to the wind's eerie whistle and the occasional rustling of the trees as a gust whipped through them. But this was a drone, gradually increasing in volume. She strained her ears, instinctively huddling closer to the ground.

From the corner of her eye, she caught a glimpse of flashing light. She spun around, her heart pounding wildly as the sky lit up briefly off in the distance. It was a car, she realized suddenly. Someone was driving up the winding road that led to the estate. She threw herself down full-length on the ground, heedless of the prickly scrub and rough stones.

The hum of the engine grew louder, and after a few minutes, the car came into sight, slowing as it neared the gate and stopping in the circle of light cast by the spotlight. A man got out, leaving the engine running. He ran over to the speaker and announced himself, and a moment later the gate

opened. As the man turned back to his car, she was able to
see his face.

It was the man she and Luke had surprised in her room at
the Hotel Azur. The man she'd punched before he'd managed to make his escape off the balcony. He maneuvered his
car through the gate, and it swung shut behind him with a
clang that echoed in the surrounding hills.

She watched as the car pulled into the courtyard. Before
the headlights were dimmed, she caught a glimpse of the car
that was already parked there. It was Henri's, as she had
suspected. The front door of the building opened and a man
stepped out, his blond hair briefly illuminated in the wedge
of light from the house. Henri.

Karen crept as close to the edge of the shadows as she
dared. Henri gestured at the other man, motioning for him
to move the car. A moment later, a light switched on in the
low building she had thought was a garage. The car slipped
around to the side and disappeared, the light going off at the
same time that the sound of the engine died away. The two
men appeared, heading for the front door. They went inside, closing the door behind them.

So far, nothing had happened to indicate that Luke's
presence had been detected. Where was he? Karen fumed.
She glanced at her watch again. Perhaps he had already returned to the car, she realized suddenly. She had assumed he
would have to pass this way again, but it was possible that
he had found another way back to the grove of cypresses.

Her heart began to hammer in her throat as she made her
way through the silent darkness back to the car. She stopped
suddenly as something rustled the brush off to her right, the
tiny hairs rising along the nape of her neck. She froze, and
then went limp with relief as she caught the silvery gleam of
a pair of eyes near ground level. Just a rabbit, she realized,
as she made out its form. It watched her for a moment and
then loped off into the night.

Breathlessly she arrived at the car, desperately fumbling for the door handle. She knew the car was empty even before she had the door open. Still she peered into the back seat, clinging to the hope that Luke was already there ahead of her.

She climbed into the driver's seat and groped in her pocket for her keys. Her hands shook and a deep-seated trembling, born of fatigue and desperation, threatened to overwhelm her. Where the hell was Luke? He'd promised to be back here in two hours. For a moment her memory mocked her. "Do you always keep your promises?" she'd asked him and his answer had been, "Nearly always."

*I'll give him one more hour,* she decided reluctantly. *But I can't wait here in the car.* She got out again, taking care not to slam the door. Then she took cover under the trees, choosing a spot where she could see someone approach the car from any side.

An hour later she conceded defeat. Luke wasn't coming. Something had gone wrong. She waited until she was safely inside the car and driving rapidly toward the main road before she allowed herself to think.

It was nearing two in the morning now. She fought down a rising sense of hopelessness. There had to be something she could do. The main road loomed before her, dark and empty. The tires swished against the road as she pushed the speed higher and higher. The world spun in a sickening lurch as she rounded a curve too quickly. She forced herself to ease back on the gas.

When she reached Sospel the streets were empty. She slid the car to a halt in St. Michel's square and jumped out, leaving the door open.

A sob tore at her throat as she neared the door of the police station. The knob twisted futilely under her touch. The door was bolted shut. Obviously the station was deserted.

Nevertheless, she pounded the door with her fist. The only response was a mocking echo from across the square.

Now what? She ran back to the car, this time heading toward the *auberge*. She was more than a mile away from the inn when the car began to sputter. Treading harder on the gas pedal, she urged it forward. The car gained power momentarily and then subsided into stony silence. Karen guided the car with numb hands as it coasted to the side of the road.

As the car shuddered to a halt, she glanced down at the gas gauge, tapping it with her finger. It registered a quarter of a tank, but she was almost positive that it had just run out of gas. She pulled the latch under the dash and leaped out of the car, running around to open the hood. Pumping on the throttle, she examined the carburetor, noting that no gas squirted into its throat. "Damn," she cursed, then paced to the side of the car and kicked the tire in frustration. "Why couldn't you at least have gotten me to the *auberge*. Yvonne is my only hope of finding Inspector Ronet before morning."

She left the hood up but locked the door on the driver's side after retrieving her keys. There was no alternative other than to start walking.

She had progressed only a few hundred yards when she heard a car coming along the road behind her. Instinctively she slipped back into the shadows, not sure she wanted to reveal herself until she saw who it was.

The car came into sight, a tan Ford Panda. It slowed to a crawl as it passed the Renault and then backed up before stopping alongside it. The headlights dimmed and a man got out, his large frame silhouetted against the night. Gunther Werrmann. She recognized him immediately, but she said nothing, waiting to see what he would do.

He leaned over to look under the hood and then strolled around to the driver's side, peering into the car's empty interior. Then he looked up, his gaze searching the shadows at the side of the road. Before she could retreat, he strode toward her, calling out to her. "Mademoiselle St. Clair? Monsieur Donovan? Are you there?"

With a wall of rock behind her, Karen had no hope of eluding him. More important, she had no reason. Nothing except the same vague uneasiness she'd felt two nights ago at the *auberge*.

He seemed to spot her even before she stepped out into his view. "Mr. Werrmann? Is that you?"

He smiled at her and leaned forward in an oddly old-fashioned bow. "May I be of assistance? It appears that you've run out of petrol."

Despite his genial manner, Karen couldn't quite dismiss her mistrust. "You're out late," she commented pointedly.

"And so are you." He peered past her into the shadows. "Is Mr. Donovan with you?"

"N-No," Karen stammered.

"Then it's lucky I've come along." He moved closer, and she could smell the odor of his pipe tobacco. "It's taken me longer than I expected to drive home tonight."

"Where were you?" Karen's voice was unsteady, but he seemed to notice nothing odd about it.

"Piera Cava." At her blank look, he gestured toward the southwest. "As the crow flies, it's not far from here. A charming ski resort. Deserted at this time of year, but none the less an interesting place." As he spoke, he grasped her elbow in a friendly manner and urged her back toward his car.

"Unfortunately I spent too long chatting with one of the local innkeepers. I don't recommend the drive back at night. The roads are treacherous. I feel quite fortunate to have made it this far in one piece."

Karen felt herself relaxing. She walked beside him, her eyes on his car. If he gave her a ride to the *auberge*, she'd be able to contact Yvonne that much sooner. Before she could change her mind, she turned to him. "Could you give me a lift back to the *auberge*?"

He hesitated. "Of course. But do you think you should leave your car here?"

"It should be all right until morning."

He looked distressed. "But..." He paused for a moment. "I don't want to sound as if I'm telling you what to do, but I don't really think you should leave the car there. I myself could have hit it if I had been going at a faster speed. For the safety of other people, why don't you let me take you into Sospel. It shouldn't take us more than ten minutes to bring petrol back for your car."

"I've just come from there," Karen objected. "I saw nothing open."

"On the Braus Pass road there is a station open," Gunther said. "It's the only service available during the night."

"I hate to keep you up," Karen demurred.

"I insist." Gunther gave a short laugh. "At my age, nothing is more thrilling than helping a beautiful woman in distress."

Karen gave in gracefully. Perhaps it would be better to have her own car running again, she realized. That way, if she needed to go into town to meet with Inspector Ronet, she would be able to do so.

Gunther insisted on coming around to open the door for her. Karen managed a smile, but inwardly she fumed at the delay this cost them. Once he was inside the car, his large frame seemed to fill the small interior. It wasn't until he had turned the car around and headed toward Sospel that he spoke. "Your boyfriend isn't with you tonight?"

Karen cast a sidelong glance at him. Hadn't he already asked her that question? "We don't spend all our time together," she said shortly.

"So he didn't return to Sospel with you?"

Karen stared at the road ahead, willing the car to go faster. She had no desire to confide in Gunther Werrmann. Her nose wrinkled as her nostrils were assailed by the heavy lingering scent of his tobacco. She saw that his pipe lay in the ashtray, still smoldering.

"I was speaking of Mr. Donovan," Gunther reminded her.

"We returned to Sospel together," Karen admitted. "But we're not together tonight."

He said nothing more. Karen wound down her window to let in fresh air. The wind whined through the opening. Ahead of them, a few stars gleamed faintly in the dark sky, and soon the buildings of Sospel swung into view on either side. Karen breathed deeply, feeling oddly relieved to be away from that isolated road.

As Gunther had promised, there was a service station open on the far side of town. For a moment the bright lights blinded Karen as they drew up to the pumps. Gunther reached for the door. "You wait here. It should take me only a moment to arrange for some petrol."

Karen reached automatically for her purse, then stopped abruptly as she remembered that she had left her passport and wallet in the glove compartment of the Renault. In her haste to get to the *auberge*, she had never even thought of it. "I hate to ask you." Karen looked sheepishly at Gunther. "I've left my money behind. If you'll trust me until we return to my car..."

Gunther's lips curled in a curiously unamused smile. "Trust you, *mademoiselle*? But why wouldn't I trust you?"

Karen's gaze followed him thoughtfully as he closed the door and walked away. His remark had seemed odd. But then, he'd left the keys in the ignition, so he certainly must trust her. Her nerves were starting to play tricks on her again.

She glanced at her watch, and her pulse quickened with concern as she noted the time that had passed since she'd left the estate. "Hurry, Gunther," she murmured aloud. She leaned toward the driver's side, trying to see out the window. Gunther wasn't in the office, she saw. After a moment, she spotted him. Near a dimly lit street lamp, his bulky frame leaned against a phone box as he spoke urgently into the receiver.

Her heart began to pound. She leaned back abruptly, knocking the pipe out of the ashtray as she moved. Without looking down, she reached for it. As her fingers groped in search of the pipe, something small and sharp dug into her palm. She leaned forward, at first unable to see anything on the dark floor. Gingerly she felt around again, picking up the sharp object when she encountered it again.

For a moment she stared uncomprehendingly at the tiny object in her hand. Panic clawed at her throat, choking her, making it difficult for her to breath. "Oh, my God," she whispered. She opened her hand again and stared, wondering if somehow she'd imagined it. But no, the delicate silver filigree earring, in the shape of a butterfly, was unmistakably real. And just as real was the realization that it was one of the pair she had given to Diane less than a year ago.

Driven by a desperation born of fear and anger, Karen thrust the earring into her jeans pocket, cast one last glance at Gunther and then maneuvered herself into the driver's seat. With clinical detachment she turned on the ignition key and forced the car to life.

As she swung the car in a violent arc and tore out of the station, she saw Gunther shoot a startled look in her direction and then throw down the phone. He ran after her but she easily left him behind, casting one quick glance into the rearview mirror before she took off into the night.

By NOW she was growing familiar with the clump of cypresses. She plunged the Panda into the tunnel of trees and
then slammed on the brakes. The car lurched unsteadily and
slowly settled to a full stop. Karen searched frantically under the seats, hoping to find a flashlight. Nothing.

She jumped out and ran to the lift-back, unlocking it and
then thrusting it open with uncaring haste. Her hands fumbled in the darkness, groping into the recesses of the small
compartment. There was nothing round or smooth like a
flashlight. Nothing at all except a frighteningly familiar
tweed material. Unsteadily she drew it out, reeling back
from the odor of dry-cleaning fluid and what she now recognized as the scent of Gunther Werrmann's pipe tobacco.

It had been him, then. Gunther Werrmann had choked
her in the train compartment. An overwhelming rage sent
the blood pounding to her temples, and she threw the jacket
to the ground.

All her thoughts now centered on finding Luke. He was
the only person she could trust in this confusing mess. An
icy control settled over her, and her movements became de-
liberate, unhesitating and purposeful.

She retraced her steps through the scrub and brush until
she was even with the wall that ran around the estate. For a
moment she stood there, assessing her options, and then,
remembering that Luke had headed around to the back, she
made her way in that direction.

At the back of the estate, the wall loomed closer to the
house itself. Dodging patches of reflected light, she wove her
way through the shadows, scanning the wall. From this
vantage she could see that the large garage was connected to
the house on one side by a roofed walkway. The roof of the
garage came within a foot of the wall at one point. Now if
she could only find a way to scale the wall.

She crept back along the base of the wall, the plan becoming clear as she discovered several bushes that grew high

against its rough surface. The gnarled branches clutched at her sweater, scraping her face and the backs of her hands as she pushed at them. She was almost to the top when the bush gave way beneath her. Frantically she dug her fingernails into the wall's coarse surface and clung with all her strength. Inch by inch she was able to pull herself upward, despite the grueling pain that shot through her shoulder muscles.

The wall was nearly a foot wide. She lay on the top, panting and fighting to regain her breath. When at last she felt ready, she crawled on her hands and knees toward the garage roof, keeping a careful eye on the house.

The garage presented a new problem. The tile roof was slippery and as she tentatively tested her weight on its surface, the tiles shifted loosely and noisily beneath her. Again she was forced to make her way on her hands and knees. Each time a tile crunched beneath her, she cringed, wondering if the noise was audible inside the building.

The distance seemed endless. When she finally reached the narrow ledge that skirted the windows along the second floor of the main building, her whole body was trembling. Beyond the windows, the second floor was in darkness. Below her, patches of light shone on the ground, reflections from the windows downstairs. Gathering her nerve, she forced herself to put aside her fear and look for a way into the building. As noiselessly as possible, she groped her way along the ledge, pushing at first one window and then another. After a brief moment of resistance, the third window opened under her pressure.

Quietly, moving as lightly as a cat, she let herself into the house. Her pulse roared against her eardrums. She was in a long, dark passageway, interrupted on both sides with doors. Steeling herself against her growing fear, she tried the knob of the door nearest her. It was locked. Rapidly she moved down the hallway, trying the next two doors, screaming soundlessly with frustration as she found that they too were secured against her.

A faint light at the end of the hallway drew her attention. She paused when she reached it, staring down at what appeared to be a narrow staircase. Without a moment's hesitation, she tiptoed down the steps. At the bottom, she found herself in what at one time must have been a butler's pantry. The cabinets that lined the room still held a motley collection of crockery.

The light was coming through a partially open door, which she surmised must lead into the kitchen. A heated conversation was in progress on the other side of the door. Suddenly there was a muffled thud, as if someone had closed a refrigerator door, and then a chair scraped across the floor. Karen froze where she was, straining her ears to make out what they were saying.

One man's voice dominated the conversation. The fact that he was speaking in English surprised her. As she listened more carefully, she recognized the accent to be American. Was the speaker Henri Verna?

In a matter of seconds she was across the room, her feet barely touching the floor. She crouched in the shadows beside the door, peering through the narrow opening that led into the next room.

It was a narrow view, giving her only a glimpse of the corner of a battered wooden table and the man who sat beside it, tipping his chair back as he spoke. Henri lifted a glass to his mouth and took a sip, then spoke. "We'll wait for Gunther," he insisted.

Another voice cut in. This one had a heavy Italian accent that didn't mask the speaker's fear. "We can't stay here. Let's take the Americans somewhere else, hide them—"

A new voice entered into the exchange. This one had a guttural accent similar to Gunther's, and Karen had trouble making out all of his words. "No more games. We don't need the Americans. The operation can still take place as planned. The poisoned oysters are already on their way to France. Even without the Americans, everything will work beautifully.'' A heavy fist slammed against the table. ''If you two are too squeamish to do the job, I will kill the Americans myself.''

Karen stifled a gasp, pressing the back of her hand against her mouth and holding her breath.

Henri's tone was clipped but coolly even. ''Why kill them now? As you say, the operation is a success. If you do away with Garrett and Turner, you lose a valuable part of the whole plan.''

''It's not only those two we have to worry about now,'' the Italian put in sullenly. ''If this St. Clair woman is on her way here or to the police, as Gunther suggests, we've more trouble on our hands.''

Another chair scraped across the floor and heavy footsteps came around the table. A shadow blocked Karen's view of the room. She didn't dare breath. Whoever the man was, he was too close.

''Don't forget that I am in charge here until Gunther's return,'' the shadow man stated bluntly. ''If he doesn't get here soon, we'll go to him. And we'll take the Americans with us.'' He laughed shortly. ''In a place like this, there must be many places to hide a body.''

Soundlessly Karen inched her way backward until she felt the bottom step behind her. She had ascended three steps before her gaze fell on the bundle of keys. There were seven or eight of them, old-fashioned skeleton keys, tied together and hung over a peg near the partially open pantry door. She wavered, unable to decide whether obtaining the keys would be worth the risk of going back down the steps.

In the end she had no choice. Somewhere in this house, Diane and Mark Turner were held prisoner. And where was Luke? The men in the kitchen hadn't mentioned him and yet he must be here somewhere. Biting her lip, she crept back down the steps and, with a silent prayer, lifted the keys from the peg. The men were still arguing, their voices raised, but she didn't stop to listen.

As she turned back toward the steps, a board creaked under her left foot. Instantly she froze, sure that at any moment she would be discovered. Blood thundered in her ears. Sweat beaded on her forehead, but she made no move to wipe it away.

There was no break in the conversation on the other side of the door. The man with the guttural accent was trying to make himself heard over the Italian's nervous protest. Someone set a glass down hard on the table.

Karen finally decided that no one had heard her. She bolted stealthily up the stairs and paused on the second-floor landing. She approached the doors this time in a methodical manner. Of the eight keys on the ring, she tried seven before finding the one that unlocked the first door on her right.

The rasp of the key in the lock seemed to cannonade off the walls. Gingerly she pushed the door inward. The room contained very little in the way of furnishings, and there was no sign of human occupancy. An old trunk was pushed against the wall beneath the window, and on the other side of the room, several unmatched chairs and a broken table were shoved together haphazardly. She closed the door carefully, making sure to lock it behind her.

Diagonally across the hall lay the next door. This time, the third key provided her entry. In size and general disarray, this room was similar to the previous one, with one major difference. In this room there was an iron bedstead whose stained mattress was only partially covered by a tattered sheet.

Diane was lying on that bed, clad in a faded pair of jeans and a loose plaid shirt. Karen slipped into the room and closed the door quietly behind her.

Diane's breathing was slow and even, but as her face was turned toward the wall Karen could not tell whether she was actually sleeping. All too aware of the men downstairs, Karen did not call out to her. Instead she tiptoed across the room until she was standing beside the bed.

Up close, she could see that Diane's fine, dark hair was grimy and tangled. The jeans were tattered and the shirt was far from clean. Her eyes were closed, her lashes making shadows on a face that seemed even thinner than usual.

As Karen took in the scene, she noticed something else. Diane's fine-boned wrist was circled by a heavy metal handcuff, its twin clamped firmly around the iron bedpost. A mingling of compassion and outrage kept Karen from waking her immediately.

Karen thought back to the conversation she'd overheard in the kitchen. As Luke had suspected, Diane's and Mark's disappearance was somehow linked with Gilbert Industries. One of the men had said something about poisoned oysters being on the way to France. What did it all mean?

Karen placed one hand over Diane's mouth before she tried to wake her. If Diane cried out when she woke, it might bring one of those men to investigate. She had to shake Diane several times before she opened her eyes.

Diane blinked groggily and then rolled over onto her back, her eyes widening when she saw Karen. Her mouth opened beneath Karen's palm, but Karen shook her head urgently. "You mustn't make any noise," she whispered as softly as she could. Slowly she raised her hand from Diane's mouth. No sound emerged. Diane seemed to be stunned into silence.

"Karen," she whispered at last. "Where did you come from?"

"I've been looking for you." Karen sat down on the edge of the bed so that she could speak without raising her voice. "What's going on? How did you get here? Are you okay?"

Tears welled up in Diane's brown eyes. Her mouth worked convulsively, and it was a moment before she could speak. "I've been such a fool, Karen. I was tricked. All those letters were fakes. There is no minister." Her breath caught on a sob, and she snapped her mouth shut, swallowing hard.

Karen pressed her shoulder reassuringly. "Who are these people? Why are they keeping you prisoner here?"

"They're Soviet agents, Karen. There's a man named Gunther Werrmann who's in charge of them all. He's an East German but he works for the Soviets."

"But what on earth does this have to do with you?" Karen strained desperately to make sense of what Diane was telling her.

"It's all tied up with Gilbert Industries." Diane tried to sit up, but couldn't because of the handcuffs. "You know, the big oyster-packing plant that Dad was so opposed to."

"I heard them say something about poisoned oysters," Karen prompted.

"Gilbert Industries sends most of its oysters here, to France. The Soviets apparently want to cut the United States out and take over the export market."

"So they're going to poison the oysters..." The whole crazy mess was starting to make sense to Karen.

"Yes." Diane nodded excitedly. "To discredit the U.S. suppliers. The Soviets know that if people here in France die from eating those oysters, no one will buy from the U.S. for a while."

"I still don't see what possible connection this could have with you." Karen's brows drew together, mirroring her bewilderment.

"It all started with that stupid ad Ron Ferguson ran. You know, the minister who wrote the letters." Diane's face fell and tears glinted in her eyes. She went on, stumbling in her haste to tell Karen the story. "Only there is no Ron Ferguson. Soviet agents wrote those letters. They were just using me. I think they're going to somehow make it look like I poisoned the oysters."

"Of course," Karen hissed. "Is there another American here? A man named Mark Turner?"

"How did you know?" Diane regarded her blankly. "How did you find me, Karen? I didn't even know you were in Europe."

"There isn't time for that now." Karen stood up abruptly, going around the bed to take a closer look at the handcuffs.

"It's no use, Karen. I've tried and tried to get them off, but there's no way."

Karen frowned. "So Mark Turner is here?"

"Yes." Diane watched Karen as she came around to stand beside her. "I haven't seen him for two days now. But I think he's still here."

"How did Mark get involved in this?" Karen asked.

"He answered a fake ad, too. I was shocked to find out he was here."

"You'd met him before?"

Diane nodded. "Mark started working with the coalition last fall."

"The two of you didn't come to Europe together?"

"Oh, no." Diane shook her head. "Until Gunther brought him to the estate, I didn't know he'd been tricked."

"Why did you leave your suitcase behind at the hotel, Diane?"

"I brought too much with me," Diane said sheepishly. "By the time that man called me at the hotel in Nice, I was tired of dragging my suitcase around. I thought I'd meet

Ron Ferguson and make sure I liked him before I checked out of the hotel." Her eyes clouded. "The man said Ron would be waiting, but when I got there, it was in a rotten part of town. Two men forced me into a car and brought me here. I don't even know where we are." Her voice ended on a wail, and Karen moved hastily to quiet her.

"I'm going to have to go for help, Diane." Karen tried to reassure her, even though her own panic threatened to overwhelm her. She hated to leave Diane behind, but even if she found some way to break the handcuffs from Diane's wrist, the noise would almost surely bring those men upstairs to investigate.

Her only hope was to try to reach Inspector Ronet. "Has there been another American here today?" she whispered suddenly. "A man named Luke Donovan?"

Diane shook her head. "I don't think so. But they've kept me in here all day and night."

Karen refused to allow herself to speculate about the fate of Luke. He had to be here somewhere. She had no time to look for him. With the men downstairs arguing over whether to kill Diane and Mark, she had to go for help immediately.

"Are you sure you can't wriggle your wrist out of the handcuff?"

"No, it's useless. You must leave, Karen. I don't know how you got in here, but if you could get out and call the police . . ." Diane's voice trailed off pleadingly.

"I'm going now." Karen hesitated at the door. "I promise I'll be back soon."

She let herself out carefully into the hall, locking the door behind her. There wasn't time to replace the keys downstairs. She'd just have to hope that the men would blame one another for their absence. Suddenly her heart stopped. Someone was coming up the pantry staircase.

Karen tiptoed as quickly as she could to the window and eased herself out onto the ledge. Only seconds after she closed the window behind her, the hall light came on. Flattening herself against the house, she waited to make sure that no one came to the window.

After several minutes, she forced herself to start moving. When she reached the spot where the garage roof met the stone wall, she paused. Everything in her screamed out against leaving Diane behind. Surely there was something she could do. But what? Undoubtedly those men were armed and she was sadly outnumbered. If they caught her, who would there be to go for the police?

An idea flashed through her mind and she considered it, weighing her options. Dare she risk trying to get into the garage? At least she could prevent them from leaving the estate until she got back.

Before she could lose her nerve, she scrambled to the edge of the roof and scanned the ground below. In the shadow near the end of the covered walkway were two garbage cans. If she could lower herself to the ground, she would probably be able to use the cans to get back up on the roof.

The muscles in her arms strained to the breaking point as she levered herself downward. For a moment, she swung helplessly, her feet dangling and her heart in her throat, before she dropped to the ground. She moved stealthily along the back of the garage until she reached the corner farthest from the house. A heavy metal door, closed now, provided entrance for cars. In the shadows alongside the larger door was another door. The knob twisted easily beneath her fingers and she crept inside, pausing until her eyes adjusted to the darkness.

There was only one car in the garage, the one she'd seen arrive earlier in the evening. As quietly as she could, she opened the passenger door and leaned in to release the hood. It took less than a minute for her to remove the distributor cap and spark plug wires. Then she carefully lowered the hood, letting it rest against the latch instead of closing it fully.

When she emerged from the garage, she stuffed the distributor cap beneath some shrubs and tossed the spark plug wires over the wall. She had reached the garbage cans before she remembered Henri's Mercedes. Was it still parked in the courtyard?

A moment later she had her answer. She crept into the shadows cast by the lotus tree, measuring the distance that lay between her and the Mercedes. There was nothing to shield her from view, no hiding place in the bare courtyard. Still, she couldn't leave without doing something to disable the car. She eyed the front door and then made her decision. Lowering herself to her hands and knees she started to crawl toward the car.

The driver's door was unlocked. Karen opened it a crack, shielding the courtesy lights with her body, then twisted around until she could slip her hand upward into the opening. Her fingers sought and found the small switch that controlled the interior light and she held it in, making sure the light did not come on. Slowly she eased the door open and reached with her free hand beneath the dash.

A grim smile of satisfaction curved her lips as she carefully withdrew the fuse box. As soon as she had the box fully disconnected, she was able to let go of the switch for the light. She carried the fuse box with her as she crawled back toward the garage.

Suddenly a noise caught her attention. She hugged the ground, ignoring the sharp jab of stones as she molded her body tightly against the hard-packed earth. Footsteps crunched nearby, and then two men came into view at the end of the covered walkway. They moved quickly around to the side of the garage and stood near the door that she had just used to enter that building.

Karen rolled sideways until she could shield herself behind a bush. One of the men spoke, and she recognized Henri's voice.

"You understand what you're to do?" Then without waiting for an answer, he added, "What about your girlfriend? I'm afraid she'll cause trouble."

"Karen?" A familiar voice said, following the word with a short laugh. "I've been taking care of her up to this point. Don't worry, I'll keep her out of the way."

The shock was so sharp, so intense, that the darkness blurred around her. Karen shut her eyes, pressing her fist against her mouth. *No!* her mind screamed.

A slow rage began to build inside her as she realized how easily she had been duped. From the very first, Luke had been underfoot wherever she turned. Their meeting on the train, seemingly a coincidence, now appeared in a different light. He'd gained her sympathy with his talk of Mark Turner but never once, she realized, had he voiced that concern to the police. He'd turned up at the flower market right after that man had been killed. And despite the fact that he'd fought the enemy a few times, he'd never managed to actually win any of those fights.

The two voices faded as the men moved around the garage. Karen strained to catch a glimpse of Luke, but the shadows concealed him. She lay in the bushes for what seemed an eternity. Then footsteps sounded in the covered walkway and a door opened and closed. After that, the night was silent.

Fueled by her anger, she retraced her path to the garage and went around to the back. Karen eyed the metal garbage cans warily and then felt around the lids carefully, making sure they were secure. Satisfied, she clambered upward, scrambling to gain a firm hold on the roof before hoisting herself over the top.

This time she didn't bother to retrace her path along the top of the wall. It would be easy enough to simply drop to the ground. She shifted her weight to the outside can and then began to lower herself down the side.

As she released her handhold on the wall and dropped to the ground, she caught a glimpse of movement out of the corner of her eye. A moment later, she was caught and held by a pair of strong masculine arms.

"What the hell are you doing here?" Luke growled against her ear. Before she could answer, he dragged her with him away from the wall. Consumed by rage, Karen kicked wildly at him, fighting him every inch of the way.

Suddenly he released her. "Dammit, what's the matter with you?" His voice grated harshly. "I'm trying to help you."

Karen whirled to face him. "I don't need your brand of help, you—"

Luke reached for her arm. "Get control of yourself, Karen. Calm down."

"You were in on this the whole time." Karen advanced toward him, her eyes glittering furiously.

"That's crazy." Luke shot her a startled look. "What are you talking about?"

"I heard you talking to Henri. You can't fool me."

"You don't understand." Luke stepped closer.

Karen's last vestige of control broke. As if in slow motion, she raised her fist, remembering instinctively to keep her fingers loose and her wrist straight. With a quick snap, she caught him square on the ridge of his jaw. Luke was unconscious by the time he hit the ground.

# Chapter Eleven

Gunther's car was in the clump of trees where she'd left it. Karen's breath came in short bursts as she struggled to get the keys, which were still wedged deep in her pocket. She was just about to unlock the door when she sensed that someone was moving up behind her. Before she could turn around, something hard and cold pressed against her waist. She'd never felt the barrel of a gun before but she knew instinctively that that's what it was.

"You did a very foolish thing, Miss St. Clair." Gunther's voice conveyed an unmistakable note of triumph.

Karen steadied herself against the door.

"Where have you been?" He jabbed her viciously with the pistol and she winced.

When she didn't reply, he answered for her. "To meet with your accomplice at the estate? Who is he, Miss St. Clair? Who are you working for?"

Karen's mind raced frantically. "I don't know what you're talking about," she whispered.

"I think you do."

"Who are you?" Karen countered. "Is your name really Gunther Werrmann?"

He ignored her. "We'll go to the house now, I think. Move away from the car, slowly and carefully." He paused for a moment and then added, "Don't challenge me. Remember your friend at the flower market? I wouldn't hesitate to do the same to you."

"My friend?" Karen stalled for time. The situation seemed utterly hopeless, but she refused to concede defeat. She had to keep Gunther talking in order to give herself time to come up with a plan of escape. If only she could get the gun away from him.

"Jean Alard. One of your American agents."

Karen struggled to understand. The man who'd been killed at the flower market had been an American agent? She searched for something to say. "So it was you who attacked me on the train."

"Yes. I must be getting old. I should have killed you then." He sighed heavily. "I thought you were a friend of the Garrett woman's. So I merely tried to frighten you into going home."

She heard him move behind her and then he spoke again. "We'll walk, I think. You'll forgive me if I've decided to keep a close eye on you." He barked a short, mirthless laugh. "Come, Miss St. Clair. I want you to walk slowly ahead of me."

Karen took a step away from the car. "I'm not an agent." She tried to speak calmly. "You don't have to be afraid of me. All I want is for you to release Diane."

"Surely you don't expect me to believe that." She sensed from the amusement in his tone that he was smiling. He was close behind her now and she could smell the acrid scent of his tobacco. In an effort to put some distance between them she started walking as he had directed. His left hand gripped her elbow, his fingers biting cruelly into her flesh. "Not so fast. You'll make me think you're trying to escape."

Karen fought to maintain control. She breathed deeply, making a conscious effort to relax the tense muscles in her shoulders. His hand dropped away from her elbow. The darkness around them seemed less dense now, and she risked a glance upward. A touch of pink edged the sky, and it glowed with the first faint light of dawn.

She walked as slowly as she dared. Once they reached the estate, all chances for escape would be gone. She had no doubt that Gunther would not hesitate to kill her and Diane. Time was her only ally. "What did you plan to do with Diane?"

For a moment he didn't reply. Then, as if it mattered little to him what she now knew, he spoke. "My plans for her took months to develop. That's the problem with you Americans. You're always too impatient. Foolproof operations require lengthy and careful consideration."

"You planned to make it look as if she and Mark Turner poisoned the oysters." She ventured the statement as if she knew more than she did.

"Very good." Gunther laughed complacently. "But then that would be easy to figure out, wouldn't it?"

"But why Diane and Mark?"

"The two of them were almost too perfect," Gunther said. "They're so devoted to that citizens' coalition of theirs, so determined to save the environment. I knew it would be easy to make it look as if they would poison the oysters in an effort to subvert Gilbert Industries."

"You went to a lot of trouble to set them up. It must have taken months." Karen tried to make her voice sound reluctantly admiring.

"It was a matter of slow, patient work. We had many replies to our ads." Gunther warmed to his subject. "We checked out each one, looking for people who were lonely and isolated. When we found out that Diane and Mark were both known for their opposition to Gilbert Industries, we knew we had the right people."

"That worked out really well, didn't it," Karen prompted. "But how did you plan to make it look as if Diane and Mark were responsible for poisoning the oysters?"

Karen heard his soft laugh of triumph. She stumbled over a rock, regaining her balance almost immediately. Gunther appeared not to notice. "One of our own agents has a job at the oyster-processing plant. He's the one who will actually put the cyanide into the cans of oysters. Only a few cans need to be poisoned. Once those oysters reach France and people begin to die..." He let his words trail off.

Karen's steps faltered as she considered the implications of his words. "Keep moving," Gunther ordered, jabbing the gun into her back.

Karen started walking again, her mind racing. "What made you think anyone would believe that Mark and Diane poisoned the oysters? If your own man is actually the one who is doing the job..."

Gunther laughed. "We've planted evidence in their houses, papers that prove the two of them actually hired and paid someone inside the plant to poison the oysters. Everyone will believe they did it to discredit Gilbert Industries. Once the oysters reach France, the two Americans will conveniently be killed in a car wreck."

"But how will you explain their presence in France?"

"That's easy," Gunther replied. "Haven't you ever heard that it's human nature to want to watch the results of one's crimes? Like the arsonist who returns to watch the fire he set. People will believe they came to France so they would be able to witness the outcome of their plan. Perhaps it can even be made to seem that they hoped to focus media attention on the poisoned oysters."

"Then you plan to make it look like Diane and Mark poisoned the oysters so that adverse publicity would put Gilbert Industries out of business." Karen shivered at the cold thoroughness of the scheme.

"Exactly." Gunther sounded smug and self-satisfied.

"So why did you send them first to Rome and then on to Nice?" Karen asked. "Why make it difficult to trace their whereabouts? Wouldn't that defeat your purpose?"

"I wanted to know if anyone followed them," Gunther explained. "Apparently my security measures paid off, because someone did follow them. You, Miss St. Clair. But Giovanni made a mistake. He didn't realize that Diane had left a forwarding address."

"Giovanni?" Karen's heart raced as she caught a glimpse of the estate ahead. She tried to slow her pace gradually so that Gunther wouldn't notice.

"He called me after he followed you from the hotel in Rome. The fool, he should have taken care of you himself." Gunther's voice was harsh now.

Karen sought to piece together the facts. So the man Luke had seen watching her at the hotel in Rome was named Giovanni. And he was the one who searched her room at the Hotel Azur. "Why did he search my room in Nice?"

"To find out more about you, of course." Gunther added, after a moment, "It wasn't until then that he bothered to tell me you had a man with you."

"You didn't know?" Karen asked the question carefully, not trusting herself to hear his answer correctly.

"Even I make mistakes, Miss St. Clair."

"Luke Donovan isn't working for you?" Disbelief edged her voice.

"Come now. You don't need to pretend ignorance any longer. I've told you that I know you're an agent. Or is it Donovan who is the agent? You are merely his cover, perhaps?"

Karen stumbled again, as her tears threatened to blind her. Luke wasn't working for Gunther. Had she been wrong about him? "You keep saying that I'm an agent. What do you mean? What kind of agent?"

Gunther grunted harshly. "Do you think I'm stupid? An American agent, of course. Don't you and this Luke Donovan work for the CIA?"

Karen drew in her breath with a sharp gasp. "I've told you. I'm not an agent." She bit back her words, not wanting to say anything that might anger Gunther. Perhaps it was better not to argue with him. Did it matter now if he thought she was an agent? "Were you following us that day we came to Sospel? Was it you who hit Luke at the church?"

Gunther rejected that immediately. "Do you think I am so stupid? That was the work of Giovanni. If he was not such an idiot, he would not have been so conspicuous."

"He's not the only one of your agents who's stupid," Karen shot back. "What about the man you sent to talk to me at the museum? And Irene Miller?"

"Museum?" Gunther repeated the word. "I sent no one to talk to you at a museum."

Karen bit her lip. His denial sounded genuine enough. But if the man at the museum, the same one whom she had seen talking to Irene in Menton and who later had fought with Luke in the alley, was not working for Gunther, then who was he? If he was an American agent, why hadn't he identified himself? Why had he threatened her with a gun? "What about Irene Miller?" Karen asked abruptly.

For a moment, Gunther was silent. When he spoke, his voice sounded heavy. "I couldn't be sure about Irene Miller. I suspected she was working with Alard. That is why I stayed at the *auberge*. I followed her there the day we brought the Americans to Sospel, but I lost track of her when she left. I waited to see if she would come back, but you came instead." He sounded distracted now, almost as if he was no longer paying attention to her but was piecing together his own puzzle. "She did send you, didn't she? You were together on the train. Tell me, Miss St. Clair?"

"No." Karen didn't need to hear his low laugh to know that he didn't believe her. She squeezed her hands into fists to keep them from trembling. It seemed she had been wrong about everyone. Irene wasn't working for Gunther, after all—in fact it appeared she was an American agent of some sort. As for Luke, she didn't know what to think. Has she misjudged him? But what about his conversation with Henri? They were almost to the front gate now. Desperately she asked another question. "Why have you gone to so much trouble over oysters?"

"We go to great trouble over many matters," Gunther pointed out. "And for a prize like this, we will work hard."

"You want the oyster market?"

"Is that so difficult to understand? Oyster production is a billion-dollar industry worldwide. Right now, your country has cornered the market. And most of your oysters come from Chesapeake Bay, harvested and processed by companies like Gilbert Industries."

"So you decided to poison some of ours in order to discredit us in the world market." Karen had slowed her pace almost to a crawl.

"The Soviets have built up their oyster production in the Black Sea and the Baltic Sea, but they need an entry to the world market. Unless they get that, they'll have to go on throwing them out and losing billions of dollars in the process."

"And France looked like a good market?" Karen asked to keep him talking.

"France is the best market." Gunther's voice held a note of resentment. "It's time the United States had some competition."

"So the Soviets hired you to provide that."

"You Americans have your business methods," Gunther's voice came from right behind her. "We have ours."

Karen realized that he would not be talking so freely un-less he planned to kill her. She contemplated stopping and trying to struggle with him for the gun. As if he could read her thoughts, Gunther jabbed the pistol against her back. "Hurry. No more talk."

Karen hunched her shoulders and continued walking. Gunther held all the cards at the moment. What chance did she have against him as long as he held that pistol? But per-haps inside the house, she would be able to stall for more time. Luke wasn't working for them. If he was an Ameri-can agent, surely he was planning to do something about Diane and Mark. If he regained consciousness in time.

THE FURNITURE in the parlor was old but comfortable. Karen had been alone in the room for almost an hour now without noticing that. Gunther had brought her to the par-lor as soon as they had entered the house. For the first time, she had seen the third man who'd been in the kitchen. He was taller than Gunther, and thinner, but they were very much alike in manner.

Just outside the parlor door, the man Gunther referred to as Giovanni was staring at Karen. He'd only spoken once—when she had left her seat on the sofa and walked toward the room's only window, he'd warned her to sit down, pointing a businesslike pistol straight at her.

Suddenly there was a noise outside in the hall. Gunther was talking to Giovanni, and a moment later he came into the room. Ahead of him walked a handcuffed man. He ap-peared to be in his late thirties, but it was hard to tell. His face was unshaven and his eyes sat in hollow shadows that spoke of no sleep for several days.

He looked briefly at Karen and then looked away. Gunther motioned him toward the sofa. "Sit down," he ordered briefly. The man obeyed.

Gunther went back into the hall. He spoke angrily to Giovanni, and Karen heard him warn the man to keep an eye on them. For a moment after that, the room was perfectly quiet. Karen risked a sidelong glance at the man beside her. "Mark Turner?" she whispered tentatively.

His head turned toward her. "Who are you?"

"A friend of Diane's. You are Mark Turner, aren't you?" Viewed up close, his face was pleasant, and kindness showed in his light brown eyes. "I didn't realize they had someone else trapped in this scheme of theirs." His tone was bitter.

"I'm not," Karen said, and then added, "at least not in quite the same way. I came here with Luke Donovan." She looked closely at him to see whether he recognized the name.

His eyes registered shock and then interest. "Luke's here?"

"You know him?"

He ignored her. "Where is he? Have they got him, too?"

"I don't think so." Karen bit her lip. "At least, I hope not."

"I think they're going to kill us," Mark said abruptly.

"You know about their plan to make it look like you and Diane sabotaged Gilbert Industries?"

"Only what I've been able to figure out for myself."

Karen's mind had been working on a problem since her conversation with Gunther. "What about Henri Verna? What do you know about him?"

Mark shook his head. "Not much. He's been kinder than the others, but he's one of them."

Karen glanced over at Giovanni and then lowered her voice to a whisper. "Is he in charge or is Gunther?"

"Definitely Gunther." Mark's voice held that note of bitterness again. "Apparently Henri's only in on this because he arranged for Gunther's use of this house."

"But who is he?" Karen asked insistently.

Mark shrugged. "From what I've been able to gather, he's an American who's adopted France as his home. He's got a gambling problem. I've heard Gunther arguing with him about money. Henri's an opportunist of the worst sort. He doesn't care what he does, as long as the pay is high enough."

"Does this house belong to him?"

Mark frowned. "I think he just rents it."

Giovanni's voice interrupted them. "Shut up. No talking."

Karen moved back into her own corner of the couch, giving Mark a wry look. Giovanni stood up as someone else came into the hall. A moment later, Diane stumbled into the room. Mark got to his feet immediately. "Diane!"

"Sit down." Gunther's sharp bark boomed into the room.

Diane cast a quick glance over her shoulder at Gunther, then scurried over to a chair and sat down, rubbing her wrists. Karen was surprised to see that they had removed Diane's handcuffs. Obviously they thought Mark was the biggest threat.

As glad as she was to see Diane, Karen was disturbed by the fact that Gunther had brought them all in here together. Was he planning to take them all somewhere and kill them? Karen cringed, not liking to imagine his wrath when he discovered that she had disabled the two cars within the compound. But that wouldn't stop him. He still had his own car.

Pushed to desperation, Karen tried to think of some way that they could escape. There were three of them in this room, with only Giovanni to watch them. He had a gun. And the other men had to be nearby, probably in the kitchen. Still, anything was worth a try.

Diane had sat down in the armchair across from the sofa. Karen cleared her throat and when the other woman looked up, she nodded her head toward Giovanni. Frantically Karen tried to communicate by gestures that she was planning something.

Diane's eyes darkened but she gave no other sign that she had understood. Karen watched Giovanni for a moment. He was obviously bored, and the hand that he constantly raised to push back a recalcitrant lock of hair trembled as if he were nervous.

A moment later, Karen groaned, faintly at first, but then with gradually increasing intensity until she doubled over on the couch, holding her stomach. Giovanni stood up and looked at her sharply. Karen risked a quick glance up at him and then moaned again. "I'm going to be sick."

Giovanni looked helplessly behind him and then advanced a couple of steps into the room. "What's the matter?"

Karen clutched her abdomen. "I'm going to be sick, I tell you." She leaned over and held her head. "I feel dizzy," she said weakly.

Giovanni walked over to her, impatience marking his every movement. He stopped in front of her, standing between her and Diane. Beside her, Mark shifted. Karen didn't dare look at him. Would he guess what she wanted him to do?

It was Diane who made the first move. Suddenly she lunged at Giovanni, throwing herself against his back. Caught off balance, he stumbled forward, catching himself on the edge of the sofa to keep from falling on top of Karen.

Mark jumped up, bringing his handcuffed arms down with a violent blow to Giovanni's arm. The pistol spun out of Giovanni's hand and Karen went after it, pushing past him and dropping to her knees. Her fingers closed over the cold metal. She grasped the gun firmly and rose to her feet, whirling to find that Diane and Mark had managed to subdue Giovanni.

Karen raised the pistol and leveled it at Giovanni. "Don't make a sound," she ordered. Too late, she heard the quick rush of footsteps at the doorway. Before she could turn to face him, Henri Verna was beside her. He grabbed her wrist, his fingers biting into her soft flesh while his other hand wrenched the gun away from her. As Diane and Mark looked up at her, Giovanni seized the moment to start struggling against the hold they had on him. Restrained by the cuffs, there was little Mark could do to stop him.

Karen tried to break away from Henri but was no match for his strength. He locked his arms around her and dragged her backward. "Don't fight me, you fool," he whispered against her ear. "You're blowing this whole operation."

"That's what I'm trying to do." Karen made an attempt to kick him.

The blow didn't faze him. He tightened his grip as he dragged her with him out into the hall and toward the front entry. There was a square intercom panel set in the front wall near the door and Henri headed straight for it. He shoved her against the wall in the corner and then blocked her with his body. His fingers fumbled with the controls on the panel and a moment later he spoke into the intercom. "You're out there," he whispered urgently. "Good, I thought you'd never get here."

There was a crackle of static and then a voice that Karen recognized replied. "We got here as fast as we could, Henri." Inspector Ronet's tones were crisp and cool.

Karen stared at Henri. "Who are—"

He cut her off abruptly. "Come on. I've got to get you out of the way." He grabbed her arm and Karen allowed him to lead her back toward the parlor.

"What's going on?" Gunther Werrmann stepped out of a doorway on their left. The pistol in his hands was aimed at Henri.

Henri tightened his hold on Karen. "She was trying to escape, Gunther. Luckily I stopped her in time."

Gunther eyed him suspiciously. "I thought I saw the light on the intercom panel go on. Is someone at the gate?"

There was a brief pause. "Apparently someone pressed the bell. But when I answered, no one was there."

Gunther frowned. But Karen noticed that his grip on the pistol had loosened. The man who'd been talking with Henri and Giovanni earlier came into the hall. "I'll go check," he offered.

Gunther looked relieved. "Yes." He waited until the man had moved past them and headed for the front door before he spoke again. "Take her back into the front room."

Karen suddenly realized that she'd seen no signs of Diane or Mark or Giovanni in the past few minutes. Apparently Henri's thoughts were running along the same lines. He glanced at Karen, his expression sober as if to warn her to be quiet. "All right, let's go."

Karen went along docilely with Henri. She could feel Gunther watching them as Henri led her back toward the parlor. They had almost reached the parlor doorway when the front door opened and the man who'd gone out to check the front gate stood there, an odd expression on his face. A moment later, she saw why.

"Put down your weapon," Inspector Ronet's crisp voice ordered from behind him, stepping around him and into the hall. Gunther lifted his pistol, but before he could shoot, someone tackled him from behind. Karen flattened herself against the wall as Henri released her and dashed into the fight.

The man who had tackled Gunther was the man who had been talking to Irene at the railway station in Menton. He and Henri managed to subdue Gunther within seconds.

"So we meet again, Karen," a woman's voice said, and Karen whirled around.

"Irene!" Karen stared at the pistol in the woman's hand. "What are you doing here?"

"Meet Special Agent Miller," Henri said from behind her. He waited while Inspector Ronet and two other policemen led Gunther back toward the kitchen. "And this is Pierre Benoit." He introduced Irene's friend from the railway station. "You've given us a rough time, Miss St. Clair."

Karen stared at them. "What's this all about?"

Pierre Benoit walked over and put his hand on her shoulder reassuringly. "It's a long story. But at least we can finally tell you about it."

At that moment, Luke came in the front door, stopping abruptly when he saw them. His eyes narrowed on Pierre Benoit, and a frown creased his face. Benoit's hand dropped away from Karen's shoulder but it was too late.

"Let go of her, you bastard!" Luke yelled. He rushed forward, taking Benoit by surprise and landing a punch on his jaw. The sound of the impact echoed through the hall and Karen winced.

"No, Luke!" she cried.

Benoit crumpled to the floor and Luke stood over him, dusting off his hands. "It's about time I evened the score." Satisfaction was evident in the look on his face.

"Oh, Luke, how could you?" Karen wailed.

"What?" His gaze met hers.

"You hit the wrong man, Luke. He's on our side."

"ACTUALLY, YOU'VE been a great help to us." Oliver Young addressed the words to Karen and Luke later that morning. They were in the lounge at the *auberge* and Yvonne had just finished serving coffee and rolls. On the sofa across from Karen, Henri Verna leaned back and stretched out his legs. Irene sat next to him, her blue eyes filled with amusement.

"Henri told me I almost blew the whole operation." Karen looked at Oliver as she spoke.

"You did cause us quite a bit of trouble." Pierre Benoit pulled his chair closer to the group. He rubbed his jaw and looked accusingly at Luke.

"But what did you mean about Karen and Luke helping you?" Diane asked quietly. Mark Turner sat in the chair next to hers, and Karen had noticed the attentive way he treated her.

Oliver Young had appeared at the estate soon after Inspector Ronet's entrance. Karen hadn't quite managed to sort out his exact position in all this, but apparently he wasn't a consular official at all, but a CIA case officer. From the way the others had treated him, Karen surmised that he was the man in charge of this particular counterintelligence operation. Oliver took off his glasses, this time revealing eyes that weren't quite so cold and harsh. "Gunther Werrmann became convinced that Karen and Luke were American agents, especially after Karen met with Jean Alard at the flower market. The two of you managed to divert suspicion from our people."

"Why did Jean Alard contact me?" Karen took a sip of her coffee. "And what did he mean by that message he gave me?"

"You've already figured out that he meant for you to find Henri." Oliver paused to take another roll from the tray Yvonne offered. "When he told you to tell Henri that the dog was barking, he must have been trying to warn us that Gunther had grown suspicious. We'll never know exactly why he risked talking to you. We had intended to tell you nothing."

"But why?" Luke asked. "Wouldn't it have been easier to let us know what was going on?"

Henri looked slightly uncomfortable. "Easier, perhaps. You'd probably have objected to our allowing Gunther to continue holding Diane and Mark. We needed more time to make sure we identified all Gunther's agents before we moved in on them."

"We were surprised when you turned up at the hotel in Rome," Irene broke into the conversation. "Oliver told me to keep an eye on you, Karen, but apparently Gunther managed to attack you during the time I was away from the compartment."

"I took over for Irene in Menton," Pierre Benoit added. "Watching the two of you was the hardest assignment I've had. Maybe we should put you to work for us."

"What did Jean Alard mean when he told me to find the Sospel connection?" Karen frowned.

"That's me," Henri explained. "The agency assigned me that code name when we started this operation. One of our informants told us what Gunther was planning, so we leased this house and put our own plan in motion."

"How did you get Gunther to trust you?" Luke shifted closer to Karen on the couch, and she glanced quickly at him.

Oliver answered the question. "Henri's one of our best undercover operatives here in Europe. He's developed quite a reputation for dealing in unsavory business, and until now, we've never had to reveal his part in any arrest. He's known for being able to supply arms, safe houses, anything for a price."

"I spent a lot of time at the casino in Monte Carlo, running up some gambling debts and letting it be known that I was running short of cash," Henri added. "Gunther took the bait just as we'd hoped. He needed a place to hide Diane and Mark until the time came to set up their accident."

"Then he really did intend to kill us." Diane's face turned pale. She leaned forward, her expression anxious. "Is it really all over now? Are we going to be able to go home?"

Henri nodded. "You'll be safe now. We'll be keeping an eye on you for a while, but we don't anticipate any problems. Gunther Werrmann and his operatives will be out of the picture for a long time. We managed to arrest the man they'd planted at Gilbert Industries, as well."

"And the poisoned oysters?"

"We got him before he was actually able to taint them. We've had our own man at the plant all along, watching his every move."

"Did they really think anyone would believe Diane and Mark were responsible?" Karen glanced at Diane.

"Gunther's plan could have worked. He'd managed to plant a good deal of evidence against the two of them." Henri shook his head. "If we hadn't gotten word of his plans from our informant, Mark and Diane would have been in a lot of trouble."

"I feel like such a fool." Diane looked down at her hands.

"That makes two of us." Mark put his arm around her. "I answered one of those ads, too. Mine was placed by a lonely widow, or so I thought."

Oliver stood up. "I've got to go to the police station. Inspector Ronet will be needing me." He walked toward the door and then turned back. "By the way, how did you find Henri? I told you I'd never heard of him."

"Your secretary helped us." Luke rose to his feet.

"Renée?" Oliver looked disbelieving. "She knows nothing of Henri. In fact, she thinks I'm a replacement for the guy who usually has that job."

"She didn't actually tell us about Henri. She just lent us her clipping file. We did the rest ourselves, after finding a photo of Henri in the paper."

Oliver shook his head. "I should have known. In this business, it's always the little details that trip you up."

IT WAS EARLY AFTERNOON before Karen had a chance to talk with Luke alone. She and Diane had gone upstairs to rest, but Karen had been too restless to sleep. Going downstairs, she found the lounge empty so she went outside.

There was a small garden behind the *auberge*. Karen sat for a while on a stone bench that looked out over the town of Sospel. The gravel pathway crunched as someone else entered the garden. "Luke." Karen met his dark hazel gaze, her cheeks flushing under his scrutiny.

"I get the feeling you've been avoiding me." Luke sat down beside her. His thigh pressed against hers, and he slipped his arm around her shoulders. When she didn't say anything, he cupped her chin, turning her face until he could brush her lips with his own. "Karen?"

"How's your jaw?" Karen stroked his skin with her fingertips.

"After all the punches I've taken this week, I hardly noticed it." Laughter and tenderness mingled in his voice.

"You shouldn't have taught me how to punch."

"I had a feeling I'd regret that." Luke's arm tightened around her and when he spoke, he sounded serious. "It wasn't the punch that hurt, Karen. It was the fact that you didn't trust me."

"But I heard you and Henri talking about me," Karen protested. "What was I supposed to think?"

"So that's why you punched me?" Luke replied. "Henri caught me prowling around the estate. He explained what was going on and then made me hide until he could arrange a way for me to escape. I was on my way to find you so you wouldn't dash in here and interfere at the wrong moment."

"Which is exactly what I did," Karen said wryly.

"I should have known you would." Luke's reply sounded amused.

Karen avoided looking at him. She wasn't quite sure how to explain her feelings when she'd overheard him talking to

Henri. She felt as if her emotions had been on a roller coaster these past few days. "We don't know too much about each other," she said hesitantly.

"I know that I love you."

"You're going too fast for me," Karen objected. "I'm a cautious person, Luke. I can't rush into things."

Luke laughed deeply, his body pressing against hers. "That's not the impression I've gotten this week."

"Has it only been a week?" Karen lifted her gaze to meet his.

Luke nodded. "I think we're off to a great start, don't you?" He pulled her closer, bending his head until he could kiss her again. His lips moved fiercely over hers, then gentled as his tongue began a leisurely exploration of her mouth. It was awhile before his lips left hers long enough for her to speak.

"I should have trusted you, Luke. But I was afraid..."

Luke kissed her gently. "You don't have to explain." His eyes darkened. "Just promise me that you won't push me away. I know you need more time, but my feelings aren't going to change. I knew the minute I saw you in that hotel in Rome that fate had caught up to me."

"Well, you do seem to need me," Karen said slowly, her eyes warm with laughter. Then she relented, giving in to the tide of feelings rising inside her. "I think I love you, too."

"You think!" Luke crushed her to him, his mouth searching for hers. "How can you just think you love me?"

"I told you, I'm cautious." Karen slid her arms around his neck.

"I'm prepared to wait," Luke replied, just before his lips covered hers. "But not too long..."

It was awhile before Luke lifted his head. "Maybe it's better that you are cautious. I rather enjoy having to persuade you."

"Does this mean I'll be seeing more of you?"

"We make a great team, Karen. Admit it." Luke's hand stroked her hair. "Ever thought about going into the private investigation business? I could use an assistant. You could specialize in art fraud cases, and I promise you'd have plenty of time to paint."

"Assistant?" Karen lowered her lashes, pretending to give the matter some thought. "I wouldn't consider anything less than a full partnership."

"In everything?" Luke asked playfully. "I might agree to that if it meant you might think about marrying me. I promise I'll give you time to get to know me better." He caressed the nape of her neck, letting her hair spill over his hands. "As long as you don't take too long, that is."

"I'll give the matter some thought," Karen teased. "Partners?"

"Partners," Luke agreed.

"In that case," Karen said, just before she raised her lips to his, "you can start by paying half my towing and storage fees when we get back to the States. I left my car illegally parked."

Luke was too busy kissing her to protest.

# New This spring
## *Harlequin Category Romance Specials!*
## New Mix

## 4 Regencies—for more wit, tradition, etiquette...and romance

## 2 Gothics—for more suspense, drama, adventure...and romance

### Regencies

***A Hint of Scandal*** by Alberta Sinclair
She was forced to accept his offer of marriage, but could she live with her decision?

***The Primrose Path*** by Jean Reece
She was determined to ruin his reputation and came close to destroying her own!

***Dame Fortune's Fancy*** by Phyllis Taylor Pianka
She knew her dream of love could not survive the barrier of his family tradition....

***The Winter Picnic*** by Dixie McKeone
All the signs indicated they were a mismatched couple, yet she could not ignore her heart's request....

### Gothics

***Mirage on the Amazon*** by Mary Kistler
Her sense of foreboding did not prepare her for what lay in waiting at journey's end....

***Island of Mystery*** by Margaret M. Scariano
It was the perfect summer job, or so she thought—until it became a nightmare of danger and intrigue.

### Don't miss any of them!

# Six exciting series for you every month... from Harlequin

## *Harlequin Romance*
### The series that started it all

Tender, captivating and heartwarming...
love stories that sweep you off to faraway places
and delight you with the magic of love.

◆

## *Harlequin Presents*
### Powerful contemporary love stories...as individual as the women who read them

The No. 1 romance series...
exciting love stories for you, the woman of today...
a rare blend of passion and dramatic realism.

◆

## *Harlequin Superromance®*
### It's more than romance...
### it's Harlequin Superromance

A sophisticated, contemporary romance-fiction
series, providing you with a longer,
more involving read...a richer mix of complex plots,
realism and adventure.

# Harlequin American Romance™
## Harlequin celebrates the American woman…

…by offering you romance stories written about American women, by American women for American women. This series offers you contemporary romances uniquely North American in flavor and appeal.

◆

# *Harlequin Temptation*™
## Passionate stories for today's woman

An exciting series of sensual, mature stories of love…dilemmas, choices, resolutions… all contemporary issues dealt with in a true-to-life fashion by some of your favorite authors.

◆

# Harlequin Intrigue™
## Because romance can be quite an adventure

Harlequin Intrigue, an innovative series that blends the romance you expect… with the unexpected. Each story has an added element of intrigue that provides a new twist to the Harlequin tradition of romance excellence.